OH, CHRISTMAS TREE

WRITTEN BY

BRIAN HERALD, BRANDON GRAY,
AND DANIEL THOMPSON

Cover Design and Illustration by Carissa Bowser of Victory Garden Studio
Developmental Editing by Bryn Donovan
Photos by Holly Fite of Mellonberry Photography

ISBN 978-1-7344659-4-5 (print)

1st edition October 2025

DEDICATION

To family. Specifically, found family. I'm looking at you Rippy.
Benny. Rigg. Trace. Turtle (swim, swim). Henrick. Cockroach &
Venom. Baby Jack. Lil Puppy Jack. Theo. Joey. Darrel Strawberry
(and the whole Strawberry Family). Decanter. Brett Debbie.
Whale Guy.

Cody Frizz wanted to let you know about the 9v9 ultimate frisbee
match happening on the Holy Cross quad over break.
Kindly, BYOF-FFS.

CONTENTS

CHRISTMASTIME IN GREENVILLE, MAINE

ELLIE - MONDAY

During the holidays, downtown Greenville, Maine, was as picturesque as the most charming small town in the most typical rom-com story. Ellie loved the way shop owners decorated their windows with fresh fir garland and strung them with softly twinkling lights. The tall lamp posts up and down Main Street were wound with wide red-and-white ribbon, earning the strip the nickname Candy Cane Lane, at least until all the decorations came down in late February.

Inside Tay's Hot Choffee Shop, the local coffee/hot chocolate fusion shop, the atmosphere felt like a Christmas movie. The air was filled with the scents of coffee and hot chocolate and the sounds of festive music, jovial conversations, and laughter. Specialty holiday drinks had taken over the menu, and while Tay's Dark Choco-Gingerbread Latte and Cocoa-Spiked Eggnog Cold Brew were gaining in popularity, the Peppermint Mocha remained the star atop the Christmas tree of holiday drinks.

Working at Tay's shop, Ellie had access to all the flavorful creations she wanted. She's had a taste for custom beverages ever since she tried her first hot choffee in middle school. Her best friend, Taylor, prepared the cup of hot chocolate with a shot of coffee, and it was a burst of flavor and a jolt of energy Ellie never wanted to live without. Over the years, Ellie adjusted the hot chocolate-to-coffee ratio to increase the caffeine boost, and sometimes she replaced coffee with something a bit stronger for that warm, fuzzy feeling on an extra cold wintery night. One way or another, the drink remained a staple in both Ellie and Tay's lives. The two of them were sort of like hot chocolate and coffee, actually. Ellie was warm and sweet, but could take a long time to cool down, while Tay brought an energetic enthusiasm to every situation and was quick to refill your cup with empathy, encouragement, or whatever you needed at the time.

Ever since they were kids, Ellie encouraged Tay to follow her dream of serving her imaginative drinks at a place of her own. So, when Tay had the opportunity to buy the small coffee shop where she worked throughout high school, she decided to forgo college and try to make her dream a reality. Ellie and Tay went their separate ways for the first time when Ellie left for college. While Ellie was away developing her skills as an artist and earning a Bachelor of Fine Arts, Tay grew the choffee shop to fill out two suites along Main Street, with plenty of room for customers to linger and maybe catch a poetry slam, or maybe even an all-kazoo performance of "A Christmas Gift for You from Phil Spector." Tay's shop turned out to be the perfect place for Ellie to land when she moved back home last Christmas after getting laid off from her graphic design job at a popular clothing and outdoor recreation equipment retailer. The timing turned out to be perfect, though, as it gave Ellie the chance to be back home with her mom, who was experiencing some health struggles, and to help Tay with her busy business. Plus, spending girl time with her bestie almost every day was priceless.

Ellie brushed the crumbs off a table in the back corner of the shop and swept them into the palm of her hand. She took off her winter hat and dropped it on the table to reserve the spot for herself. The late afternoon rush had subsided, so Ellie's shift was about over. "I'm clocking out, Tay," she said as she breezed behind the counter and returned the "12 ounces of Christmas" coffee-themed apron she had been wearing back onto the community coat rack.

"Thanks for your help today," Tay said. "Will I see you back here tomorrow?"

"I think so," Ellie leaned against the counter. "I'm happy to pick up shifts whenever I can. It's fun hanging out here."

"That's right. Love that—" Tay stopped short when she noticed Ellie with her winter hat off. "What is happening? I feel like I haven't seen your hair in months. Can I make you a hair appointment right this second? I mean, I still love your hair." Taylor fluffed Ellie's hair with her hands. "So jealous of this fierce auburn color."

"This pale, sun-forsaken skin creates quite the contrast, doesn't it?" Ellie added.

"The freckles help. They definitely help lessen the blatant lack of vitamin D you got going on here."

Ellie laughed. Her wavy auburn hair had grown three or four inches past her shoulders, where she normally kept it, and the highlights from the summer sun had faded. "I know, I know. I had to cancel my last appointment." She had a welcoming, familiar face, deep brown eyes, and a button nose. Her lips curled up at the edges and her cheeks filled out even more when she smiled, which was almost all the time. She could easily turn fierce and even slightly intimidating when she pulled her hair tight and added dark eye make-up.

"Seriously, though," Tay continued. "You have to make time for you, El."

"As a matter of fact, I'm about to get in some me time right now. I'm going to sit in that corner with my tablet and sketch until you kick me out."

"Well, we close in an hour, so consider yourself warned. Wait a second, are you sketching for fun or is this a freelance project?"

Ellie squirmed. "Both?"

"Work is not you time, Ellie Holden!"

"It's a work project, but it's also fun. I like doing freelance gigs. It's getting the project that's the real work."

"Any other fun ones lined up?"

"I've put out a bunch of bids recently, but no bites so far. When I got laid off, I really liked the flexibility of freelancing, but I've been spending too much time with proposals that I just don't hear back on. It's another job all on its own."

"Thinking of getting back in the rat race? Maybe find something full-time again?"

"I don't know. I came back here to be available for my mom. I want to make sure I have the time to keep her on track and make sure she's doing all the things she needs to do to feel healthy."

"Well, you can always pick up hours here in between graphic design gigs, you know that."

No sooner than Ellie put in her earbuds did her phone ring. "Hey, Taniyah. Everything okay?"

"Hi, Miss Ellie. I'm sorry to disturb you but I need to leave a little early. Is there any way for you to come home after work? I know you planned to go out—"

"No problem, Taniyah," Ellie cut her off. "You can leave whenever you need to. I will head home shortly."

The weather outside was frosty and cold, and Ellie could feel a chill sitting by a window. As she packed up her things, she decided to make a hot chocolate to-go.

"Leaving already?" Tay asked.

"My mom's nurse Taniyah needs to leave early. I don't want to leave my mom too long, so I'll just head home."

Ellie opted for a large hot chocolate instead of her usual small size. She sprinkled in a few white chocolate flakes and even added a pump of peppermint for good measure. "Here's to me time," Ellie said as she raised her hot chocolate in a sarcastic toast. She pulled her winter hat down and zipped up her coat to her nose. "See you tomorrow, Tay! Love you, bye!" Ellie said over her shoulder.

"I'm making us a hair appointment!" Tay shouted through a cloud of nutmeg.

The bell atop the door jingled as Ellie stepped outside. Her thick coat, knitted hat, and mittens were no match for the frigid dusk air. Despite the bone-chilling cold, Ellie always parked a few blocks away when she worked downtown. She felt like she was inside of a snow globe strolling down Candy Cane Lane. It even sounded like a snow globe, one of the wind-up musical ones, thanks to the jingly, jolly, holiday music the town piped through speakers hidden inside bushes to create the ultimate festive atmosphere.

♫
Deck the hall with boughs of holly,
Fa, la, la, la, la, la, la, la, la!
'Tis the season to be jolly:
Fa, la, la, la, la, la, la, la, la!
♫

Fresh cinnamon wafted through the air as she passed Pies 'N Fries Pizza Shop. They always amped up the cinnamon-sugar/dough ratio in their famous, limited-time seasonal dessert: Cinnamon Snough Balls, which were most definitely not the same as the Cinnamon Dough Balls that Pies 'N Fries offered the rest of the year.

Ellie had to increase her pace as she passed Rousseau's Candies because fresh candy apples were being set out, and she could hear the grill sizzling inside Rex's Grocery as he prepared the ready-to-take steak tip dinners. She had to keep walking. Otherwise, she could easily spend the tips and wages she had earned that day, week, or even month on these impromptu purchases.

As much as she loved the walk, Ellie looked forward to getting home and into some comfy clothes. Her festive flannel shirt was mostly protected by her work apron, but some collateral cream splatter on the sleeves was unavoidable. As long as she could make it to her car without a gust of wind blowing her into a snowbank, she'd be in an oversized sweater with her hands tucked into the sleeves before the sun set completely.

Ellie drove extra slowly through her neighborhood, just a few blocks away from downtown. Even though the speed limit was only twenty-five miles per hour, that still felt too fast for those streets. Plus, the slower speed made it easier to take in the beautifully decorated houses and snow-covered lawns. The mix of Cape Cod, colonial, and garrison-style homes had enough space between them that neighborhood kids could easily run to each other's yards to play whiffle ball and build snow tunnels, but the houses were not so close that families could hear each other struggling with their kids' homework in the evening. The low roofline on the Cape Cod houses, like the one Ellie grew up in, made it easy to string lights along all of the edges; the ones with wreath-clad dormers were a special treat. Neighbors with garrison-style homes, like Aunt Ruth's, took advantage of the bonus space where the second floor jetted out to string two rows of lights across the front, in addition to outlining all the windows and hanging wreaths on their shutters. The colonials that had a portico over the front door offered entryways of garland, bows, and lights that even Santa Claus himself would appreciate. It looked just like a postcard. *This neighborhood gets it*, Ellie thought, admiring the effort from her fellow Greenville residents.

Every time she arrived home, her heart grew a little bigger at the sight of the glowing spruce tree in Aunt Ruth's yard next door. Ellie trudged across her yard through the snow and made her way to the mature blue spruce. The tree had grown strong for over sixty years, its branches nearly reaching over into Ellie's yard. Sure, there were some spots on the tree where the branches were sparse, but you couldn't see that at night when the tree was lit up. That was what mattered most. Steady red and green lights swirled up from the base of the tree while white lights softly faded in and out. The handmade ornaments outnumbered the store-bought ones, as they should. As the sun quickly dropped below the horizon, the lights on Aunt Ruth's spruce tree twinkled brighter and brighter. Much like the tree, Ellie and Aunt Ruth's relationship had also grown strong. First as neighbors, then as friends, now as found family. Ellie had tried calling her Miss Ruth, Ms. Matthews, Ruthie...but none of them felt as right as Aunt Ruth. Ellie pulled out an expertly made angel ornament, her handmade creation for this year. "This one's for you, Aunt Ruth," Ellie said as she looped it onto a branch. "Can't wait for you to see it when you get home."

Ellie could see the light on in her mom's kitchen window from the tree outside. Growing up, she could always see her mom, Evelyn, bounce in and out of view through the window as she bopped around the kitchen while Ellie played in the snow with their family's foster dog, or decorated the tree, or did this, that, or the other thing. Her mom moved slower now, using a wheelchair to move around more easily. Ellie couldn't see her mom from the tree outside anymore, but she could tell she was there.

Inside, her mom's kitchen was warm, and the scent of something cooking reminded Ellie of the dozens of times she'd come in from the cold, looking for something to help her warm up. The kitchen smelled toasty and...maybe even a bit smoky...? Her nose was not wrong. The scent was getting stronger, and the air was getting smokier. Ellie's eyes darted around the kitchen looking for the culprit before she spotted it. The stream of smoke was a quick giveaway.

"AHH! SOMETHING'S BURNING!!!" Ellie shrieked.

She rushed to the toaster and quickly popped up two extremely charred pieces of toast. The whole scene looked like it had been co-opted for a volcanic science experiment. Ellie shot her mom a stern, knowing look.

Evelyn shook it off. "Oh, there's nothing wrong with that toast. Just scrape it off a bit."

"Mom, you try to do too much. I'm here to help with things like this," Ellie reminded her.

"A new toaster might be helpful..." Evelyn said with a hint of sarcasm.

"Keep it up and I'll move the toaster back out of reach," Ellie joked. "Why are you making toast anyway? Let me make you something to eat. How are you feeling today? Have you done your exercises? Taken your meds? Would you like a heating pad?"

Evelyn mostly ignored the progress note inquiry. "How's that toast coming along? I'm fine. Nothing to report, Dr. Holden," she said sarcastically.

"That does have a nice ring to it. I should at least get an honorary doctorate for helping out around here, right?"

The two sat for a quiet moment at a table with a view of Aunt Ruth's spruce tree outside.

"The tree is looking good, El," her mom finally said to break the silence. "All that time you're spending out there decorating is really paying off."

"Thanks," Ellie said, still staring out the window. "It's been my favorite tradition ever since she moved in next door. I feel like it's the least I can do for her right now, you know? And when she gets home from the hospital, she'll have a beautifully decorated tree waiting for her.".

"It shouldn't be too much longer," her mom confirmed. "Ruthie said was just having some tests done. And she'll love that tree, dear."

Ellie sipped what was left of her hot chocolate and quietly hummed the tune to "O, Christmas Tree," admiring the tree out the window.

CHRISTMASTIME IN DANVERS, PA

JOSH - MONDAY

GOLIATH INVESTMENTS TOOK UP two entire floors inside a nondescript commercial office building on the outskirts of a sleepy suburb in northeastern Pennsylvania. As the largest tenant, Goliath got to have their sign on the building, as well as most of the reserved parking spots near the front entrance.

Inside the cubicle farm maze on the second floor, Joshua Hanson sat at a tidy desk with a notebook at the ready next to his desk phone, a three-compartment pen holder with plenty of pens, pencils, and highlighters, organized into separate compartments, of course. His usual dark blue blazer hung neatly on the DIY coat rack he had attached to his cubicle wall. Everything in its place, optimized for efficiency and predictability. Just the way he liked it.

While Goliath's dress code was "business casual" on paper, most people around the office liked to add their personal touches, accessorizing with skinny ties, square-toe dress shoes that looked like a platypus bill, and silly duck socks fully on display within the three inches between the tops of their shoes and the bottoms of their pants. Josh opted for a comfortable version of business casual: blazer, dress shirt, chinos, squeaky clean sneakers. He followed the L-M-D method, always wearing a light-colored item, a medium-colored item, and a dark-colored item. If it was good enough for Ryan Reynolds, it was good enough for Josh. Like Ryan Reynolds, Josh had more of a runner's physique than a boxer's build. His milk chocolate eyes sparkled when he flashed his smile—a friendly, genuine smile with dimples that he had a hard time hiding even with the slightest smirk. His dark, medium-length hair typically had a windswept look even though he spent most of his time indoors. Occasionally, he'd put some product in to style it, but much preferred the low maintenance, natural, tousled look.

Sounds of clacking keyboards and phone conversations were the droning soundtrack around the general office space, but the conference rooms were the rowdiest spots. When two or more analysts gathered, meetings typically devolved into exaggerating golf handicaps and exchanging funny videos that the meeting participants had seen online. In a recent meeting about how Goliath would comply with upcoming tax code changes, Josh also learned about the *Top 10 Dumbest Motorcycle Accidents, Most Awkward Interactions with Former High School Classmates,* and *What Not to Do Next to a Lion's Cage.*

The hum of investment activity was interrupted by a booming voice that got louder as Pam, the HR Director, marched down the aisle towards Josh's cubicle pod with an unknown woman in tow. "The first floor of Goliath's offices are mostly administrative staff and human resources. That's where my office is," Pam explained as she approached Josh's desk. "The second floor is *The Big Show,* as our CEO, Jerry, likes to call it. The directors and executives have their offices along the windows, and this is where all of the account managers, equity traders, analysts and the like sit. Like Josh here," Pam paused next to Josh's desk. "This is where you'll sit, Mia. Josh, meet Mia. Mia, Josh."

"This is where all the real work happens," Josh joked as he reached out to shake hands.

"Josh is the senior-most investment planner in this pod of desks, and one of the best at the firm," Pam smiled at Josh. "Today is Mia's first day, and she just wrapped up training for the afternoon." Pam continued introductions with the other analysts seated nearby. "Mia, this is Dave. He's a financial analyst, and he's also a musician. Hence the..." Pam motioned with her hands a gesture that referenced Dave's long hair.

"Actually," Dave said, as he tossed his hair and tucked it behind his ears, "I'm more of a musician who happens to be a financial analyst."

Mia chuckled. "Well, it's nice to meet you both."

"Isn't there another who sits here?" Pam asked, looking around for the missing team member. "No matter, these boys can introduce you to him later. Unless you have any questions, I'm off." And with a large, dramatic wave, Pam and her giant smile made their way back down to the first floor.

As Mia settled in, the absent cubicle mate appeared. "Hey! Who's this?" Scott asked as he approached and assumed his signature intrusive lean over the cubicle wall.

"Scotty, this is Mia. She just started," Dave said. "Don't weird her out."

"Welcome to the team, Mia," Scott offered a fist bump. "Name's Scott. Friends call me Scotty for short." Then he turned his attention to Josh. "So, 'Shua, you catch my live stream last night?"

"Oh man, was that last night?" Josh said. "Shoot. I missed it."

"Ooh, what do you live stream?" Mia asked.

"Yeah, Scotty," Dave teased with mocking interest. "What do you live stream?"

"First off, I don't need it from you," Scott said, pointing a finger at Dave before turning his attention to Mia. "I'm somewhat of a gamer."

"What's your screen name?" Dave asked, again, mockingly.

Scott stood up straight and pushed back his shoulders, "SupMan71309."

"How old were you when you started, thirteen?" Mia mocked.

"Wow," Dave said as he nodded with approval. "You'll fit in just fine here, Mia."

"Anyway..." Scott turned his attention back to Josh. "Last night I faced off against my nemesis, PlasmaBoy. It was epic. PlasmaBoy is diabolical. Join later tonight. We're going head-to-head again. You coming for happy hour?"

"Ahh," Josh hesitated. "I don't think so. I might have a call in a few minutes."

"You *might* have a call?" Scott tilted his head and raised an eyebrow in disbelief.

"Yeah, I have a client, Mrs. Lewis, who likes to call near the end of the day when the account statements are mailed out. I've managed her retirement accounts for years, so I like to be available."

Boos echoed among the crew as Dave, Scott, and Mia began packing up for the day.

"How about you, Mia?" Dave offered. "You in for some apps and drinks with the boys?"

"Sure!" Mia said. "Maybe Scotty can explain what Dungeons and Dragons level he's at."

"Not funny," Scott said from behind his cubicle wall. "That's actually a pretty sensitive subject for me."

A look of horror appeared on Mia's face. "I'm sorry, Scott! I didn't mean to offend you!"

"He's fine, Mia," Dave assured. "His Dungeon Master just banned him from the next three campaigns."

Scott stood up. "The wound's still fresh. But I'll come back stronger than ever."

Just like Josh predicted, his phone rang as Dave, Scott, and Mia headed out.

"Good afternoon, Josh Hanson speaking."

"Hi Josh. It's Gloria Lewis."

"Hello, Mrs. Lewis, what can I help you with today?"

"I am having the hardest time remembering my password, and I want to get into my account."

"Well, Mrs. Lewis, I can certainly help you with that. Click the button that says, 'Reset My Password.'"

"It's hard to remember so many passwords..."

"I know. I know, Mrs. Lewis. It is hard to remember so many passwor—"

"Well, now, do you have a suggestion for a new one? You must have some good ideas."

"How about your favorite song, Mrs. Lewis? Or a former address?"

"I've lived at the same address my whole life. Can you believe that?"

"Really? Wow. Your whole life, huh? Well, I'm sure you can come up with something. Just don't choose something like 'Password 1 2 3.' That's one of the most commonly stolen—"

"Password...1...2...3...that worked!"

"Oh, that worked, huh? Okay, well, I'll do my best to forget this conversation. You have a great day now, Mrs. Lewis. Buh-bye."

Josh sensed that his boss was nearby as soon as he hung up the phone by the cloud of cologne that preceded him. He wasn't interested in another dreaded conversation, so he debated pretending to be extremely busy and perplexed by the spreadsheet displayed on his computer screen. It wasn't long before he could see Jerry's shiny, slicked-back hair coming into view over the top of his cubicle wall, followed by his giant, perfect smile and contrast collar dress shirt. Somebody must have seen Michael Douglas in *Wall Street* at a very impressionable age.

"Josh-u-a! Burning the midnight oil. I love it. You helping a client reset their password again, Josh?" Jerry continued before Josh could respond. Though he tried.

"Well, the thing is Jerr—," Josh started to say before Jerry interrupted him.

"You gotta send that stuff to the call center, my man!"

"I just think that—"

"I pay you too much to do that kinda work, Josh."

It was no use. Jerry wasn't interested in listening.

"Right. But Mrs. Lewis is one of my longest-standing clients. She has the majority of her investments with this firm. I just feel that she deserves the utmost attention, no matter the question. You know what I mean?"

Josh couldn't tell if Jerry was weighing the argument in his mind or trying to decide between a three-way parlay and taking the over on the game tonight.

"Plus," Josh continued, seizing the opportunity to speak to a captive Jerry, "the online system can be very confusing, especially when it's getting redesigned every month."

"You gotta keep it fresh with those standard maintenance updates, Josh! Those S.M.U.s! Those SMUUUUs! That's what I hear on all the business podcasts over and over. But listen, I came over here to talk to you about something," Jerry paused, tapping a finger on his chin before admitting, "but I forgot what it was." Without another word, Jerry walked away. Normally, forgetting what he wanted to say didn't stop him from trying.

Josh packed up his laptop, daily planner, and empty lunch cooler before Jerry had a chance to remember what he wanted to say. He still had a few sips of his coffee left from earlier that day, so he drank that down and tossed the cup.

On his way home from the office, Josh stopped at the local grocery store near his condo. He grabbed the few items that he needed, and a few he didn't, before finding an open check-out line.

"Hey, Josh!" a friendly voice called as Josh loaded his items onto the conveyor belt.

"Oh, hey, Christina! I'm surprised to see you here working at a register. Weren't you just promoted to Assistant Manager?"

"Yes! Good memory," Christina beamed as she scanned Josh's items while he added them to his reusable bag. "We're a little shorthanded tonight, so I'm jumping in to help out." She held up a small jar of red pepper flakes soaking in oils with garlic and spices. "Chili crisp? Yum! What's this for?"

"I'm trying a new chicken recipe I found online. I've been kind of crushing it with random recipes lately. I found an orange chicken recipe that I've pretty much perfected. It uses freshly shredded ginger and orange marmalade–"

"Ahem." Their conversation was interrupted by a loud, throat-clearing sound from the person in line behind Josh.

"Sorry..." Josh muttered as he quickly bagged up the last items.

"Let me know how it comes out!" Christina said as she handed Josh his receipt.

"Will do. Maybe I'll make a vegetarian version someday so you can try it."

Back at home, Josh made his dinner, meal-prepped for the next few days, and even had enough energy left in the tank to make one of his favorite desserts: raspberry crumb bars. Josh had learned to cook from his Aunt Ruth. She always had a few new recipes for them to try when he visited her in Maine over school breaks. It was a tradition he continued throughout college and as a working professional. His co-workers certainly never minded when he left a plate of an experimental cake or extra fudgy brownies on the counter to share.

Around lunchtime the next day, Dave and Scott started their daily back-and-forth about where they would eat.

"Pizza?" Dave suggested.

"I had pizza for dinner," Scott said.

"Burgers?"

Scott looked intrigued. "A burger does sound pretty good," he said.

"You coming today, Josh?" Dave asked.

Josh leaned back in his chair. "I don't think so–"

"Boo!" Scott shouted towards Josh.

Josh continued, "I just have some stuff to do–"

"BOO!" Dave and Scott taunted as they left their cubicles and headed out for lunch.

Josh thought he'd have a quiet lunch hour to work in peace, but then he noticed Jerry approaching, holding a paper plate with three raspberry crumb bars on it. *He must like them,* Josh thought, glad to see someone enjoying them.

"Hey Josh," Jerry said, still chewing. He pushed a cascade of well-organized papers into a pile as he sat on Josh's desk. "I remember what I wanted to talk to you about yesterday." Jerry tossed the paper plate and two uneaten crumb bars into Josh's wastebasket. He lowered his voice and continued. "I noticed that you sold a handful of general market funds over the last couple months. You're supposed to be pushing the new Goliath-branded funds, Joshua. You know that. They're going to give the investors those returns they're looking for. Tech is SO hot right now."

Josh had repeated this rebuttal so many times, he probably said it in his sleep: "But, Jerry, Goliath-branded funds have higher fees than other market funds and they just didn't meet the needs of those clients. They were looking for a more diverse portfolio of investment–"

"Yeah, yeah...more diverse portfolio of investments. Yeah, sure. You sound like my old Teddy Ruxpin doll. Except all you talk about is your clients' needs and your–" (Jerry made air quotes with his fingers and then completed his grand mocking finale) "–fiduciary responsibility."

Josh sat up a little straighter. "Hey, that's a real thing, you don't need to use air quotes. The Employee Retirement Income Security Act protects–"

"Anyways..." Jerry announced, signaling that he was done listening. "Goliath's funds are so diverse. They might be the most diverse–" Jerry froze mid-sentence. "This gives me an idea. What if I create a new fund that is all about diversity..." Jerry was transfixed in thought as he walked away, mumbling to himself. "Diversity is SO hot right now..."

Josh sat, shaking his head, staring at his unappreciated hard work disposed of at the bottom of his wastebasket. If only being good at his job and baking sweet treats was enough to get ahead here. If he wanted to keep progressing his career to the next level, he had to play along. He walked to Jerry's office.

"Jerry, hey. I'm sorry about the funds. I'm just not much of a salesperson. But I'll make sure to include them in my strategic plans going forward. I know it's good for the business."

"Josh, look, you're valuable here," Jerry said without looking up from his phone. "You're great at your job. Alan in Compliance loves you. Sure, you won't participate in Monochrome Mondays. It's fine. Though, no one understands why..."

"Jerry," Josh pleaded, "I can do Monochrome Mondays if you think it's important to the business—"

"No." Jerry shook his head profusely as he looked up. "You can't patronizingly participate in Monochrome Mondays. It knows when you mean it."

Josh hesitated. "Who...or...what knows...?"

"I know it's gimmicky, alright?" Jerry said as he walked toward Josh. "I know you're Mr. Serious over here," Jerry motioned like he was typing on an oversized keyboard with just his index fingers, "over here calculating your cost basis and counting your dividends or whatever you're doing. I'm sure you have your reasons for not doing Monochrome Mondays. It's fine. We're all fine with it. I mean, we'll deal with it. Your client roster is rock solid, and the returns are stellar. That counts for something. You just keep doing your thing. We'll check in again soon, ya?" Jerry nodded a few times, and Josh took it as a dismissal, so he headed back to his desk.

He could hear the disappointment in Jerry's voice despite Josh having one of the most valuable client rosters at Goliath. The management fees Josh earned for the firm in one month probably covered the cost of the sushi lunches Jerry liked to host for himself and other executives, and the rounds of drinks he liked to order at the high-end bars where he was supposedly schmoozing 'potential clients'. By the time he returned to his desk, Josh had three missed calls and a voicemail from his mom, of all people. She rarely called with good news. In fact, she rarely called at all. Josh listened to the message before calling her back.

> "Hey Josh, it's your mom. Can you call me when
> you have a chance? It's about your Aunt Ruth."

Josh's heart sank into his stomach. He wasn't close with his parents. He hadn't spoken with his dad in a few years, and he only talked to his mom every few months, and never for long periods of time. But Aunt Ruth? He felt closer with his Aunt Ruth than anyone in his family, maybe anyone in his life. They had just spoken last week. What had he missed? Why wasn't she calling herself? His stomach turned, and before his imagination could spiral out of control, he dipped into an empty conference room and called his mom.

> "Josh, hon, I'm sorry to call you like this," his
> mom said. "Something's happened with your
> Aunt Ruth."

He didn't hear much after she told him that Aunt Ruth had passed away unexpectedly. All the noises blended into a muffled sound as he watched co-workers walk by him outside the conference room like nothing had even happened. They were having conversations and going on like usual, but his whole world just changed. His chest hurt. Josh realized that he hadn't taken a breath since his mom told him.

> "Josh? Are you there?"
> "Yeah, sorry. I'm here. I gotta go because I'm at
> the office, but I'll give you a call back later."

He hung up the phone and felt completely alone. He had no idea what he would do without Aunt Ruth in his life, but he knew that he had to get to Greenville, Maine, as soon as possible.

3

AROUND TOWN

ELLIE – MONDAY EVENING

ELLIE ARRIVED HOME AFTER WORK and found her mom sitting at their kitchen table looking out the window at Aunt Ruth's tree. It was unusual for her to just sit without a book in her hand or some music in the air. "Everything okay, ma?" Ellie asked.

When her mom turned to look at her with tears in her eyes, Ellie knew something was wrong.

"Oh no, Mom." Ellie rushed to her side. "What's wrong? Are you feeling okay? Did you hear something from your doctor?"

Evelyn took a deep breath to compose herself. "It's Aunt Ruth," she began.

Ellie felt her legs go weak, so she sank into the chair next to her mom and listened intently about how Aunt Ruth had driven herself to the hospital a couple days ago when she was having chest pains. Ruth hadn't told anyone about the cholesterol medication she was on or how she was at risk for heart disease. When she said she was staying overnight at the hospital for some tests, she had left out that those tests were related to the mild heart attack she had just experienced.

"She didn't want anyone to 'worry' or 'fuss' over her, is what the nurse told me," Evelyn said to Ellie. "She went to sleep last night and just...didn't wake up again. It was peaceful."

Ellie had so many questions and had so many things she wanted to say to Aunt Ruth. Most of all: *Why didn't you tell me???* But she knew why. Aunt Ruth was not the type to burden others with her troubles. When Ellie would spend time with Aunt Ruth, it was all about Ellie. She made Ellie feel so special. Right from the first day they met. One of her favorite memories was of twenty years ago when Ruth had first moved in. Ellie was only eight years old and played with sidewalk chalk in her driveway. Next door, a new neighbor puttered around her yard and waved at Ellie. Ellie waved back and admired the tall tree in her neighbor's yard.

"It's like a big Christmas tree, isn't it?" The new neighbor walked towards Ellie until they were just a few feet apart. "It looks like it belongs in the center of town decorated with lights and ornaments, but it's right here for us to enjoy.

"It's pretty," a young Ellie observed.

"It's a Blue Spruce," the new neighbor explained excitedly. "It's not native here, but neither am I. HA! My name's Ruth. What's yours?"

"Ellie," she answered. "What's native?"

"It means it doesn't normally grow here unless someone puts it here. The environment has to be just right for it to grow. How tall do you think it is?"

"Um, like six feet?" Ellie guessed.

"Six feet? That's a good guess. I'm going to guess more, just in case. I'm going to guess it's closer to thirty feet."

Ellie's eyes widened. "Thirty?? That's a lot."

"Let's find out! We need two sticks," Ruth said as she scoured the ground. "Find one that's as long as your arm and I will, too."

The two met back near Ellie's driveway with sticks in hand, and Ruth had grabbed a tape measure, too.

"Now hold it in your hand and stick your arm straight out and walk backwards until the top of the stick lines up with the top of the tree," Ruth said. "You might need to close one eye. When they line up, put the stick down on the ground right where you're standing."

They both stopped and dropped their sticks.

"Now we just measure from the tree to the sticks."

Ruth stood at the tree while Ellie pulled the tape measure to the spot where their sticks lay.

"Twenty feet!" Ellie shouted.

"Twenty feet tall! Wow!" Ruth said as she walked towards Ellie with the tape measure.

"You were so close! That was fun. How do you know how to do that?" Ellie asked.

"It's kind of what I do. Or, did."

"You measured trees?"

"No," Ruth chuckled. "I figured out answers to questions and solutions to problems. It's called being an 'engineer.' But I just say I like to figure stuff out," she smiled at Ellie.

Ellie sat quietly with her mom at their kitchen table, lost in the memory. She held her mom's hand and stared at the tree out the window. It was the closest thing she had to Aunt Ruth now.

The next morning, Ellie had woken up with a hole in her heart, so she stayed in her bed longer than usual. When she finally made her way downstairs, her mom already had coffee ready in the kitchen. Normally, Ellie spent a few quiet moments in the morning to meditate and prepare for the day. Now, though, she waited, wishing Aunt Ruth would step out of her house for her morning walk, look over at Ellie in the window, and wave like she had done so many times before.

"How are you feeling this morning, El?" Evelyn asked as she wheeled into the kitchen.

Ellie patted her eyes with a tissue. "Okay, I guess." She continued through tears. "I just miss her."

Evelyn rested her hand on her daughter's back. "I miss her, too. We'll keep her spirit alive."

Ellie sniffled as she nodded. "Right. She'll always be with us."

"You know," Evelyn said. "Something that seemed to help me when your dad passed was talking about him and hearing about him from other people. It helped me feel close to him. Hearing people talk about him made me smile. I know it's soon, maybe too soon for

you, but it might help lift your spirits to talk about Aunt Ruth."
Evelyn pulled a piece of paper from a nearby drawer and handed it
to Ellie. "This is a list of errands Aunt Ruth asked me to run for her
a few years back. She told me to keep it in case I needed to again; she
always went to the same places each week to see her friends. I could
tell they all cared about her very much. Maybe you should visit some
and let them know about Aunt Ruth. It'll give you a chance to grieve
a bit and also let the people she cared about hear it from you."

Ellie held the paper in her hands. Aunt Ruth's handwriting
looked so neat and familiar on the worn piece of paper.

*Candy Shop, Book Store, Rex's Grocery, Wine Store, Hardware
Store*

"That sounds like a nice idea. I think I'll do that. Thanks, Mom."

Ellie prepared to set out to visit Aunt Ruth's favorite places and
tell her friends the sad news. She bundled up against the cold and
wind chill in her knitted scarf, mittens, winter hat, and leg warmers,
and then stuffed her coat pockets with lots of extra tissues.

Ellie's first stop was Rousseau's Candies. Ellie had shopped there
somewhat regularly but was not close with the owners. She stood
outside the candy shop looking through the large glass window
display that featured oversized lollipops wrapped with LED rope
light that changed colors. The store wasn't busy inside yet this
morning, and she could see someone putting candies into a glass
display. Ellie realized that she was about to disrupt whatever was
going on in this person's life. She thought about how difficult this
was going to be. How she didn't want to do it. Maybe she could just

make a phone call, or write a letter, or maybe they could hear it from someone else. Then she thought of something Aunt Ruth often said. Instead of saying that she 'had to' do something, Aunt Ruth would say that she 'got to' do something. It was a common mind trick, but Aunt Ruth made it a habit, and she tried to look at everything as an opportunity. Ellie decided that she would, too. She felt a responsibility to do this as delicately as possible. She got to honor Aunt Ruth in this way. Ellie stepped into the candy shop and was greeted immediately.

"Hey there! Morning!" said a voice from behind the counter. "Come on in. We're open." A man who looked like he was built more for catching touchdowns than candymaking popped up from behind the glass display case. "I'm just running a little late putting out the candy today. I'm Mike. Just give me a shout and I'll help you when you're ready."

"Hi," Ellie said, making her way to the counter. "I was hoping to speak with..." She realized she didn't know who Aunt Ruth was most friendly with here. "Well, I'm not sure exactly. My Aunt liked to come here pretty often but I am not sure who she saw regularly. She, my Aunt Ruth—"

"Miss Ruthie? Of course!" Mike said. "I recognize you. You're down at Tay's shop a lot, too, right? I have Ruthie's regulars right here." Mike grabbed a paper bag from behind the counter. "I keep a box of coconut cremes set aside for her. I threw in a bag of the milk chocolate Santas, too. She loves the seasonal chocolates. She hasn't been in for a few days, so I figured she'd be here any time." Ellie's expression must have given away that she had bad news to deliver because Mike's expression suddenly became concerned. "Wait, is Ruthie okay?"

"Well, not exactly," Ellie began. "I know you're busy, but can you spare a few minutes to talk?"

Mike led Ellie to one of the wrought iron bistro sets by the front window and pulled out a chair for her to sit.

"Aunt Ruth, Miss Ruthie, she um...she had some health issues that she kept pretty quiet. The other day, she started feeling not great, so she went to the hospital. It was her heart. They did what they could but, unfortunately, she passed away in her sleep very early yesterday morning."

Mike's head dropped. "Oh, poor Miss Ruthie. Bless her soul." He looked up. "You must be heartbroken. She talked about you all the time."

"We were next-door neighbors, but I pretty much grew up with her in my life, so I considered her family."

"Well, I am so sorry for your loss, Ellie. Miss Ruthie was a regular here. One of the bright spots of my day was when she would come visit. I met her through my mother-in-law, Margery. They've been friends for years."

"I didn't realize you were related to Margery," Ellie said. "She spends a lot of time at Tay's."

"Right, the Lunch Ladies Club," Mike chuckled.

"Yes, the Lunch Ladies. They're a fun group. I guess Aunt Ruth would be considered an honorary member of the Lunch Ladies, but she didn't hang around the choffee shop like Margery, and the other ladies."

"Miss Ruthie was too busy around town for that. Even when she would come in here, she would chat for a while, really talk, too, not just 'hey, how are you?' but she'd actually want to know what was going on with me and she would ask about things we had talked about before," Mike explained. "Sometimes it felt like she was digging for a problem to solve, or something she could help with. She would always ask about my candy-making process and the machines I used and then offer ideas to make the process more efficient, or mention a manufacturer in Germany or Belgium that I should look into."

Ellie snort-laughed, "That sounds like Aunt Ruth. She was the best person to talk to about anything."

"The absolute best," Mike agreed. "Her loss will be felt by a lot of people because she had such an important impact while she was here. We are so lucky to have known her, and I know that I am a better person for having known her."

Mike's words really touched Ellie's heart. She knew Aunt Ruth was special, but hearing about her from a stranger made her emotional. Ellie pulled a tissue from her pocket. "Can I hug you?" she asked.

"Of course," Mike stood and gently wrapped his big arms around Ellie.

"I'll try not to cry on your work shirt," Ellie said.

"Oh, you're fine. Thank you for coming to tell me."

The door chimed as a customer walked into an unexpected scene. "Mike? Is that you? Everything okay in here? Have you captured an intruder?"

Mike moved his head to look beyond Ellie. "Laura, hi. Come on in." Mike stepped back and held his hands on Ellie's shoulders. "You can sit back down and stay as long as you'd like."

"Ellie, dear? Is that you?" the woman asked.

Ellie recognized Laura. A bona fide Lunch Lady. "Oh, hi there, Laura."

"Right," Mike said. "You two know each other from Tay's."

Ellie and Mike made eye contact, and both said, "Lunch Ladies Club."

"Oh, that silliness," Laura waved off the both of them as she walked to the counter. "Mike, I need some more of those weird things you make that I put out at my register."

Mike stood with his hands on his hips. "Weird things? You mean the spicy mint chocolates with chili flakes? Those aren't weird, they're a delicacy."

"Well, they're all gone. I think the kids are daring each other to try them."

"I can get you some more," Mike said, then looked at Ellie. "But there's some news you should hear."

"What's going on?" Laura was concerned.

"I have some news about Aunt Ruth." Ellie explained what had happened as the three of them sat in chairs at the front of the store. It was the quietest Ellie had seen Laura, maybe ever.

"I'm just so surprised, and sad. And kind of angry?" Laura said, finally. They sat quietly for a few minutes. "She knew this was the best way," Laura broke her silence again. "But this, gosh, this is hard."

Ellie had always known Laura as a jokester, silly, loud, fun, playful. This was the first time Ellie had ever seen her emotional and serious.

"Well," Laura said as she slowly stood. "I need to get back next door."

"Oh, right," Ellie perked up. "You own the book shop next door, right? I'm sort of following Aunt Ruth's daily routine to let people know about Aunt Ruth's passing, and I was going to stop to see you next."

"Come on over when you're done here," Laura said before leaving.

Ellie walked into Laura's Little Book Store on Main with a bag of chocolate mint chili drops for Laura. "Here you go," Ellie said, holding out the bag of candies. "Mike sent me with these." Laura's eyes were puffy, and she had a box of tissues next to her.

"What a guy," Laura said, taking the bag. She placed two books onto the counter in front of her. "Ruthie had ordered these books a couple of weeks ago but hasn't been in to pick them up. I think you should take them. They're already paid for, so, I guess technically they belong to her estate. But I won't go calling the lawyers on you or anything."

Ellie looked at the covers. A Healthy Heart and Tango in Transylvania.

"Ruth had gotten really into this romance series about dance competitions in remote locations," Laura explained. "It's a quickly growing subgenre called romantango. Anyway, I think she'd want you to have them."

"Thanks. So, she spent a lot of time here with you?"

"Oh yeah. Ruthie was here all the time. She was one of my best unpaid employees. She spent more time helping other people find books than she did for herself. I'll miss her a lot."

"So will I," Ellie said. "I have a few more stops that I want to make. I want to tell some of her other friends in person before they hear it from somewhere else."

"That's a nice thing you're doing. I know Ruth would be proud of you for doing that."

Ellie left the bookstore holding Aunt Ruth's books close to her heart. When she got onto the sidewalk, her phone rang.

"Hi, Mom. Everything okay?"

"Hey, El. Yes, just calling to check in on you and see how everything's going."

"Pretty good. I think this is really helping. I'm off to see Rex next. You know, I always kinda thought Aunt Ruth had a little crush on Rex."

"A little?" her mom exclaimed. "Hon, I feel like she had been making eyes at Rex since he was just a butcher, so a few years, at least."

"That doesn't make this any easier." Ellie hustled along the sidewalk through the cold as quickly as she could. "I'm here now, Mom. I gotta let you go. Love you."

Ellie stepped into Rex's Grocery and took in one of the most familiar and comforting scents: bacon and burnt toast.

"Morning, Ellie," Rex said as he peeked over his shoulder. "Did ya eat yet?" He was working the griddle and stacking up his famous breakfast sandwiches. "Got a bacon, egg, and cheese with your name on it right here." Rex must have sensed that Ellie needed to talk to him because he came around from the grill to check on her. "You looking for something in particular today, Ellie?"

Rex's Grocery had grown into something really special over the last couple years. What started as a small corner store had blossomed into a unique grocery shopping experience. It had become a custom food market, with freshly made food and products from around the world that you couldn't find in other stores in town. Most of the people who came into Rex's spend more time than they expected perusing the aisles. Ellie's favorites were the double-sided breakfast pastry and dirty chai crispy rice treats. Maybe that's why Rex came right over. It was unusual for her to linger around the register counter right away.

"I came to talk to you about something," Ellie began. "I don't want to interrupt but it's kind of important." She continued to explain about Aunt Ruth to Rex. His eyes welled up as she spoke. Ellie offered a tissue.

Rex walked back to his griddle and turned it off, then fiddled around with some utensils just long enough to compose himself. "I know how much your Aunt Ruth liked to talk about herself," he glanced at Ellie with a sarcastic look," but in case she had never mentioned it, Ruthie and I were a little more than friends. Not too much more, we both liked our own space, but we cared about each other quite a bit."

"I had my suspicions," Ellie admitted. "Did she tell you anything about her health, or share any concerns at all?"

"You know, looking back now, maybe she did it her own way. When you get older, you end up at the doctor's office for things you never had before. The last couple years, I suppose she mentioned appointments more than she had in the past and mentioned tests more than before. I assumed it was all just part of the deal of getting older. I guess I just missed it. Maybe I wasn't paying close enough attention."

"No," Ellie assured him. "I don't think that's it. Aunt Ruth always kept some distance from people. I think she probably wanted you to know as much as she told you. She was never the type to make things about herself."

Rex looked at Ellie with his big, bright blue eyes and deep wrinkles. "I'm sure she would appreciate you letting people know like this. I know I do."

"Thanks. I have a few more stops, so I should get going."

"Okay, come back soon. You'll get Ruth's special cut of ribeye on the house next time."

Ellie was feeling fulfilled. She knew this was the right thing to be doing. Her next stop was to the wine, beer, and liquor store, Pour It Up. Aunt Ruth had never been much of a drinker, not from what Ellie had seen, anyway. She did love giving special bottles as gifts, though. Aunt Ruth was always a great gift-giver. Ellie took a deep breath as she stepped into the store. *Mmm.* It smelled like cloves, cinnamon, vanilla, and all the warm winter spices. *No wonder Aunt Ruth loved it here*, Ellie thought.

"Good morning!" Sandra welcomed Ellie before she did a double-take. "Ellie? Is that you?"

"Hey there, Sandra. I know, it's strange seeing me outside of Tay's, isn't it?" Not only did Sandra run the Pour it Up, she was also the sassiest of the Lunch Ladies crew, and probably their unofficial ringleader.

Sandra stopped what she was doing and walked over to Ellie. "How's Ruth? She home yet? I haven't heard from her in a few days."

"Well, that's why I'm here..." Ellie told Sandra about Aunt Ruth and the two sat and chatted for a while. "You know, I never really saw Aunt Ruth drink much, but she was in here an awful lot. Was she just visiting with you?" Ellie asked.

"Ruth loved coming here for tastings. She would learn all about the wine or liquor being sampled, then buy a few bottles, or more sometimes, and then give them as birthday gifts or holiday gifts. She always recalled what she learned at the tastings, explained to the gift recipient all about the drink like she had made it herself in her own kitchen. She was one of a kind," Sandra said.

Ellie's next stop on Aunt Ruth's list was a tough one: Hardware Store. Even though the hardware store wasn't in that building anymore, Ellie knew what it meant. She stood outside the two-story brick building and admired how well-maintained it had been, even though it had changed owners three or four times since her father sold it. The building represented patience, sacrifice, hard work, generosity, and following your dreams. All qualities she saw her dad demonstrate from the time he bought the building until the day he handed her a check that would help cover about half of her college tuition.

When he retired, he had meticulously planned his expenses so he could live comfortably and support his family for years to come, and he had set aside enough that he could afford to help Ellie with college. She tried to refuse it, wanting him to save it for himself, but he insisted and said that he could 'sacrifice a few cruises to the Bahamas to help her with her education.' That was always his joke. 'I guess that's one less cruise to the Bahamas this year.' Property tax went up again? 'One less cruise to the Bahamas.' You see how much we're spending on the plow guy this winter? 'Guess no cruise to the Bahamas.' He passed away unexpectedly before planning even one cruise in his life.

Ellie stepped inside the now home of *Juniper Lee's Home and Decor*. She explained to Juniper that she was stopping by all of the places on Aunt Ruth's errands list and letting people know in person that Aunt Ruth had passed away. Juniper Lee was Estelle's daughter, who was one of the Lunch Ladies, and a good friend of Aunt Ruth's. From talking with Juniper, they put together that all of the places Aunt Ruth would frequent were either owned by her friends or related to her friends. She really did all that she could to support and hold up those who were close and important to her.

"You know," Ellie said, "maybe we should all get-together. We could meet at Tay's Choffee Shop and just spend time with each other."

"That sounds really nice." Juniper said. "I'll let my mom know and bring her, too."

"Yes, please do. I'll backtrack and let everyone I saw this morning know."

That afternoon, a group of acquaintances and friends got together. Ellie and her mom, Evelyn, were the first ones there. Juniper Lee and Estelle got there at the same time as Laura and Sandra (who snuck in a few bottles of cabernet from her store). Rex came, too, with a giant charcuterie board that he assembled from the meats and cheeses in his deli. Finally, Margery arrived with her daughter and son-in-law, Mike, who carried two baskets of candies and chocolates. It wasn't long before word spread about Aunt Ruth's passing and the impromptu celebration of her life. Ellie hugged, cried, and laughed more than she had in a long, long time.

4

A COLD, SUNNY DAY

JOSH – SATURDAY MORNING

THERE'S NEVER A PERFECT DAY for a funeral, but the day of Aunt Ruth's funeral was as close to perfect as it could be. Her favorite kind of day was cold and sunny with snow on the ground.

"It was a lovely ceremony," Josh's mom said. "She was probably yelling from heaven, 'hurry up and put some snow back on there!' while we were tossing handfuls of dirt onto the casket."

"She sure did love the snow. My siblings couldn't make it, huh?"

"They said they would try, but you know how it is. They're busy, and it's a lot to get all the way up here."

"I know, but still," he said.

"You were closer to Aunt Ruth than anyone in the family, though. They didn't spend nearly as much time here as you," his mom said as she searched in her purse.

"Every school break since I was ten." Some of the best times of his life, but he kept that part to himself. There was hardly a better time in a ten-year-old's life than that stretch from the end of December to early January. The hallowed end-of-the-year holiday break. For Josh, this meant nearly two weeks off from school, visiting his Aunt Ruth in Greenville, and getting to see Ellie, the girl who lived next door and was just about Josh's age. It didn't take long for the three of them to establish their tradition of doing all the festive holiday things together while Josh visited. They decorated with handmade ornaments; they baked cookies, pies, fudge, and cakes; they tried daring new recipes; they went caroling around the neighborhood; they wrapped gifts at the community center; and, of course, they attended the downtown Christmas tree lighting. Josh was feeling nostalgic being back in Greenville after so long. "Do you want to stay for a little while, maybe go through Aunt Ruth's things, check on her house or something?"

His mom checked her phone. Her inability to be present in the moment was something that Josh noticed a long time ago, and was something that bothered him about himself, too.

"I'm pretty sure Ruth had everything taken care of. If they need me for something, they'll call. I think I'll just head out this afternoon. It's good to see you, Josh." She hugged his neck and disappeared into the crowd.

As the rest of the funeral gathering dispersed and Josh made his way through the crowd, his heart skipped a beat when he saw a striking, familiar face in the distance. Ellie. He immediately changed direction and started to walk towards her when someone stepped in his path.

"Pardon, sir...Joshua? Joshua Hanson, I presume?" A compact man with nervous, awkward energy stopped Josh in his tracks.

"Umm, yes, I'm Josh. Do I know you?" Josh said, distracted, as he gazed beyond the man and saw Ellie move in the opposite direction.

"Hello. Hi. No, sir, not yet. My name is Jasper McGillicutty,

Esquire," Jasper said as he dug through various pockets in his pants and coat.

"My friends just call me Jasper. My clients do, as well. Really, everybody I meet calls me Jasper. You're welcome to as well." Jasper handed Josh a crinkled, dated business card that surely was part of the first and only batch of cards Jasper ever had printed. "I'm glad I ran into you," Jasper continued. "I'm a lawyer here in town and I have some papers related to Miss Ruth's...your Aunt Ruth's estate that I need you to sign. Do you think you could find the time to pay a visit to my office this afternoon? Say, in an hour? My office is just over that way," Jasper said as he pointed in the direction across the street.

With a warm smile and a nod, Jasper was gone. Josh looked beyond the lawyer, where he had spotted Ellie before, but she was nowhere in sight.

It had been a long time since Josh last strolled down the festive Main Street, which was currently in its Candy Cane Lane era. All the storefronts had frosted windows to match the piles of snow on the sidewalk. Shoppers were all smiles, carrying bags of beautifully wrapped gifts and lattes filled with nutmeg and peppermint. *Mmm...a coffee did sound really good right about now.*

Josh stopped into a local coffee shop. It was tactfully, yet beautifully, decorated for the holidays. The bulletin board was full of fliers for local services and events: Dog walkers, snow shoveling, babysitting, guitar lessons by Seth, better guitar lessons by Matt. *Rock on, Matt.* There was even a poster for the Downtown Christmas Market. Josh stepped up to the counter, where there was a nearly full tip jar, and was greeted by a barista named Craig.

"Hi. Welcome to Tay's Hot Choffee Shop. Are you more *hot* or more *choff*?"

Josh chuckled at how adorable it was that Taylor still made the new employees say that. Craig should catch on in a week or two.

"Hi, Craig. You know, in my younger days I thought I was pretty *hot*. But nowadays, I'm feeling more *choff*. You know what I mean?" Craig must not have gotten many actual responses to that question because he stared at Josh without responding. "I'll take a flat white reversed red eye with oat milk, please."

Josh reached for his wallet and checked to make sure he had some small bills to toss in the tip jar. When he looked up with his credit card in hand, Craig was staring back at him, frozen in time. He hadn't moved since Josh ordered.

Craig scratched his head. "Um, I *think* that was a coffee order, but I haven't heard those words together like that before."

Josh realized he needed to provide a little more detail. He added, "It's a—"

"I got this one, Craig," Taylor said as she stepped up to the register and smiled at Josh. "Up until now, Craig has dealt with mostly the same, simple drinks that are, you know, on the menu."

Josh smiled at the familiar face. "A flat white has to be *somewhere* on your menu."

"You know," Taylor continued, "if we add Skittles to that drink, I think we could get the rest of the rainbow colors in your order."

"It's nice to see you, Taylor. Business looks good. Your shop is busy. You feel like you've got everything under control here?"

"Heeeeyyy, Josh. Yup, eight years in and I feel like I'm starting to figure it out." Tay glanced at her menu of specialty holiday drinks and then back at Josh. "What, our Eggnog Hot Chocolate Fusion Latte not boujee enough for you? It's brand new this season. Maybe a PSL? PML? JBRML?"

"What even is a JBRML?"

"It's obviously a Jingle Bell Reindeer Mocha Latte."

"How do you say that with a straight face? Nah, I'm not quite in the Christmas fusion drink spirit."

"I know...I'm sorry to hear about your aunt, Josh." Taylor clasped her hands together and closed her eyes.

Josh's eyes darted around the room, unsure of what he should be looking at. Should his eyes be closed, too...?

Taylor continued in a softer voice, "When someone you love becomes a memory..."

Josh squinted, both eyes closed.

"...the memory becomes a treasure."

Josh opened one eye to see Taylor mouthing a silent prayer with her eyes still closed. He closed his eye again. He took a deep breath. This was actually quite peaceful. It had been a long time since—

"Your drink will be right up."

Josh opened his eyes to see an empty register, as Taylor had left to work on his drink. He tried to flag down Craig to pay for his drink.

"This one is on the house, Josh." Taylor said from her espresso machine.

"Thanks, Tay." Josh pushed a twenty-dollar bill into the tip jar on the counter.

"I think Ellie would really love to see you while you're here," Taylor continued as she prepared Josh's drink.

"Yeah, I'll be in town a few d—" A coffee grinder erupted and interrupted Josh. He waited for it to stop. "It's been quite a while. I'll be in town a few days. I hope to run into her."

Taylor looked up. "Absence diminishes small passions and increases great ones. Just as the wind extinguishes a candle, it also enkindles a bonfire."

"A Taylor original?"

Taylor smiled and attended to the drink again. "It's François de La Rochefoucauld."

Josh snapped a finger. "I was so close."

"One flat white with oat with a shot of coffee?" Taylor handed Josh his to-go cup.

He smiled and nodded before taking a small sip. "Mmm...delicious, Taylor."

"Au revoir, mon ami."

"Rochefoucauld?"

"*That* was French."

"Of course," Josh conceded.

Outside in front of the coffee shop, Josh breathed in the fresh, cold air. There was a sweetness to it that he was not used to since he spent almost all his waking hours indoors and in front of a computer screen. It could be that. It could also be from the steamed milk that was currently freezing to the tip of Josh's nose after he sipped his drink without the lid on.

As he approached a bell-ringing Santa, Josh reached for a dollar to add to the collection and pulled out Jasper's business card. He looked in the direction that Mr. McGillicutty pointed earlier and found a window with fading gold lettering: JASPER L. MCGILLICUTTY, ATTORNEY AT LAW. *That must be the place.*

Josh found the nearest crosswalk and respectfully waited his turn as traffic moved in front of him. As soon as the WALK sign lit up, Josh stepped into the crosswalk. Suddenly, he heard a panicky voice in the distance that sounded like, "*something's left*" or "*that has some heft,*" but he couldn't make it out. Josh looked all around as the words got louder and were repeated faster. He started to panic a bit himself. After a couple of confusing seconds, he heard it loud and clear: "*ON YOUR LEFT!!!*" He hopped out into the road just as a cyclist zoomed past him in the bike lane and ran through a red traffic light. *Typical cyclist.*

During all this commotion, the crosswalk signal changed from WALK to DON'T WALK, and the traffic signal turned green, but Josh hadn't noticed this. He was in the road blocking traffic with a heart rate of about 200 beats-per-minute. As if he hadn't experienced enough torment, a car waiting at the now-green light honked a quick *BEEP-BEEP*. An exasperated and frantic Josh yelled towards the traffic, "I'm sorry! My life just kinda flashed before my eyes! I'm a little shook up—" Josh did a double-take at the driver in the first car waiting at the light. The driver stared at him in disbelief. He was struck by the immediate attraction he felt towards her. He squinted for a closer look. "*Ellie*? Is that you?"

Ellie popped her head out the window of her compact SUV as Josh made his way over to her. "Joshua Hanson!?"

"Wow, I can't believe it!" Josh said as he leaned down for an awkward through-the-car-window hug. "How are you? You know, I saw you at the funeral. I tried to say hello, but—" He figured he would spare her the details of his interaction with the lawyer. "I'm really glad to bump into you."

"Yeah, me too!"

The driver behind Ellie honked their horn at the traffic disturbance. Ellie glanced at them in her rear-view mirror. Josh could see that she was getting anxious by her tentative smile, tightened grip on the steering wheel, and her nervous chuckle.

"This is nice...um...I saw you at Aunt Ruth's service, too—"
BEEP! BEEP!

Both looked at the car behind Ellie.

"I'm sorry, Josh. I've—"

"I know. You gotta go. I'm going to pop over to Aunt Ruth's house tomorrow. Maybe you can stop by?"

"Okay, yeah! That sounds good. It's really nice to see—"
BEEEEP!! BEEEEP!!

"Okie dokie..." Josh said as he stepped away from the car so Ellie could pull away. "Later gator!"

Ellie smiled fondly at the inside joke. "Not if I see you first!" she said as she drove past Josh.

As the car behind Ellie pulled up, the driver rolled down their window. A woman with deep red hair wearing a bright red blouse smiled as she lowered her sunglasses and said, "In a while, crocodile..." She winked before replacing her sunglasses and then drove off. From a distance, she offered one final, soft:

BEEP-BEEP.

As Josh approached the law office, he took in the rest of Main Street. Something seemed off. Was he still shaken up from the traffic incident? It wasn't *that* big of a deal, was it? No, that wasn't it. Something else—and then it hit him. As he peered at the end of Main Street, something was conspicuously missing. He was expecting to see the pride of downtown Greenville: the signature seventy-foot balsam fir lit up like a, well, like a Christmas tree. Each year, the town workers spent a day stringing lights and hanging decorations. You could see the tree all the way from the opposite end of Main Street, but not anymore. *Hm, that's strange.*

A bell jingled atop the door as Josh entered the law offices of Jasper L. McGillicutty. The office space was small and quiet. There were just a couple of desks, each with a laptop and papers scattered on them. Two chairs were positioned in front of each desk, where many sensitive legal conversations had probably taken place, hopefully none at the same time. Filing cabinets and legal boxes lined the walls to create mini towers around the office. There was no one in sight.

"Hello? Jasper? Anyone here?" Josh said loudly.

Suddenly, from a door Josh hadn't noticed in the back, Jasper rushed out with his sleeves rolled up and a napkin tucked into his collar, still chewing whatever he was eating in the back room. He recognized Josh right away.

"Yup, yup, yup. I'm here. I am here. Oh! Joshua! I am so glad you are here."

Jasper shuffled over to Josh and shook his hand.

"Hi, Jasper. Is now a good time? I know I'm a little early, but I saw your sign and just thought I'd stop in rather than wait outside."

"Yes, this is great. Thank you for coming by. Um...it was a beautiful ceremony today. For Miss Ruth. Your Aunt Ruth, I mean."

"Yes. Yes, it was. Hey, Jasper, let me ask you something. The tree, the downtown Christmas tree, what happened to it? I couldn't see it standing down at the end of the street. I feel like I always used to be able to."

"Oh, yes, the tree. Well, we had that tree, what, 70 years? Unfortunately, it did not survive the holiday season last year, so the tree is no more. A real shame."

The two got quiet and stood awkwardly for a moment. Josh wondered what could have happened to the tree. Was it a lightning strike? Did a plow truck drive into it? Did someone chop it down for firewood?

"Well," Jasper said. "There is no good way to transition into this, so I will just do it, if it's okay with you now?" Jasper yanked the napkin out of his collar, then made his way to a desk and opened the laptop. He pointed at a chair to invite Josh to sit at the front of the desk. Josh took a seat across from Jasper.

"Your Aunt Ruth appointed me the trustee of her assets. I have the duty, but also the pleasure and the honor, of helping distribute the items from her trust to the proper recipients."

The doorbell jingled again, and Jasper looked beyond Josh towards the door.

"Oh! You made it right on time!" Jasper said.

Josh turned around to see who had entered the office and then jumped to his feet. He was surprised to see Ellie.

MEETING WITH MR. MCGILLICUTTY

ELLIE – SATURDAY AFTERNOON

ELLIE LOOSENED HER SCARF and unbuttoned the top of her coat as she stepped into the law office, anticipating the warmth inside.

"Ellie! Wow! What are you doing here?"

She heard the voice before she even had a chance to take in her surroundings. She looked around and then locked eyes with Josh, standing next to Mr. McGillicutty at a desk across the room. Warmth? Yes. But this? This was not something she had anticipated. "Josh?" Ellie had no idea that Josh would be there. "This is so funny!"

"Come on in, please. Come in." Jasper took her scarf and coat and hung them up for her. "I assume you both know each oth—"

Ellie stepped towards Josh, and he met her halfway. They shared a warm, extended embrace. The kind of hug where you closed your eyes and, no matter where you were or what was going on around you, it felt like home. As Ellie pulled back, her hands lingered in his. This was the first time they had seen each other in person in nearly ten years. At least, the first time without a car horn beeping at them.

"Well, now," Jasper said. "I suppose you do know each other indeed. Very well. I do suppose." He cleared his throat and ended up in a coughing fit. Jasper leaned onto the desk and punched at his chest with a closed fist. His face reddened as he coughed.

"Oh my goodness!" Ellie noticed him struggling. "Are you choking? Let me help."

As Ellie moved closer, Jasper swallowed whatever was blocking his breathing and began to catch his breath again. "Phew! Sorry about that, folks," Jasper said with relief across his face. "Thought that was the big one for a second there."

"I'm just glad you're okay," Ellie said, also relieved.

"I was attempting to subtly interrupt the moment you two were having so we could get started with these legalities. I guess I need to chop up that tuna salad a bit more finely next time. That was close." Jasper motioned towards the chairs in front of him. "Please. Take a seat. Let me explain why we're all here."

Josh pulled back a chair for Ellie, and she took a seat.

"Miss Ruth filmed a video of her last Will and Testament." Jasper leaned back in his chair and folded his arms. "So many people doing that these days. Hers is a hoot, that dear Miss Ruth...but I digress. Your Aunt Ruth, rest her soul...."

"May she rest in peace," Ellie added.

Josh nodded solemnly with pursed lips.

"Well," Jasper continued, "she also made some additional recordings to be played for specific people, and so I have one for Josh, but it's for both of you, actually. You'll see why in a moment."

Jasper turned the laptop on his desk to face her and Josh and then pressed the "Play" button for them.

The scene looked familiar. It was Aunt Ruth's living room. At first, Ellie could only see the room with Aunt Ruth's couch in the center of the screen. She couldn't see Aunt Ruth but she could hear her fiddling with the camera equipment.

"Is this thing even on?" Aunt Ruth said. "I see the red thing flashing... okay, I think so. Okay. Here we go. And action!"

Finally, Aunt Ruth came into view. Ellie got emotional when she saw her on-screen. Ellie could sense Josh tighten up, as if he was holding himself together.

Aunt Ruth was the same upbeat and animated Aunt Ruth Ellie had spent so much time with. She looked so happy. It was probably a cold, sunny day, her favorite kind of day. As soon as she sat down on her couch, she began talking directly to the camera.

"Well, Josh, if you're seeing this,"

Aunt Ruth looked down solemnly and then back up fiercely.

"I've been selected for a secret task force with a mission so critical to the survival of the planet, it would melt your ears."

She broke into a smile.

"Not really. But if I had, I couldn't talk about it. Anyway, while I'm gone..."

She winked at the camera.

"I'd like you to have my house, Josh. There's a catch, though. Well, a few. More than a few."

Aunt Ruth looked off camera.

"What's shorthand for like, six things? More than a handful...oh, half a dozen. Duh."

She looked back at the camera.

"I've got half a dozen things you need to do first. I've put together a Christmas scavenger hunt of sorts around town: caroling to embarrass my friends, baking my favorite cookies, volunteering at a toy drive, and a couple more. Some sort of food challenge like on TV where they have to eat a live scorpion. It doesn't have to be alive or even a scorpion, just something a little off-putting. But first, the tree."

Ellie looked over at Josh, and they shared a nervous glance before looking back at the video.

"Josh. You and Ellie need to decide, collectively..."

Aunt Ruth looked off camera.

"Can it be considered 'collectively' if it's just two people?"

She looked back at the camera.

"You two need to decide together what to do about the tree in my yard. It's an important tree, Joshie. I cared immensely about that tree...Maybe I still do, while I'm covertly collecting enemy secrets off the shores of the Galápagos Islands..."

She held a finger to her lips as if to shush them to keep the secret.

"I want to know that proper thought and attention is given to what should happen with this tree. I know that this tree is important to Ellie, too, and she will want to know that it's going to be taken care of for years to come. Once you two sort out the future of our Christmas tree, then the house is all yours,

Josh. If you don't want it, or for some reason you can't handle all this right now, then the property will be auctioned off and proceeds split between you, Josh, and my favorite charities. Jasper can handle all that."

Jasper paused the video. Both Ellie and Josh sat quietly and stared at the laptop screen where Aunt Ruth's image remained frozen on the screen.

Josh shook his head. "What am I supposed to do with a house?"

"Live in it, sell it, say that it's haunted and rent it out to ghost hunters," Jasper suggested. "Whatever you want. She owned the property free and clear, so it is really up to you. And you're welcome to stay there while you're in town. Her trust is covering the expenses until there's a decision."

"This is all so unexpected." Josh processed this out loud. "Let me get this straight. Aunt Ruth wants me to have her house, but we need to do a bunch of Christmas traditions first...?

"Don't forget about that tree," Jasper said. "You and Miss Ellie need to come up with a plan for it. Worry not, Ellie, this isn't all work and no play for you." Jasper pulled an envelope from a folder and handed it to her.

"What's this?" she asked.

"It's a gift from Miss Ruth. In that envelope is a portfolio statement and a letter from your Aunt Ruth. She had a substantial amount of stock in her former company and has gifted you a portion of her holdings."

Ellie peeked inside the envelope at the stock statement. "Quantity 3,000. Aunt Ruth is giving me $3,000 worth of stock? That's incredible!"

Jasper cleared his throat and shifted in his seat a bit.

"Could I take a look at that?" Josh offered. "Do you mind?"

"Please do!" Ellie handed Josh the statement. "That's actually 3,000 shares, not $3,000. And the last price per unit was $165."

"What's that mean?" she asked. "So more than $3,000?"

"A little bit more," Josh said, handing her back the paper. "That's 3,000 shares of stock in her previous company at $165 per share."

Ellie did some quick math on her phone. She gasped. "She left me..." Ellie lowered her voice to a whisper. "Almost five hundred thousand dollars!? How much money did she have?? That's incredible!"

"She was a mighty generous woman," Jasper said.

"I'm really happy for you, Ellie," Josh added.

This was more money than Ellie had ever imagined having. It was almost inconceivable. She pulled a sealed envelope out of the folder and held it in her hands as she ran her thumb over her name, which was written in Aunt Ruth's handwriting.

"Are you going to open it?" Josh asked.

"I will. Later." She tucked it away.

"So," Jasper said. "Any thoughts on the tree? You can come back after you've had some time—"

"Well," Josh started slowly. "I feel like that's pretty straightforward, right?"

Ellie looked at Josh and they both nodded knowingly. She looked straight towards Jasper and said, "We should keep the tree and treasure it forever," Ellie said at the same time that Josh said, "We should donate the tree as the town's Christmas tree."

Ellie snapped her head towards Josh, surprised at his response. "You want to cut it down?"

"And donate it to the town, Ellie, as the community's Christmas tree, to honor Aunt Ruth!"

"Cut it down like some infected pine and leave it to die on display in front of the whole town?"

"Yeah," Josh paused. "I guess it's not as romantic of an idea as I first thought. Now would be a good time for it, though. I mean, the tree is showing some signs of decay and could easily be infected by bugs. Maybe you're right. Maybe keeping it would be a more honorable memorial to Aunt Ruth."

Ellie felt a wave of relief that Josh was coming around.

"On the other hand," Josh continued.

Her heart sank.

"Tree maintenance could be an unpredictable expense. It's an uncertainty that could be avoided. In terms of risk avoidance, limiting exposure to asset hazards and the consequences of unforeseen and unplanned for…"

Ellie couldn't bear the thought of chopping down Aunt Ruth's tree. She also didn't have much leverage. If Josh inherited the house, he could do whatever he wanted with the property, including the tree. But Aunt Ruth said they both had to agree on what to do with the tree before he got the house. So, she had a little leverage. She couldn't just fold and go with what Josh wanted. The tree was too important to her.

"No," Ellie said. "I don't want to cut down the tree. It's too special. Too important. I think you'll realize that, too, Josh. You have so many memories around that tree. We both do. Besides, if we can't agree, then you don't inherit the house." She turned to Jasper. "Right, Jasper? I don't have to do any of it and then he doesn't get the house?"

"Technically," Jasper said, "the only thing Miss Ruth stipulated was that you both must agree on the tree."

"You'll help me with the traditions, right?" Josh looked panicked. "I don't even know anyone here, really. I don't need to inherit the house. I mean, it would be nice, but I'd also be happy with a charity getting a big donation."

Ugh. Ellie couldn't imagine anyone else living in that house, though. The thought had not even crossed her mind until that moment, actually. "You should have the house," she said. "It feels right. I will help you, Josh. Because I am not spiteful enough to make you do the traditions alone. Why would I deprive myself of a wonderful holiday experience?"

"It has nothing to do with me?" Josh smiled.

"Very little," she smiled to herself.

"Well then," Jasper jumped in. "It appears you two need a little more time vis-à-vis the topic of the tree."

Ellie noticed Josh clasping his hands together, a telltale sign that he was stressed out by this situation. She responded the way she always responded when she didn't know what to do— with an exorbitant amount of enthusiasm.

"This is kind of exciting! It could be fun. Plus, it's for Aunt Ruth. We're gonna figure it out, and it's gonna be fun."

"Right." Josh said flatly. He forced as much enthusiasm as he could. "Fun. It could be fun."

Jasper put away the laptop and shuffled through papers on the desk to find a manila folder. "I will share a link with you to Miss Ruth's video. Here is a copy of the paperwork." Jasper handed Josh the folder. "You and Ellie need to both agree on what to do with the tree, then you both need to sign a form with your agreed-upon intention. I can be the witness. Just let me know when you are ready."

"Thanks," Josh took the folder. "Do we need a notary to witness the sign-offs or anything like that?"

Jasper shook his head and threw his hands in the air. "It's like 'esquire' means nothing anymore!" Jasper escorted them towards the door. "I don't know whether you intend to keep the property or sell the property, but I can recommend the real estate agent about three doors down, after you complete the Christmas traditions and get this tree business sorted, of course." He shook each of their hands and then glanced at his wrist. "I do have another appointment, so I have to skedaddle. You don't have to leave, but you can't stay here!" Jasper paused. "Actually, you do have to leave."

Ellie glanced at Josh and smirked. The door jingled again as she and Josh left. "Was he even wearing a watch?" Ellie whispered, hoping she was out of Jasper's earshot.

Outside, she strolled with Josh down the sidewalk along Candy Cane Lane. The downtown was decorated like a little Winter Wonderland; shops had Christmas lights and wreaths in their windows, and light posts had been transformed into giant candy canes with white, red, and green ribbons wrapped around them.

"So..." Josh started. "The tree..."

"Yes. The tree. We could thumb wrestle for it," she joked.

"I think the stakes might be a bit too high in this case for a best-of-three thumb war battle."

"Best of seven? Stanley Cup style?"

"Lord Stanley would never," Josh said. "Hey, what happened to the town's tree anyway? Jasper said it died last year or something?"

"That is kind of a funny story. Last year, the town decided to do a '12 Days of Christmas' theme for the tree decorations. It was really hard to find ten lords a-leaping, ladies dancing, and maids a-milking, you know? A lot of people made their own ornaments to put on the tree, and you know what ends up being super heavy and not good for a tree? Homemade swans and geese and gold ring—" Ellie paused, "actually, someone stole the gold rings, and they were never replaced."

"The ornaments were too heavy?" Josh asked.

"Yeah, so, the tree started leaning because of the weight, and so we added more ornaments to the other side to balance it out."

"Let me guess, that didn't work?"

"Good guess," she said. "It did not. The tree fell completely over. Luckily, it happened overnight, so no one was hurt. It was quite traumatic."

"Yikes. Sounds it."

"Back to our tree situation," Ellie said. "I think we'll figure it out.

It sounds like, assuming you do want to inherit the house, we can just get started with the Christmas traditions while we argue about the tree."

Josh nodded. "Right. We can do that. I'll be in town for probably a week or so. Are you just visiting for the funeral or..."

"Actually, I am living back in Greenville now," Ellie was still not fully comfortable saying it. She loved Greenville, but hated having to explain the backstory of how she was laid off and her mom's health issues. *Maybe he wouldn't ask*, she thought.

"Really? Did you come back after college?"

"No, I moved back here a little over a year ago. I'm back at my mom's house," she sighed heavily. "A bunch of stuff happened...my mom needed to transition into a wheelchair to help her get around...I got laid off from my job...it was just a good opportunity to come home, reset, help my mom."

"That's really cool. Well, I mean, I'm sorry about your job and that it's been tough for your mom, but it must be helpful that you can be around like this. Is she doing okay?"

"She's pretty good most days. There are days when the arthritis is just wreaking havoc, but we've done as much as we can to make her comfortable and make things accessible. She tests my limits sometimes, though."

"R.A., right?" Josh asked.

"Yeah, how'd you know?"

"Aunt Ruth kept me updated."

"Aw, that's sweet. Once my mom started having trouble with mobility, we saw some doctors and have been doing everything we can since then. It sounds like you know all of this, though."

"Is she still fostering dogs?" Josh asked. "I loved when I'd visit and we'd have a companion to throw snowballs at."

Ellie smiled at the memory, but her smile faded as she realized how different things were now. "No. No dogs in the house right now. I think my mom's a little nervous with all the changes." Ellie hadn't talked to her mom about having a dog again. It was an interesting idea, though. Her mom used to love bringing a dog home and letting them run around the house, watching to see how long it took for them to discover the basket of toys that were there for them to play with, introducing them to the most spacious dog bed available on the market, though, Evelyn had a hard time not letting them sleep on the couch if that's where they preferred.

"What about you?" Josh asked, interrupting Ellie's train of thought. "What else have you been up to?"

"Oh, I've been working with Taylor at her shop part-time. You remember Tay."

"Of course. She's great."

"She is great," Ellie agreed. "Sometimes I pick up freelance graphic design gigs here and there, so I can keep the resume fresh, you know?"

Josh chuckled. For a few moments, the only sounds were their shoes crunching rock salt on the sidewalk and a tinny-sounding version of "The Little Drummer Boy" coming from a speaker hidden in a winterberry shrub.

"Christmas is going to be so different this year without Aunt Ruth," Ellie sighed. "She was young. I thought I'd have so many more Christmases with her. At this point, I'd take just one more year together. A little bit more time."

She looked at Josh. He nodded solemnly.

They come upon a bench in front of Turnkey Real Estate's office. It was adorned with a plaque that read:

THIS BENCH GENEROUSLY DONATED BY JANNIE
TURNKEY AND HER CONTRACTOR HUSBAND
TUCKER. VALUABLE AND RESPECTED MEMBERS OF
OUR COMMUNITY.

Josh sat and motioned for Ellie to sit as well.

"She loved this time of year," Josh said. "I'll miss her a lot. It's kind of special that we have this little assignment to work on in her honor, though." He looked around. "It feels good to be back here. I feel closer to her here. Lots of good memories."

"Honestly, I'm still a little shocked to be sitting here with THE Joshua Hanson. In the flesh."

"You didn't think I'd come back here, even to honor my favorite aunt?"

"No, no, no...that's not it. Of course you'd come back for this. I just can't imagine you staying very long. I would think that you'd be trying to get out of town and get back to work."

"You know me, work-work-work."

"Probably right on track to conquering the investment world, right?"

"Yeah...well..." Josh paused. "I've sort of been in a rut lately, you know? I'm looking forward to clearing my head while I'm here. I need to go through some things at Aunt Ruth's house, so it should be a nice change of pace."

"Are you thinking of making a change?"

"I don't know, seems a little soon to be thinking about making changes to her house—"

"No, I mean in your *life*. You said you're in a rut. Are you going to be making any changes in your life?"

"I don't know, maybe? I don't really know what that would even look like. To have something like this happen, Aunt Ruth passing away, inheriting a house, it's kind of overwhelming to think about major changes on top of that."

"If you could be doing anything right now, in your wildest dreams, what would it be?" Ellie loved these types of questions and knew Josh didn't.

"I hate these types of questions," he said.

"I know. Humor me."

"I love what I do. I don't think I'd want to change that. I'm not really a beach person, so I'm not dreaming of being a beach bum. I guess maybe I'd work for myself. Have my own investment firm."

"What's stopping you?"

Josh sat quietly. "Oh, you know, I guess, just the regular stuff. I don't want to throw away all the years I've put into my job. I have bills and expenses and, I guess, just general uncertainty. That's a big part."

"What if you didn't, though? I mean, you could live in Aunt Ruth's house, you could meet with clients anywhere until you could afford an office; you're not throwing away all your experience, you're just rolling it into something new."

"Having Aunt Ruth's house does kind of open up some new possibilities, I suppose."

Ellie didn't love his use of the word 'possibilities' there. Like when you have something you don't want, so you frame it as a 'great opportunity' for someone else. Ellie looked sharply at Josh. "You wouldn't sell it, would you?" She watched his reaction with an eagle eye.

Josh looked at her and then looked away. "I mean, it would be fiscally irresponsible not to explore the market. That's just the nerdy finance guy in me. It's who I am. I'll have to look at that." He glanced at Ellie. "But, in the name of thoroughness, I should consider keeping it, too."

Josh Hanson the diplomat. "That is, assuming you have a house to stay in." Ellie smacked Josh on the leg and stood up. We still have to agree on what to do with Aunt Ruth's tree before that house is yours."

Josh stood up, too. "And apparently some cookies to bake and some carols to sing..."

"Don't forget about the scorpions!"

They laughed at the memory from Aunt Ruth's video.

"So," Ellie said, getting serious. "Are we doing this? We're gonna figure this out?"

"I think so...I think we should," Josh sounded weary and like he was trying to convince himself.

"I'm gonna need a little more enthusiasm from you. Come on, pretend you just checked your Financial Times e-zine or whatever, and commodities are in the tank in Asia."

"I think you mean commodities are rising in Asia, but yeah, I gotcha." Josh hopped up and down a few times to pump himself up. "Okay...okay...let's do this! Christmas Traditions! Let's go!"

"Go Team El-osh!"

Josh froze, confused. "Team El-osh? What is that?"

"Yeah, that's, like, one of those celebrity couple names, but for our mission. Like a team name."

Josh thought hard for a second. "How about Team J-Ellie? That's better, right?"

"Way better. They're not ready for Team Jellie!"

Ellie checked the time on her phone. "It's getting late. I've gotta run. I told Tay I'd help her at the choffee shop this afternoon."

"It was great to see you, Ellie."

They hugged, a familiar, comfortable embrace. Josh stretched out his hands as Ellie stepped back, and they held hands for an extra second.

"Later, gator," she said as she strolled away.

6

TURNING A NEW KEY

JOSH - SATURDAY AFTERNOON

JOSH COULDN'T HELP BUT SMILE as he watched Ellie turn and walk away. He knew he had some big choices to make in the very near future. He had to consider all options. He also needed the reality check he got from Ellie. She could see things so simply sometimes and help him sort through the layers of what-ifs and conditions that swirled around a single decision. She was a breath of fresh air.

Josh looked around downtown. He noticed the Turnkey Real Estate window behind him, which was plastered with FOR SALE and SOLD property fliers. *Hm. Let the decision fatigue begin.*

A bell jingled atop the door as Josh entered the real estate offices. The Turnkey Real Estate office was tidy with a small reception area that doubled as a storage area for signs and a life-sized cardboard cutout of "Jannie Turnkey: Greenville's Most Trusted Agent," a seemingly successful big shot businesswoman who was holding an oversized golden key and wearing a giant, confident smile.

Josh walked in during what sounded like one of the greatest real estate pump-up speeches of all time. From the reception area, Josh could see into each office through the glass walls. A woman, around his age, sat at a desk, hurriedly packing papers and manila folders into her work bag, which looked like it could double as an equipment bag for the Boston Bruins back-up goaltender. She had familiar-looking, deep red hair, a bright red blouse, and was trying to soak up as much confidence as she could from another woman who resembled the cutout figure in the reception area.

"You've got to be a *killer*, Shelb." the real-life version of Jannie Turnkey said. "You know this market better than *anyone*. This is your deal."

The woman Josh presumed was Shelb nodded affirmatively.

"It's a huge deal, Shelb. This is no time to be timid."

Shelb shook her head 'No.'

"Walk in there like you own the place," Jannie continued. "You know what needs to be done, and you just need to *tell* them what it is."

Shelb stood up confidently. Jannie made a circular motion with one hand and then excessively sprayed perfume in Shelb's direction with the other hand as she twirled around and around and around.

Jannie put down the perfume bottle and handed Shelb her bag. "Go get 'em."

Shelb stiffened her posture and marched confidently towards the door with her bag and paperwork, protected by a thick layer of Estee Lauder armor.

"That's my girl," Jannie said under her breath.

All of the built-up momentum was quickly halted when Shelb noticed Josh in the reception area.

"Hello. I'm sorry, I didn't hear you come in."

"No, I'm sorry," Josh said. "I didn't mean to interrupt. You seem busy. I can come back another time."

As she walked closer, she froze. They both seemed to have the same flashback to the traffic incident earlier that day.

"Hey," Josh said, realizing she had been in the car behind Ellie at the stoplight. "You beeped at me."

"You were blocking traffic!" she replied, crossing her arms in front of her.

"Now, now, Shelbie," Jannie said as she joined the conversation. "Let's not scare away potential customers." Without skipping a beat, she turned to Josh and reached out her hand. "Hi, I'm Jannie Turnkey of Turnkey Real Estate. This is my daughter, and associate agent, Shelbie. Say hi, Shelbie." Shelbie offered a tight-lipped wave and Jannie continued. "What brings you in today Mr....?"

"Josh. My name's Josh," he began, "I recently learned that I've inherited a piece of property in town."

"How great! Congratulations!" Shelbie turned on the enthusiasm.

"It was something my aunt left to me in her will..."

"Shelbie, please, have some decorum," Jannie scolded. She turned to Josh and tilted her head sympathetically. "I am so sorry for your loss. If there is anything we can do to make this time easier for you, do let us know. Shelbie, tell him about our firm and our services. Get him an intake form to fill out. Josh, if you write down some basic information, we can put together a property analysis for you, completely free of charge, no strings. It's just one of the many complimentary services we provide to the community. Respectfully, I do have a meeting, so I have to scoot. It was so nice meeting you, Josh." Jannie Turnkey whisked out the door before Josh could say good-bye.

"Well," Shelbie said, handing Josh a clipboard with a questionnaire on it, "we're a full-service brokerage so we can help you with market research, listing photos, finding qualified buyers, all the, um—" Shelbie handed Josh a business card. "You know, all the stuff you might need to—"

Josh looked at the card and then looked at the cardboard cutout.

"That's my mom. And that was my mom," Shelbie explained, motioning towards the door. "She's really good. I mean, we're really good. I can help you. I can sell. And home values in town have held very steady due to the proximity to—"

"It's okay," Josh interrupted. "I'm really just looking for some basic market info, maybe some recently sold properties, very basic stuff. I am not even sure I am going to sell yet, honestly." Josh scribbled his contact information on the questionnaire.

"Phew," Shelbie sighed. "Honestly, I'm kinda new to this and not completely comfortable working in the family business yet. Not like her." Shelbie nodded towards the cardboard cutout. "She's Greenville's renowned real estate broker. I mean, I like some of it. I really like the home staging phase. Ever since I was little, I would tag along with my mom to client meetings and open houses."

"And now?" Josh asked.

"Now it's time to continue the family legacy," Shelbie said, unconvincingly.

"Well, I am just doing research today, so the legacy is not at risk."

"Of course." Shelbie gathered some listing sheets and handed them to Josh. "Here are a few of our recent sales and current listings so you can get an idea of the market."

"Great!" Josh said. "Well, it was good to meet you." Josh handed Shelbie the complete questionnaire. "I'll be in touch."

7

TELL TAY ABOUT IT

ELLIE - SATURDAY LATE AFTERNOON

ELLIE'S MIND WAS SPINNING. She had started her day at Aunt Ruth's funeral, and, while it was nice to be with so many familiar faces to celebrate and honor Aunt Ruth's life, she felt like she was in a fog the whole time. This was followed by the completely unexpected double whammy of seeing Josh and finding out about the gift from Aunt Ruth. She felt like, in order to fully absorb the letter from Aunt Ruth, she needed to read it in a place that was special. After saying goodbye to Josh, Ellie headed to the most special place she knew. Aunt Ruth's tree. She had to be at work soon, but this was important.

She followed the tracks she had made in the snow from her driveway over to Aunt Ruth's tree, her breath like a winter cloud with every exhale. Ellie took the envelope from her coat pocket and carefully opened it.

Dear Ellie,

As I sit and write this letter to you, I can't imagine a day without you in it. I'm sure that's how you feel reading this right now. I'm sorry to leave you, dear. Everything has a life, you know that. I've said that for years. I lived a good one. No. I lived a great one. And it was all because of the people in my life. I met some really great people. I traveled all over the world. My job kept me busy, but I got to experience so many things and met so many people because of it. I feel fulfilled. Getting to watch you grow up, and be part of your life, it felt like a bonus family. I never got married or had any children of my own. When I made that choice, part of me was afraid that I was choosing to miss out on a special part of life. I accepted that at the time. Little did I know I'd move in next door to the kindest, sweetest, most lovable little girl. (That's you!) I made another choice after we met. I chose to be a positive and reliable person in your life, if you were accepting of me. Thank you for accepting me and letting me be part of your life. It truly made each day extra special.

So, by now, you should have noticed that I left you some money. I wish I could leave you a hug or some homemade cookies. (Well, I did leave some of those, too. Just ask Josh for some.) I was able to save enough to support myself and also help some others. I was so grateful to be able to put aside some of it for you. This is all yours to do with what you please. You can let it sit and not touch it for another twenty years, or you can cash it out immediately. Just please do talk to someone who knows about these things because there are tax implications and blah, blah, blah.

Speaking of Josh—

DING

"Shoot!" Ellie was interrupted by a calendar reminder that she was supposed to be at work in five minutes.

"Sorry I'm running a little late," Ellie said as she shuffled into Tay's Hot Choffee Shop. "I had to run home for something."

"You can never be late, my dear, my first employee," Tay said. "You have carte blanche on your schedule. Wait," Tay looked at Ellie and froze. "Home? Where were you coming from?"

Ellie hung up her coat and grabbed one of the many festive aprons that the crew shared. The local hot chocolate and coffee fusion shop was bustling with activity. The bell at the front door dinged as the line of customers ordering drinks and pastry grew longer. Ellie assumed her position next to Tay and squeezed her from the side. "How are you, friend?"

"Oh, dandy," Tay said, pulling the lever on the espresso machine. Her long, braided hair was protected under a bandana decorated with peace signs. "Yourself?"

"It's been a day," Ellie helped add milk, whipped cream, and festive sprinkles to drinks.

"I know we're coffee-affirming here, but do spill the tea," Tay nudged her friend.

"Well," Ellie began. "I had a literal run-in with Josh Hanson after Aunt Ruth's funeral. I was on my way to the lawyer's office, because Mr. McGillicutty asked me to stop by around noon, and Josh came right out into traffic while I was stopped at a red light!"

"What! How funny!"

"We saw each other so he said hi, but the light turned green so..."

"You gotta go."

"I had to go."

"That was it? What a weird way to see Josh after all those years."

"Not exactly. Oh—we're out of cinnamon. I'll be right back."

"Girl, hurry!"

Ellie hustled to return with cinnamon and nutmeg and jumped back in. "So, when I got to the lawyer's, guess who was there."

"Rodney Dangerfield."

"Warm. Love the throwback."

"Rob Lowe."

'Warmer."

"Hilary Duff."

"No, Josh!"

Ellie and Taylor both stopped working on drinks to face each other.

"I was way off on Duff," Taylor admitted. "I misread that completely. That's my bad."

"It's fine. Can you believe it?"

"Josh was there? That's odd. It wasn't a family Will reading or anything, right? Just a meeting with you two and Aunt Ruth's lawyer?"

"Right. It turns out that Josh inherited her house."

"Ohmygosh, that's so nice!"

"Yeah, but there are a few conditions." Ellie smiled and stared into space, imagining the Christmas traditions with Josh. "We have to complete a bunch of Christmas traditions like baking Aunt Ruth's favorite cookies, caroling around town, and some other—"

"Wait," Taylor interrupted. "What do you mean *we*? Both of you have to do it?"

"That's the bonkers part! Aunt Ruth's Will says Josh and I have to do these Christmas traditions together, and we both have to agree on whether or not to keep the Christmas tree in her yard. Even from heaven she's found a way to have a special impact on this holiday season."

"Playing matchmaker from heaven."

"Hey! It's not like that!"

"It sure seems like that! Look at you, Ellie. All smiles and giddy again. Ohhh, Joshie...my Joshie-poo...you're so cute and good with numbers...and—"

"That was just a summer fling! We were both home for college break. Everyone has one of those."

The bell continued to *ding* each time a customer entered. Ellie looked up each time, hopeful that she'd see a familiar face.

"Expecting someone?" Tay said without looking at her.

Ellie bit her lip, trying to hold back a smile.

"You hearing this, Laura?" Tay looked over at the bookstore owner and choffee shop regular who was waiting for her order. "We may have our very own second-chance romance on our hands."

"Oooh," Laura leaned on the counter. "A rekindled romance? We could use some good news. Do tell."

"It's nothing, really," Ellie interrupted.

"Nothing...yet," Tay added as she handed Laura her order.

Ellie watched as Laura returned to her table where the other Lunch Ladies were sitting. "Great, like I need to be on the Lunch Ladies gossip agenda."

The rest of the table looked over at Ellie with intrigue. She smiled and waved.

"Right...so what happens if you don't finish all of the conditions? Or if he doesn't want to do it?" Tay said.

"The house goes to auction. He gets some of the proceeds, but the house goes to the highest bidder. I just can't imagine anyone else living in that house."

"Seems risky, no? Why would Aunt Ruth want to give her house to either her beloved nephew, or send it to auction for anyone to have? Those are such different options."

"I know. Part of me thinks that Aunt Ruth did that on purpose because sending the house to auction seems like she is just throwing it away. And she knew that Josh would never want that to happen. Maybe she thought it would make the decision for Josh that much easier? Aunt Ruth did write me a letter."

"She did? That's so sweet. What's it say?"

"I started reading it but haven't finished. Maybe it explains things a bit more."

"You what? You haven't read it yet? Ellie! How? Why? You need to read that."

"I will. I just don't want to rush through it. I want to be in the right place."

"I get that," Tay said. "So, what will Josh do when he inherits the house?"

"I don't know." Ellie hadn't thought this far ahead. "I assume he'd live in it? He already has a life somewhere else, though. He did say he's kind of in a rut and may be looking to shake things up?"

"HA! Yeah! That's the Josh Hanson we all know. The one who likes to," Tay shook their hands wildly, "shake things up!"

"Maybe we'll have such a magical time that he won't be able to imagine his life anywhere else."

"Just like one of those made-for-TV Christmas movies. Maybe Marcus Rosner could play Josh? He's a delight."

Ellie's thoughts drifted to memories of her and Josh. Rolling snowballs across the lawn until they were so big they couldn't move them another inch. Summer afternoons running through a sprinkler. Summer nights making 'smores. "Maybe he would stay..."

Ellie thought aloud.

"Ahem..." An audible groan came from the line of customers who were waiting for Ellie and Taylor to make their drinks. Someone else cleared their throat loudly. Taylor and Ellie returned to working at their stations.

"Ellie, do you remember that time in high school when the class president was going to get rid of the vending machines that had those really gross but delicious brownie cakes, and you were dead set against it? Do you remember what you did?"

Ellie smiled fondly at the memory. "I offered to help him. I made sure we ate so many snacks out of those vending machines that he couldn't bear to do away with them."

"Exactly. Do the same thing! You crush any plans Josh has to give up the house with kindness. Swoon him with sweetness."

"Right. If he's enjoying himself, why would he want to leave?" Ellie liked this idea. "It's worth a shot."

Taylor handed Ellie two to-go coffee cups. One with *Joshie* written on it, and the other labeled *JBRML*. "And it starts with coffee."

Ellie smiled as she grabbed the coffees and headed out the door to win over Josh. Or at least try to have some fun together.

The waiting customers collectively groaned and threw their hands up in the air as Ellie left the choffee shop.

Ellie sat in her car for a moment. She took out the letter from Aunt Ruth and continued reading from where she left off.

Speaking of Josh. I want him to have my house.

My dream is for him to live here, next door to your mom. And I do have some ideas of where you would live, but I will keep them to myself for now. I really want him to get to enjoy this town the way you have and I have. It's a great place to be, and I fear that he has become so consumed with working and feeling successful in his career that he'll forget how much he loved being here and how much he loves....well...He's the only one who can decide what is best for him, but I want to provide as much opportunity as I can for him to figure it out. And for you, too.

So on to the conditions. I made the house conditional on Josh doing some of my favorite traditions, and I want you to help him, Ellie. My greatest wish, beyond you and Josh living long and happy lives, is that you help him with these holiday traditions. Please do them together. It would make my soul so happy. I know it's silly. I know you two aren't as close as you used to be. Just humor me. One last time.

As for the tree, it's a special tree. It's our special tree. I can't give you the tree and then give Josh the house. Short of a special easement that carves out that part of the property, which you could look into with the town, all I can really do is make you two talk about it and agree that you want to keep the tree up or cut down the tree. I just want you to have a say and some peace of mind. Worst-case scenario, Josh clears the yard to make it more marketable and then sells the house. I know that would upset you, and that's the last thing I want. I love you so much, Ellie. You're a bright, shining star, and you brought so much joy to my life. Until we meet again.

Love always,
Aunt Ruth

Ellie started her car and turned on the window defroster. The steam from the hot coffees had completely fogged up her windows. She wanted to do this for Aunt Ruth. This was a way to respect her wishes and feel close to her this season. She folded the letter and put it back in its envelope, and then back into her pocket. For the first time in a long time, Ellie felt a glimmer of hope.

8

AUNT RUTH'S HOUSE

JOSH – SATURDAY LATE AFTERNOON

JOSH FINALLY MADE HIS WAY to his Aunt Ruth's house. He hadn't been there in a while—way too long since his last visit, actually—but it was just as he remembered it. Except it was exceptionally quiet. He could feel that she was not there. He always knew when his Aunt Ruth was around. If she wasn't hugging him, or chatting with him, she was singing or humming nearby. Or even far away. Was she clinging and clanging things in another room because she was actually looking for something or working on something, or did she just want people to know she was there? What he wouldn't give to hear her whistling The Ronettes' version of "Sleigh Ride" from another room.

Aunt Ruth was a godsend in Josh's life since he was so much younger than his siblings. For the first 9 years of his life, he had to find ways to entertain himself over winter and summer breaks. His brother and sister had their own friends, and his mom and dad were busy with their own lives. They had already done the kid-raising thing. Twice.

Josh stepped through Aunt Ruth's living room. He spent more time than he ever had inspecting the furniture and decorations that filled the space. Had he ever actually looked inside the large hutch? She had this giant hutch for as long as Josh could remember. Inside the wide, center drawer were awards and medals that Josh had won over the years and had shared with Aunt Ruth. *She kept them all.*

At the bottom of the stack of memorabilia was the first class assignment he had brought to Aunt Ruth. It was from the first week of school and titled "What I Did Over Summer" and it was about the first time he visited Aunt Ruth when he was ten.

> What I Did Over Summer by Josh Hanson
> This summer I visited my Aunt Ruth. My parents went away for work, so I went on a trip. I was supposed to go for one week. Then I stayed for another week because it was so much fun. But I didn't want to go home, and Aunt Ruth said I could stay for the whole summer! It was so much fun. We played and we talked, and we hung out. My Aunt Ruth is my best friend. I had the best summer of my life. I cannot wait to go back.

He remembered that first summer at Aunt Ruth's. They did fun stuff, sure, but mostly they just spent time together and talked. He didn't feel like a little kid when he was with her. After that summer, he spent as much time visiting Aunt Ruth's as he could.

Down the first-floor hallway was the spare bedroom Aunt Ruth used to set it up as a playroom when Josh would visit. It had been converted into Aunt Ruth's gift-wrapping room. A folding table at the center of the room, surrounded by rolls and rolls of wrapping paper, all the tape anyone could ever wish for, and gift boxes of all shapes and sizes.

Josh walked back through the living room with the big bay window and into the kitchen, where he and Aunt Ruth had spent so many hours. Her tea kettle was full of water and ready, like always. Holiday hand towels, Santa and Mrs. Claus salt-and-pepper shakers, and her Christmas tree cookie jar were on full display. Josh peeked inside, delighted to find it full of homemade cookies. He made those cookies with Aunt Ruth so many times, and they came out perfectly every time. Whenever he tried to make them on his own, they just never tasted the same. They were just missing something. He took a bite and sank into a warm kitchen on a cold day, a smile and a hug at just the right time, a tiny moment of pure joy. *Mmm.*

Josh pulled a box of pictures from the hall closet and placed it on the kitchen island. More recent photos were on top, so he dug to the bottom of the box to find the older ones and flipped through pictures of him and Ellie over the years. So few photos of Aunt Ruth, he realized. Josh felt his face relax and realized he had been smiling since he pulled out the first picture.

A sound startled Josh. A sound he hadn't heard in a long time. It was a half ding followed by a buzz. Aunt Ruth's doorbell, which had been losing its bell sound for as long as he could remember. The sound was quickly followed by a knock, and he knew exactly who was at the door.

"Ellie! What a pleasant surprise," Josh said as he opened the front door. He meant it, too. He was excited to see her again and be around someone he had been so close to in the past.

"Good afternoon! I come bearing caffeine!" Ellie smiled.

Josh noticed the coffee in each of her hands. "I hope you're not drinking one of those Jingle Bell Reindeer Mocha Lattes..."

Ellie quickly turned her cup so he could not see the *JBRML* that Tay scribbled on the cup.

"Come on in," Josh opened the door and made way for Ellie.

Ellie spotted the familiar box on the kitchen island and immediately headed that way. "Ohhh...you found Aunt Ruth's old photos."

"Yeah, I've been going down memory lane a bit here."

Ellie picked up a photo of ten-year-old Ellie and Josh during wintertime. Both kids were smiling at the camera, all dressed up in snow pants and winter coats, cheeks as red as Rudolph's nose.

"Remember that?" Josh asked.

"How could I forget? That was the year we met."

Ellie picked another photo of them at about the same age during summer, being sprayed with water from a hose. "We were drenched."

"That water was so cold."

"We'd change into pajamas and dry our clothes outside on the clothesline, then sit around the fire pit and make s'mores."

"My clothes would smell like the smoke from the fire for a week." Josh stopped short of telling Ellie how sad he would get when the smoky scent faded. He reached into a box and pulled out a photo of him and Ellie holding the "2008" handmade angel ornament that Ellie made. "Who knew these crazy kids would end up right back here in this kitchen..."

"She probably did. I'm going to miss that about her. It always felt like she knew exactly what she was doing. She always seemed to be doing exactly the right thing."

Josh was quiet for a moment. "You know, Ellie, um, we've never really talked about that summer after our first year of college. I guess the main thing I want to say is that I'm sorry I didn't try harder to make the long-distance thing work. Once we got back to school, I fell into my routine and just—I wish I had been better. Even if it still didn't work out, I wish I had been able to explain the things I was feeling to you."

"Yeah, that was hard. I transferred from Plymouth to Maine College of Art for my second year. I hardly knew anyone there. We went from full speed to pretty much zero within a few months, and not seeing each other over the holidays didn't help. It was rough. But I met Alex that second semester and we were together for a few years. Plus, you got super busy with finance and doing what you love, so we both kinda moved on."

Josh felt bad, still. He didn't mean to let things between them fizzle out like that. He also didn't know how to express what he was feeling. He wanted to give Ellie a giant bear hug and squeeze her tightly. Instead, he put an arm around Ellie's shoulders and pulled her in for a side hug.

"Thanks, Josh." Ellie sat at the dining room table with her coffee. "I felt so optimistic back then and so sure of what was to come," she said. "Now? I feel completely unsure about what I'm supposed to be doing. I don't feel the way that I thought I would."

"Well, you've made some tough choices. I think that's to be expected." Josh joined Ellie at the table. "Sometimes it's easy just to stay the course and not make a change. You're balancing lots of plates. Of course it feels a little uneasy. I think Aunt Ruth would be really proud of you."

"Thanks. I hope so." Ellie took a deep breath. "Enough about me. Let's hear about your deepest insecurities."

"HA! Well, my biggest flaw is that I care too much."

Ellie folded her hands as if she were conducting a mock job interview. "Where do you see yourself in five years?"

Josh chuckled. His smile faded slowly as he made his way back to the photos on the kitchen counter. "You know, everything has been going according to plan for me, career-wise. I always anticipated this feeling of elation when I, quote-unquote, "made it" and became "successful." But now I am at a point I always dreamed of, yet I still feel like I am chasing something. I've started having this weird desire to scale back, work more closely with people, more one-on-one, setting people up for a secure future. Getting back to the fun stuff, for me anyway. It's funny, the timing of everything. Selling this house would really provide a big cushion and the opportunity to invest for the long-term."

"Do you really need to sell the house to do that?" Ellie said. "Just start a podcast like everyone else. You'd never have to change out of your pajamas. Better yet, start a podcast about something fun like reviewing Christmas movies."

"Talk about a Hindenburg of an idea."

They both looked towards the front door when they heard that familiar half-ding/half-buzz sound. Before either could move, Shelbie burst in through the front door.

"HellooOOOooo...the door is open...it's Shelbie Turnkey...anyone home—" Shelbie spotted the two in the kitchen. "Oh, there you are, Josh!"

Josh was equally surprised and uncomfortable. "Hi...Shelbie? I didn't expect to see you today..."

"My scheduled meeting ended early. He had a duct emergency."

"A *duck* emergency?" Josh asked, confused.

"Duct." Shelbie clarified. "Air duct emergency. He's a commercial client. Always something going wrong in those buildings. So, I figured, two birds, one stone, just stop here on my way back to the office."

"Maybe even two *ducks*, one stone," Ellie offered awkwardly.

Shelbie forced a dry laugh while Josh smirked and nodded his head to acknowledge the clever wordplay. Shelbie swiftly clacked into the kitchen on her high heels. She was carrying a wreath and a gigantic handbag that would probably not even meet TSA standards as a carry-on. Her big personality and pungent perfume added a whole new dynamic to the room. As she approached the kitchen island, Shelbie moved the boxes of photos over and placed a stack of paperwork down on the counter.

"Oh, this place is lovely," Shelbie looked around the house. "Old timey, spacious, nice yard. Hopefully the neighbors keep to themselves."

"Shelbie," Josh interrupted, "This is Ellie. She lives next door with her mom."

"Oh, hey, Ellie!" Shelbie was unfazed. "So nice to meetchu!" Shelbie tossed the wreath at Josh. "Hang this on the front door. Potential home buyers love to see Christmas decorations." She noticed the kitchen oven. "Do you bake? Never mind." She took off down the hallway to explore the space.

"Well," Ellie said. "I think it's time for me to get going."

"Oh, ok," Josh noticed her do that thing with her eyes where she looks to one side. Usually that look was paired with a sing-songy 'Awkwarddddd.' He could tell she did not feel comfortable. "I'll catch up with you later...thanks for the coffee," Josh said as he chased after Shelbie.

Josh found Shelbie in Aunt Ruth's gift-wrapping room with a tape measure in one hand. "Do you know if this wall is load-bearing?" she said.

"I don't know, Shelbie. Look, this really isn't a good time." Josh followed her back towards the kitchen. "Like I said, I am not even sure I'd want to sell this place. I'm just doing some research."

Shelbie sat and suddenly appeared exhausted. "I know. I'm sorry. I'm just really trying to show my mom that I can have initiative. She says to not even step foot inside a property until you have a signed seller's agreement."

"Is that what those papers are for?" Josh said, pointing to the stack of papers she dropped on the countertop.

"Yes. Just in case. I'm not going to pressure you or anything. I'm not really like that anyhow. But I want to be the first one you call in case—"

"You would be. But no more barging in here. What if I were just wearing a towel?"

Shelbie blushed.

9

A TRUCE

ELLIE – SUNDAY MORNING

"COME ON, MOM! YOUR BREAKFAST IS READY!" Ellie called out as two pieces of perfectly golden sourdough popped up from the toaster and she recounted the impromptu visit with Josh at Aunt Ruth's house. She thought it would be sweet, and it mostly was until the real estate agent came in like a tornado. Was Josh so serious about selling the house that he had already started talking to agents? It felt like things were moving very fast. And when Shelbie started surveying the layout? *Awkwarddddd.*

Evelyn wheeled into the kitchen with a book on her lap. "I see you were sketching last night. You doing okay, El?"

While her sketchbook used to be a sign that Ellie was feeling creative and inspired, it had become more of an escape for her and a signal of stress these days. Ellie brought her mom's toast and eggs to the table and the two sat together.

"I don't know," Ellie began. She glanced out the window towards the tree in Aunt Ruth's yard. Then she explained to her mom that she had seen Josh, the meeting with the lawyer about Aunt Ruth's Will, the investment account, Josh potentially selling the house, and the range of emotions she was feeling after that roller coaster of a day.

"So that's what Ruthie ended up doing," Her mom did not seem overly surprised.

"You *knew*?" Ellie, on the other hand, was surprised.

"Well, I knew she had a plan for when she passed. I didn't know the details. She often talked about how much you kids meant to her and wanted to do something special for you both."

"Well I don't like it." Ellie knew she was being childish, but if she couldn't act like a baby in front of her mother, when could she?

"I think she knew that, whatever the outcome, you and Josh spending this time together would be fun."

"I hope she's having a good laugh at my expense."

"Okay, maybe fun wasn't the goal. Maybe she knew that you two spending this time together, grieving together, would benefit the both of you. It's been a tough few years for you."

"For you, too, Mom." Ellie hugged her mom. "Alright, I gotta run. I told Tay I'd help her through the early rush."

Ellie spent a couple hours helping Tay. Mixing drinks, clearing crumbs off tables, chatting with friends. She was feeling better. Maybe it was the customers, maybe it was the Christmas music, but she felt better. And she decided to give her positivity campaign another try.

She stood at the foot of Aunt Ruth's walkway for a moment and looked over at the tree. It was decorated, not nearly as full as it would be if Aunt Ruth were there, but it was decorated. Aunt Ruth liked to bring out the ladder to fill the branches as high as she could with strands of lights. Sometimes she'd string popcorn, but birds and squirrels would inevitably eat that. This year, though, the tree looked sort of how Ellie felt. It put forth an effort to show some holiday spirit, but there was still some space to fill in.

She looked up towards the clear blue sky, then forced a pep in her step as she walked up to the front door with a coffee in each hand. "Remember to be nice, Ellie," she said to herself. "Be super nice." Ellie placed the coffees on the doorstep, put her hair up in a high ponytail, took a deep breath, and then rang the doorbell.

DING-BZZZZ

When Josh opened the door, Ellie smiled brightly and extended one arm to hold out a coffee for Josh.

"Morning!" she said.

"Two days in a row, huh? Did I sign up for a coffee delivery service I don't know about?"

As she entered the house, she spotted a box of Christmas tree cake donuts on the counter. "Ooooh, these are great," she said.

"I know! I found them at Rex's downtown. That store is great!" Josh lifted the box to offer her a donut. "They're like a Christmas tree cake, but in a donut."

She saw the stack of papers the real estate agent left on the countertop. "So," she began her niceness campaign. "How did your real estate meeting go?"

"It was fine." He put the donut box down. "Got some good information about the market. Definitely have some things to think about."

Ellie nodded along, waiting for him to finish talking so she could move on to the real reason she was there.

"Hey, about that," Josh continued. "I'm sorry I didn't say goodbye when Shelbie showed up."

"It's okay, really," Ellie dismissed it. "But, if you are going to dip your toes into the market and have people looking at the house, I think she has a point. People really should see it decorated for Christmas."

"Yeah? I didn't think you'd be on board with the idea of listing the house for sale."

"Cards on the table...I am not, and what better way to ruin it than from the inside? Seriously, though, even if you decide not to sell it, you still need some decorations around here."

"True. It could feel a little more festive around here, couldn't it?"

"We could go to the downtown Christmas market and start looking around," Ellie suggested. "Maybe tomorrow?"

"I wouldn't dare decline, especially when you're rocking the high pony."

She caught him flashing his eyebrows in a way he used to when they were younger.

"It's a date," they said simultaneously. She wondered if he'd remember their silly jinx bit from when they were younger.

Ellie snapped a look at Josh excitedly. They both continued.

"Jinx! Pinch poke, you owe me a Coke! You're in a pickle, it's a pretty big dill!"

Ellie held Josh in an intense stare down. Finally, he broke. *Victory.*

Josh grabbed two cans of Coke from the fridge, they each exchanged cans, tapped the palms of their hands together, tapped the backs of their hands together, and shook hands. A routine they had performed hundreds of times.

"Truce," she said.

"Truce," Josh repeated. And the truce was in effect.

10

TOWN HALL

JOSH – MONDAY MORNING

JOSH WOKE UP FEELING SOMETHING he hadn't felt in a long time. He felt downright giddy. He couldn't remember the last time he woke up with genuine, unencumbered excitement. Riding the wave of energy, he brewed some coffee and grabbed his work laptop. He hadn't used it in days. It's been years since he had gone more than a day without doing some form of work.

To give Ellie some ideas of what she could do with the investment account Aunt Ruth left her, he ran some investment analysis scenarios for her. He ran some quant models, some risk models, and some allocation optimization models for her. And for fun. Her risk tolerance could be low, medium, or high, so he modeled out all three to cover the bases. *What a rush.*

Josh saved the files on his laptop and set it aside. Then, prepared for a sacred tradition he shared with Aunt Ruth. One that they repeated nearly every other morning when Josh visited. He prepared to make their favorite buttermilk pancake recipe. Not only had Aunt Ruth taught him how to read a recipe, but more importantly, she taught him how to interpret a recipe. They were both sticklers for rules and for doing something the way that it was supposed to be done. But once that was done, improvements were fair game. Auth Ruth and Josh would spend hours experimenting with recipes, adjusting the ingredient amounts, or even adding or removing ingredients altogether, trying to make a recipe that much better. All in the name of chasing that wide-eyed look from someone when they tasted something that absolutely exceeded their expectations. Cooking in her kitchen again felt so familiar, yet so lonely. Just as Josh finished mixing the pancake batter and set the bowl next to the stove to sit for about ten minutes, he heard a knock at the door.

She's early, he thought, as he opened the door. Instead, nothing. Nothing except an envelope on the welcome mat. 'To: Ms. Ruth Matthews' was scribbled on it. Josh picked up the envelope and looked around, but he didn't see anyone outside.

Back inside the kitchen, Josh opened the envelope. He read the paper carefully. It was a 2nd violation notice written on some very official-looking Town of Greenville Christmas Planning Committee letterhead. Something about a yard decoration? *But she doesn't have any yard decorations.*

He set aside the letter and returned to the pancake batter. It was just about ready.

He turned on the stove, got the pan nice and hot, and then scooped the first two ladles full of batter into the pan. Then, another knock on the door. This time it was accompanied with the familiar doorbell buzz. *That's gotta be Ellie.*

Josh opened the door and found a bundled-up Ellie. He could only see her eyes since her coat was zipped up to her nose and she had a winter hat pulled down to her eyebrows, but he was pretty confident it was her.

"Ooh, what's that smell?" Ellie said, as she loaded a chair up with her coat, scarf, mittens, and hat.

"I hope you're hungry," Josh said. "I made a double batch of pancake batter, and I don't want it to go to waste." Josh started a stack of cooked pancakes and continued to add fresh batter to the pan.

"What's this?" Ellie said, holding up the violation notice Josh had just received.

"Oh, I'm actually not sure," he said. "Someone left this at the front door this morning. I was going to ask you if we could swing by the Town Hall on our way downtown so I could ask someone about it. What's a Christmas Planning Committee anyway?"

"Oh, jeez. This town has all sorts of committees that focus on one area or another. Christmas Planning does events related to Christmas. And, yes, of course there's a Hanukkah Planning Committee. There's even a Diwali Planning Committee. Turns out, Diwali celebrations, they're a ton of fun. There's probably a bunch of finance committees for nerds like you, too."

"Oh! That reminds me." Josh disappeared to grab his laptop." I ran a few investment projection models for you." He placed his laptop down on the table in front of Ellie and leaned over her shoulder to pull up the files he had created. "I wasn't sure of your risk tolerance, so I ran some multiple times using various levels of exposure and allocation amounts. A couple stress-test scenarios. This one here is based on the Monte Carlo simulation, I like how it considers different market scenarios—sorry. I forget most people aren't as interested in talking about this stuff as I am." Josh realized that his arm was brushing up against Ellie, but he didn't move away. Instead, his eyes followed her arm all the way up to her face, passed her lips, and locked eyes with her. They inched closer, but he had forgotten about the pancakes cooking in the pan and noticed smoke beginning to billow up from the stove. "Oh no!" He rushed over to flip them, but those two could not be salvaged.

Josh stacked a few of the best pancakes onto a plate and handed them to Ellie. She added some butter then doused them in maple syrup, and then she took her first bite. Josh saw a glimpse of that oh, so satisfying, look of pure enjoyment.

"Just like heaven on earth. Maybe even..." and then she stopped short.

"You can say it," Josh said, egging her on.

Ellie chewed slowly and shook her head as she covered her lips. She wouldn't dare say it.

"They're better than Aunt Ruth's," Josh said. "You can say it. We all know it."

Ellie continued eating and she did not correct him.

The Town Hall was a brick building with a post office box and a clothing donation box out front. The GREENVILLE, MAINE TOWN HALL sign was 'proudly donated by Tucker at Turnkey Construction.'

A bell jingled atop the door as Josh and Ellie entered the small reception area. They followed a wall of portraits that displayed past mayors and the current mayor as they walked up to the long countertop that spanned the entire width of the room. There was a sign above the countertop that said 'DEEDS, GOAT PERMITS, ZONING.'

"Hello?" Josh said, tapping the bell at the empty counter. "Anyone here?"

A head popped up from below the counter. He was sporting a large Christmas tree pin on his sweater, and a welcoming smile. "Well, hello, folks. Welcome to the Greenville Town Ha—" the man froze when he looked at Josh. "Wait a minute! Is that who I think it is? Handsome Josh Hanson?" he reached across the counter and vigorously shook Josh's hand. "It's me, Todd! Todd Samsonite! Shoot, how many years has it been?"

"It's just Josh these days. I remember you, Todd. Good to see you again."

Todd had a paper route and worked every seasonal job imaginable around Greenville, so Josh ran into him a lot when he visited growing up. Sledding hill attendant, farmer's market vendor, community pool lifeguard. Was he qualified? No one asked those kinds of questions back then.

"Handsome Josh Hanson?" Ellie chuckled. "How have I never heard this?"

Todd proudly pointed to his nameplate on the counter. "Well, these days I'm known as Assistant Town Clerk Todd." It read: ASSISTANT TOWN CLERK - TODD SAMSONITE ZBM, CPCM.

"ZBM?" Josh asked. "Is that some kind of public service accreditation?"

"Zoning Board Member." Todd straightened his posture as he said, "and Christmas Planning Committee Member," pointing to the CPCM.

"Oh, perfect! Just the man I need to see!" Josh pulled out the violation letter addressed to Aunt Ruth. "I got this letter today, and I have no idea what it means or what it's for. Can you help me with this? Something about yard decorations? There aren't even any in the yard, so..."

"Let's take a little look-see here," Todd laid the letter flat on the counter. He looked at the letter and then typed in his computer. He looked more closely at the letter and then typed some more. "Oh, yeah. Okay. I see what's going on here." Todd frowned as he folded up the letter. "First of all, I'm sorry about your Aunt Ruth."

"Thanks, Todd."

"So," Todd continued. "From looking at the paper trail in the computer system, it looks like Ruth had applied to be on the Christmas Planning Committee over the summer and was accepted. And, uh," Todd pulled a promotional flier out from under the counter. "Part of the deal is that all members display a minimum eight-foot Christmas tree in their yard. So that appears to be the reason for the violation notice. But we have a bigger problem than that."

'What do you mean?" Josh asked.

"Well, since Ruth has passed, rest in peace, obviously, we now have a vacant seat on the Christmas Planning Committee." Todd paused.

"Well, I mean, I guess I could do it," Josh suggested. "What do I need to do? Attend some meetings? Bake some Christmas cookies? Put up some lawn decorations?"

Ellie put her hand on his arm and spoke under her breath, "Josh stop, you're embarrassing yourself."

Todd's demeanor changed immediately. "Put some lawn decor—okay...is that all this is to you? Is this some kind of joke to you? You come in here from the big city and just look down on all our small-town traditions?"

"Todd," Josh said calmly, "I live in Danvers, Pennsylvania. It's a town of, like, 15,000 people. We only have two Dunkin' Donuts. We're barely considered a medium-sized town."

Todd took a couple deep breaths and a short walk down the counter to put some papers away. He seemed to collect himself a bit while he took the lap. "Okay, I'm sorry. I came on a little strong there. It's just that this stuff is important to us here, and you can't join the CPC, you weren't even voted in. You're not a resident."

"CPC?" Josh asked.

"Christmas Planning Committee," Ellie whispered.

"Okay, I have to be a resident, and be voted in to join the CPC?" Josh summarized. "It doesn't seem like there is a lot of time for either of those. So, what do we do?"

"I don't know," Todd said. "But I sure hope we can figure it out before Mr. Mayor finds out—"

Just then, a commotion near the entrance drew their attention.

"Hi, Mr. Mayer!" Todd shouted suspiciously loud as Mayor Matt Mayer stepped into the Town Hall along with a cold gust of air. Mayor Matt Mayer was flanked by his Mayoral Assistant on one side and his Mayoral Photographer on the other. His assistant finicked with his coat, brushing lint off every inch. She licked her finger to scrub off a spot she couldn't brush away.

"Mom!" the Mayor scolded under his breath.

"Sorry, honey," said his Mayoral Assistant, who also happened to be his mother.

"Don't shoot that, Greg," the Mayor said to his photographer.

"Sure thing, boss," Greg said.

The Mayor stood beside his own portrait hanging on the wall. "Hi Todd. I've told you, you don't have to call me Mr. Mayer. Call me Mr. MayOR." The Mayor flashed a toothy smile. "Why so glum looking, Todd?"

"Is his photographer the Hollywood actor Greg Grunberg?" Josh whispered to Ellie.

"Sure is," Ellie whispered back. "He's taking a break from acting to reinvent himself and hone his craft as a photographer."

"Well, Mr. Mayor," Todd hesitated. "We've got a bit of a hairy situation on our hands. I was hoping to figure it out before having to involve you." Todd motioned to Josh. "This is Josh Hanson. His aunt, Ruth Matthews, recently passed away."

"Oh, Josh, I am so sorry for your loss. Ruth was a valuable member of our community and made a real impact here," the Mayor looked genuinely sympathetic.

"That's not all," Todd continued. "She was recently voted in as a member of the Christmas Planning Committee."

The Mayor grimaced twice as hard as he had when he heard Josh's Aunt Ruth had passed away. "Oh no, that is devastating news,

Todd."

"So that means that the—"

"I know exactly what that means, Todd," the Mayor sharply interrupted. He walked to a window and gazed out at the snowy ground outlined with shoveled pathways. His mayoral photographer snapped photos of the thoughtful moment.

"Not now, Greg!" The Mayor scolded.

"That is Greg Grunberg! I knew it," Josh whispered to Ellie excitedly.

Ellie tried to quietly shush Josh, but ended up drawing unwanted attention.

"What's that?" the Mayor said, turning his attention to Ellie.

"Oh, um," Josh could tell that she was scrambling for something to say.

"You look awfully familiar," the Mayor said. "Have we worked together on something recently?"

"I actually helped with some of the digital designs for the Christmas displays downtown last year. That's quite a good memory you have, Mr. May*OR*." Ellie offered an exaggerated wink to underscore the joke.

"HA! I love it!" the Mayor wailed. "Well," he quickly composed himself. "The Christmas display is one of my crowning achievements. It's super important to me, as are all the individuals who contribute. Were you about to say something?"

"Oh. Um...I was just saying," she continued. "What if I joined the Christmas Planning Committee?"

The Mayor and Todd made eye contact and they both seemed to perk up. Josh was even taken aback by this idea.

"Now that's interesting," said Mayor Mayer as he approached the counter.

"CPC bylaws do allow for proxy members under certain circumstances," Todd offered.

"I'd say this is a pretty good certain circumstance," the Mayor added, then looked at Josh. "Respectfully, of course."

"Of course," Josh agreed.

"However…" Todd said, letting the anticipation hang in the air.

"What is it, Todd?" the Mayor demanded.

"It's just that, well, we already made all the name plates for the committee, including one for Ruth Matthews."

"Oh yeah," the Mayor rubbed his chin. "Good point."

"I could make my own name plate," Ellie suggested.

Todd and the Mayor slowly and optimistically raise their heads.

"But then the name plates wouldn't match," Todd said with a sigh, deflating the room.

"I could make everyone a new name plate?" Ellie said. "Then we'll all match?"

Josh, Ellie, Todd, the Mayor's Assistant, and Greg Grunberg, the Mayor's photographer, watched Mayor Mayer closely.

"I love it!" he said finally. "Now, Greg, now! Snap a pic!"

11

A TREE CONTEST

ELLIE – MONDAY MORNING

ELLIE DIDN'T EXPECT TO BE HOLDING COURT with the Mayor when she woke up this morning. The day's been full of surprises, actually. Starting with Josh making the most delicious pancakes she'd had in a long time. And he didn't look too shabby in that festive apron, either. Then he did all that work analyzing her investment portfolio. She didn't understand most of it, but it looked like it took a while to put together. On top of all that, she had two great ideas for the Mayor on the spot. *I am crushing it!*

"Well, now, we have the CPC emergency sorted, thanks to Ellie," Mayor Mayer said, "Any other bright ideas?"

All eyes turned to her. She wanted to impress. Did she have another trick up her sleeve? *Think, Ellie. Think.* She spotted the Christmas tree pin on Todd's lapel. *Ah ha!* "How about a tree decorating contest throughout the town? Since we don't have the

Christmas tree downtown anymore—"

"Rest in peace, obviously," Todd said.

"Obviously," the Mayor added.

Ellie continued, "Then maybe residents could decorate the trees in their yards? And there's a vote for the favorite? That also opens opportunities for, uh, for a Christmas Tree Search! Yeah, a town-wide search for the best-dressed tree. You could start early in the Fall. So, it really expands the window for the Christmas season, if you think about it."

The Mayor seemed to be struggling to wrap his head around the idea. "Here, look." Ellie pulled out her phone and showed him a picture of the tree in Aunt Ruth's yard from a previous year, fully decorated and covered in lights.

This got the Mayor's attention. "That's a nice tree! Now *that* tree should be downtown!"

Todd nodded his head in agreement.

"Um...I don't think—" Ellie attempted to quell the enthusiasm she could feel rising up.

"That's actually a great idea, Mr. Mayor," Josh said. "That tree *should* be on display downtown."

"Well..." Ellie shot Josh a look. "Not that one, though. That one has to stay there in Aunt Ruth's yard."

"Todd!" The mayor shouted. "Look at that tree! Probably fine from all sides, too."

Todd admired the tree. "That's a 360-degree opportunity right there. Three hundred and sixty-*tree*-grees, if you will."

"HA!" the Mayor bellowed. "Good one, Todd. I'm gonna use that." He continued to brainstorm about the tree idea. "You know, if we did a town-wide decorating contest, we could convene a Christmas Tree Subcommittee to regulate the tree specifications and submission requirements."

"The TV station could make a whole series on it," Todd added. "Lots of radio appearances. Definitely a ribbon cutting when the final tree is chosen."

"Obviously, Todd. I mean, come on."

While Mayor Mayer and Todd continued dreaming up promotional scenarios, Ellie berated Josh the best she could using her whisper voice. "What the heck, Josh! Why'd you offer up Aunt Ruth's tree like that? You know we have to decide together what happens to it."

"What? It's a good idea. And her tree would be perfect."

Ellie tilted her head. "Come on, Josh." His brazen indifference was frustrating. He wasn't as attached to the tree as she was, so why does he have a say? The tree is on the property Josh inherited, sure, but maybe there's a way to carve out that part of the lot? She'd have to check with Todd about that. Had the real estate agents suggested he get rid of the tree, too? Ellie was spiraling. *Pull it together, Ellie.* She could just tie up the house sale in red tape. If they didn't finish the traditions in Aunt Ruth's Will, Jasper couldn't sign over the house to Josh. And he couldn't cut down a tree on a property he didn't own, right?

"Okay, I'm sorry," Josh said. "I got caught up in the moment. These guys are beyond that idea anyway. They're talking about how they could get the Budweiser Clydesdales here in time for Christmas, for crying out loud."

Mayor Mayer's Mayoral Assistant mother began the process of ushering him along to his next appointment. "Well, we're off," the Mayor said. We're excited to have you on the Christmas Planning Committee, Ellie. I'll have my people reach out." Then the Mayor and his posse rushed off.

Other than the brief period of time when the Mayor seemed ready to order Aunt Ruth's tree dug up by its roots, Ellie felt surprisingly giddy about how well her tree contest suggestion was taken. Ellie smirked at Josh. "You're gonna have to bring more than pressure from the Mayor to get me to agree to cut down Aunt Ruth's tree."

"Let's just see what the Christmas Planning Committee has to say," Josh said as he took a step closer to her.

Ellie got caught up in the little flirty fun time with Josh, so she had forgotten that Todd was still there. "Classic Handsome Josh Hanson!" Todd smirked from behind the counter.

DOWNTOWN CHRISTMAS MARKET

JOSH – MONDAY AFTERNOON

"Wow, what a trip this place is," Josh said as he and Ellie walked the couple blocks to the downtown Christmas market. Rock salt crunched under their boots with each step. "I don't think I even know where the Town Hall is where I live. Never mind having a forum with the Mayor."

'Yeah, that's the charm of Greenville," Ellie said.

Just then, Josh's phone rang. He looked at it and then silenced it.

"Who's that?" Ellie asked.

"Just some co-workers," he knew it was Dave and Scott calling. Probably heading to lunch.

"Why don't you answer? Are they your friends?"

"Yeah, I guess. I don't know. I don't usually answer calls that often."

"Well they obviously want to talk to you. Pick up. I want to say hi." Ellie reached over and swiped his phone screen to answer the call.

"Josh!" a voice yelled from the phone. "You picked up! Scott just lost a bet."

"Sorry, Scotty," Josh said.

"Hi, I'm Ellie!" she shouted towards the phone. "You don't know me but I'm Josh's friend, too."

"Who's Ellie?" another voice from the phone.

"Mia?" Josh asked. "Is that Mia?"

"Yeah," Dave said. We've all been hanging out since you've been gone. Having a way better time."

Josh chuckled.

"Okay buddy," Scott said. "Just wanted to see if you'd answer. Talk later."

"They seem fun," Ellie said. "You should talk to them more often. Do you hang out with them a lot?"

"We sit together in the office, but I don't really hang out much." His response hung in the air for a moment. "But I will," he said, attempting to preempt any pushback Ellie was considering.

"Thank you," she said with a smile.

Josh thought about the traditions they had to do together. "So, you want to keep Aunt Ruth's tree, I think we should donate it to the town. We still need to find a way to agree there. And we have to go caroling, bake something, eat scorpions..."

Ellie chuckled. "Or something scorpion adjacent."

"Then make an ornament and help at a toy drive."

"We've got our work cut out for us," Ellie said as they walked under the Tucker Turnkey Construction DOWNTOWN CHRISTMAS MARKET archway, the grand entrance to the open-air market.

The Downtown Christmas Market popped up each year at an intersection that was shut down to car traffic. Vendor booths lined the sides of the road where visitors perused homemade gift wrap, handmade decorations, chocolates, roasted chestnuts, hot chocolate, and cider. Ellie seemed to know everyone. Nearly every person he and Ellie walked by said hello to her. 'Tell your mom hi', 'Good to see you, Ellie.' Josh felt proud to be spending time with her. He felt special that she chose to spend time with him.

"Oh!" Ellie grabbed Josh's arm and tugged him across the street. "I want you to meet these two ladies."

"Josh, this is Estelle. Estelle is one of the Lunch Lad—" Ellie paused. "She is one of the ladies who has coffee and lunch with her other lady friends at Tay's regularly. Her daughter owns the building where my dad's hardware store used to be. This is Josh. He's Ruth's real-life nephew."

Josh gently shook Estelle's hand with both of his. "It's an honor to meet you, Estelle."

"You too, Josh. I'm sorry about your Aunt Ruth."

"Unfortunately, it's happening more and more at our age," a woman standing next to Estelle said.

"This is Margery," Ellie said. "Aunt Ruth was close friends with both Estelle and Margery."

"I'm sorry you've both lost such a good friend," Josh said.

"Kinda slow down here," Margery said, looking around.

"I was just thinking that this place was quieter than I had expected," Josh said. "When I hear the words 'downtown Christmas market', I imagine a bustling atmosphere."

"It's just getting going for the season!" Ellie said.

"Wait 'til you see it in full swing in a couple weeks," Estelle added.

"Right!" Ellie said. "At night, the whole market lights up. People sipping hot chocolate, shopping for the perfect gift for someone, holiday music in the air, the scent of cinnamon and fried dough—"

Josh took a deep breath. "Ahhh...cinnamon and fried dough. The way God intended."

"People bumping into you," Margery continued. "People dropping trash and not picking it up. People with sticky fingers touching things, making them sticky for everyone else..."

"That sounds like a very specific complaint," Ellie said.

"I may have some unresolved trauma from my time at the Christmas market," Margery conceded.

"Well, it was good to see you, Ellie," Estelle wrapped up their conversation. "And a pleasure to meet you, Josh. We'll see you both again soon, I hope."

He and Ellie walked a bit more into the market and stopped to hover over a table covered with handmade decorations.

"See, Josh, this is the type of stuff you need!" Ellie picked up a reindeer mug that had antlers as the holders.

"Who's that, Donner? Ehhh, she's a bit of a party animal from what I've heard."

"Yeah, you're right," Ellie said as she placed the mug back. "Last thing you need is a prank while you're trying to enjoy some hot chocolate."

"This is neat, though," Josh said. He picked up a wreath made of cork coasters.

Ellie was already on to the next booth. "Ohh! Look at this, Josh!" He joined her at 'June's Make Your Own Ornament' crafting table, where the vendor was hawking her goods.

"Step right up! Make-n-take ornaments, here! June's got everything you need! Wood, burlap, wool swatches, cotton swatches, cotton swabs..."

"I think we've stumbled upon our first tradition," Ellie said.

"Ah, yes, Aunt Ruth wants us to make a handmade ornament." Josh realized what a huge help Ellie would be in completing these holiday traditions. What would he do without her? She knows this town and all these people. He was just an outsider. But he was someone special walking around next to Ellie. She made him feel like a VIP. For a moment, Josh felt an overwhelming sense of sadness. He thought about all the years he had spent without Ellie in his life. How many import—

"June's got popsicle sticks, glue, tinsel, glitter, small wood shapes, big wood shapes, medium wood shapes, paint..." the vendor continued.

"I think we can cobble something together here," Ellie said looking over the table of supplies.

Josh followed her down the table. He realized he needed to snap out of it. The best thing he could do was be in the present.

"June's got hammers, got nails, a ratchet set, a nail gun, eye protection, a level..."

"Well, it certainly looks like I've got everything I need here," Josh said, holding a pneumatic drill. "Fifteen pounds of torque in this baby," he added.

"You wouldn't know what to do with five ounces of torque," Ellie chided.

He and Ellie set up shop next to an intently focused little girl who looked to be around ten years old.

"Hi there," Ellie said to the girl. "Mind if we join you?"

"Sure," the girl said. "I'm almost done." She was working on a stuffed snowman made from an old sweater that had been cut into usable fabric swaths.

Josh looked through the crafting supplies for something he could work with. He thought about what to say to Ellie. Something meaningful? Thoughtful? Nostalgic? Maybe it would just come to him. He didn't overthink. "Hey, Ellie," he said as he turned to look at her. She turned to face him with popsicle sticks in her mouth like a walrus.

"Ex-thh-use me, thhoo I have thhh-omething in my teethhhhh?" she joked, holding the popsicle sticks in place with her lips.

Josh collapsed onto the craft table with laughter. "I did not see that coming!"

"An oldie but a goodie," she said, holding the popsicle sticks.

"You seem really comfortable here, El. Being back in Greenville."

"Yeah, I like it here. It has changed quite a bit. Grown a lot over the years. But still feels like a small town."

As Josh worked on his super basic star made of popsicle sticks, he could feel the little girl's critical eye looking over. Ellie, ever the more creative of the two, glued a small, round, thin piece of wood to the top of a larger round piece of wood for a more rustic take on the snowman. While she was waiting for the wood glue to dry, she helped the girl tie the scarf on her snowman. This also gave Josh a little extra time to complete his masterpiece. Though he was a bit distracted. He couldn't help but watch Ellie as she looped the fabric around her finger and tied a perfect little scarf around the stuffed snowman's neck.

"So, Ellie," Josh began. "How's your mom doing today?" Josh asked Ellie.

"She's doing okay. Overall, she's not as energetic or active as she used to be, and that's okay. People change; they're allowed to be tired and lose interest in things. I'm just concerned that she's losing too much interest in things. She used to go out with friends, talk on the phone, go to the movies, you know, socialize."

"Have you talked to her about it?"

"A little, but she's stubborn, and she just brushes it off. I know there are things that she used to enjoy that she's just not doing anymore, and it makes me sad."

"You know what I think? I think you're super clever and you'll find a way to help her."

Josh and Ellie added the finishing touches on their ornaments and admired their handiwork. While Ellie's ornament looked like it belonged in Williams Sonoma, his looked like it belonged in one of those stores that moved into an empty building after a bankruptcy and tried to mimic another major brand, like Home Good Enough, Pottery Shed, or Crates and Trash Barrels.

"Should we commemorate this? Josh suggested. "I feel like we'll need some sort of evidence to prove we've done it."

"Good thinking." Ellie took out her phone and they squeezed together for a selfie with the ornaments.

"I can take that for you," said June, the vendor. "Come over this way where the light is better." She ushered them to the side of her table.

Josh and Ellie each held up their ornaments and smiled.

"Move in a little bit so you don't get cut off," June said.

Still smiling, Josh and Ellie scooted closer together while holding up their ornaments.

"How about you stand right next to each other and hold your ornaments in the other hand? I'm still not getting a good shot."

Still holding their smiles, Josh and Ellie scooted shoulder to shoulder.

"Perfect. I'll take a few real quick-like." June poked her head out from behind Ellie's phone. "There's just one thing, you two."

"We're as close together as we can get. Maybe you can back up?" Josh suggested.

"No, no, it's not that," said June. "It's just that..." She smiled and motioned above their heads.

They looked up to see mistletoe aligned perfectly above them.

"Hey," Josh said, "you knew that was there the whole tim—" But before he could finish his sentence, Ellie leaned over and planted a peck on his cheek.

"Aww," June fawned.

The smile Josh had been holding for the camera grew into a genuine, full-face beaming grin as he turned to look at Ellie. He felt like he had just won a contest.

"What can I say," Ellie shrugged. "I'm a stickler for tradition." She blushed and quickly changed the subject. "You can sell these," Ellie said as she handed her ornament to June.

"Oh, that's beautiful," said June. "Thank you so much."

"And could you throw this out for me?" Josh joked as he handed his creation to June.

"So, first tradition in the books," Ellie said. She held up her hand for a high five.

He slapped her hand gently and they briefly interlocked fingers before Ellie shoved her hands back into her mittens. Josh wondered if, had she forgotten to wear mittens, would they have ended up holding hands? "You know, I saw you help that little kid with their ornament," he said as they slowly strolled through the market.

"Oh, yeah. You would've done the same."

"Ehh...I am not so sure," Josh confessed. "If I even noticed that they needed help at all. I would probably then think about how I'd need to stop my own work, lose progress there... What if they don't even want the ribbon tied? What if I tie it wrong and mess up their ornament? What if I break their ornament? There are just so many considerations."

"I don't think you give yourself enough credit," she said. "Ooh! Look at that!" Ellie pointed to a flier advertising the Town Lighting Display. "That's tomorrow night! We should do that! Do you want to check out the light show together?"

"Um, yes. Obviously." Josh walked towards the flier and pointed to the text at the bottom where it said '$5 Eggnog Samplers.' "But only if we can do this, too. Hear me out. Instead of scorpions...eggnog chugging contest."

Ellie cringed but quickly warmed up to the idea. "Alright...okay...out of respect for the scorpions, we can do an eggnog..." She paused. "Let's call it a speed sampling, instead."

"That's way better."

Josh said, "It's a date!" at the exact same time as Ellie.

"Jinx!"

"You owe me—"

And without another word, they both started walking again. Neither had a soda on them and they both seemed to enjoy talking to each other. He smiled to himself. It had been a long time since he had so much fun with someone. "So..." he broke the silence. "How would you feel about a real date? Maybe tonight?"

Ellie was quiet long enough that Josh started to second-guess himself. Did he just make a huge mistake? He didn't want to ruin what they had going on. He just wanted to spend more time with her. Maybe he just shouldn't have said that. Why would he be so forwar—

"I think that would be lovely," Ellie said finally.

Phew! Wow, what a rush! Big risk, big reward! That's how it's done!

"Cool. Very cool," he said calmly, smiling to himself. Maybe Ellie was right about giving himself more credit.

"I have to work with Tay for a little bit today, but swing by my Mom's tonight and we'll head out?"

"Sounds great," Josh said, still smiling. "You still owe me a Coke," he joked.

13

TEA TIME

ELLIE – MONDAY AFTERNOON

"Tay, so much to catch you up on," she said. "I just left the Christmas market with Joshua."

"Okay, tell me about it, but in a haiku," Tay said.

"Hm. Give me one second to think." Ellie grabbed four coffee mugs filled with festive drinks and delivered them to the Lunch Ladies' table.

"So," Laura said, "We heard that Estelle and Margery got to meet a certain someone at the Christmas market," she winked a perfectly secretive wink.

"You've already heard about that?" Ellie put the drinks down gently.

"Looks like we have our own little *Christmas romance* story on our hands, right, Laura?" Sandra said. "That's a trope in romance books, isn't it?"

"As the bookstore owner and self-appointed trope expert, I'd say this is more of a *forced proximity* love story," Laura spoke to Sandra as if Ellie were not there.

"Oh, yes," Sandra said. "Ohhh...what if it's actually a *secret billionaire* romance story?" Sandra and Laura both looked up at Ellie with anticipation.

"Enjoy your drinks, ladies," Ellie said flatly and returned to Tay. "Okay, Tay. I got it." She recited her Christmas market recap haiku:
"The man's bad at crafts,
Or maybe he was nervous,
Mistletoe surprise."

Tay snapped her fingers. "Brava, brava. Bien joué. Now fill me in."

"We made ornaments and his was fine. He's like, an anti-craftsman, though. But then the vendor pulled this mistletoe trick, so I kissed him."

"You *WHAT*!?"

"On the cheek, calm it down, Tay."

"Prude."

"He was definitely nervous about the mistletoe. I think I surprised him. He looked like a little baby deer in headlights."

"Aw, adorbs."

"I kinda wish I didn't bring my mittens, though. We almost held hands at one point, but I had mittens on. I bet we would have held hands. And then, you'll like this, he surprised me when he asked me on a date tonight. I can't wait."

"You're right, I do like that."

"When he asked, I was quiet for a long time. Probs too long."

"The poor guy. You two haven't been on a *date* date in a long time."

"Since we were sixteen. Well, we quote-unquote dated that summer after our freshman year of college, but what stands out in my memory was that summer of puppy love when we could first drive. He borrowed Aunt Ruth's car and took me to a movie. Then we got ice cream."

"Wait a second," Tay said. "I remember this. Didn't you miss the movie or something?"

"Well, yeah, kinda."

"Say more," Tay said.

"Well, we had trouble parking, so we missed *Iron Man 3*, and had to see *Fast & Furious 6* instead."

"You didn't have trouble parking, you lying liar! You were making out in the car and lost track of time!"

Ellie laughed. "How do you remember that? Who's the prude now? I was so excited to be out on the town with a boy who wasn't from my school."

"You sparked a week's worth of gossip around school. So where will you go on your fancy date?"

"I don't know. Maybe the Italian place downtown? Knowing him, he'll make a reservation there. He's a planner like that. Oh, and I'm on the town's Christmas Planning Committee now."

"Okay, Miss Mayor. Look at you go."

"That does have a nice ring to it. I'm so sorry. I've been going on and on about me. What's going on with you?"

"Well, I am planning a reimagined reading of 'A Visit from St. Nicholas' for before the holiday double feature at the theater next week."

"How do you reimagine 'Twas the Night Before Christmas'?"

"That's what I am trying to figure out. It was the theater manager's idea."

"Your reputation precedes you."

"I pitched an idea to have this film critic from L.A. come here and speak before the movies, too. He's written a few books about Christmas movies, he has a movie podcast, he's really crushing cinema, but in a good way."

"I love that."

"So, we'll see. Can you take these muffins over to the Lunch Ladies?" Tay asked.

As Ellie made her way through the tables, her mom arrived at the Choffee Shop.

"Evelyn," Sandra called out. "Come sit with us!"

Ellie eyed Sandra and Laura suspiciously. "Ladies, what are you up to?"

"Who? Us?" Laura said with the slightest tinge of guilt.

"Hi sweetie," Evelyn said as she rolled up to the table.

"You can go now, Ellie," Sandra said as she leaned in to talk with Laura and Evelyn.

"I've got my eyes on you." Ellie pointed two fingers at her eyes and then at the ladies. "No conspiring over here, got it? This is a meddling-free zone."

14

DATE NIGHT

JOSH- MONDAY EVENING

JOSH HADN'T BEEN ON a *date* date in a while, so it felt like a good opportunity to get a little fancy. He even made a reservation at the small, albeit casual, family-owned Italian restaurant a few blocks from downtown called Mangia.

At Evelyn's doorstep, Josh pressed the doorbell. A full DING-DONG rang out. He checked his breath in his hand. It seemed fine. Does that actually ever work? It'd probably have to be pretty bad for it to register in a self-check. This blazer could have used a lint roller, though. How did I not notice this before I left—

"Hey, Josh!" Ellie said as she opened the door. "I'm almost ready. Let me go get my coat."

Ellie hurried away as Josh headed into the kitchen like he had done dozens of times before. He found Evelyn sitting at the kitchen table cutting vegetables. The kitchen looked mostly like he remembered it. There were some new contraptions on the counter, like an air fryer. A single-cup Keurig coffee machine had replaced the old 12-cup coffee maker, but the same holiday mugs were still there, and the holiday hand towels had been hung around cabinet handles with care. He took a few grapes from the bowl by the sink, then peeked inside the Mrs. Claus cookie jar and stole one of Evelyn's famous Snickerdoodle cookies. "I see you've been keeping the cookie jar stocked," he said.

Evelyn wiped her hands on a towel as Josh approached. He leaned down for a hug and squeezed Evelyn tight as she patted his back. "It's so good to see you, Josh."

"You too, Mrs. Holden." Josh paused and looked at her curiously. "Did you do something different with your hair?"

"Oh, you!" She whipped the hand towel at him. "Such a jokester. Yes, I got this free haircut when I bought this wheelchair."

"Maybe that's what looks different. But really, how are you feeling? You look great."

"Just fine. I have good days and not-so-good. Today is a good day."

"Has Ellie been staying out of your way?"

"It's been a big help having her at home, but don't tell her I said that. I don't need her using that against me."

"Our little secret." Josh bit into the snickerdoodle and a wave of nostalgia hit. This wasn't just any homemade snickerdoodle. The cinnamon was sprinkled by the hands that hugged Josh after he skinned his knee in Evelyn's driveway. They came from the bowl that he and Ellie had licked clean so many times after the last batch went into the oven. The kind of cookie that you ate until you felt sick, but always went back for more. "These cookies are heavenly."

"It's a good thing I've been able to stay in this house. That old oven is my secret ingredient."

Josh chewed slowly, letting every taste bud in on the experience. "What that's you have there?" Evelyn acknowledged the vase in

Josh's hand.

"This," Josh placed the vase on the counter in front of her, "is something of Aunt Ruth's that I thought you should have."

"Josh, I couldn't—"

Josh put up his hand. "No, this vase belongs in this house. Aunt Ruth brought this back from a Christmas market in Germany. Look," Josh spun the vase to show Evelyn the design. "This was hand-painted. It may have even been custom-painted. Look at how similar the Christmas town scene looks to yours and Aunt Ruth's house. It even has the big tree in between them."

"It does look strikingly similar to our houses. So, you think she had it painted?"

"Possibly. If not, I can see why she had to have it."

"I can't accept this, Josh. This is too important."

"Please accept this and consider it a gift from Aunt Ruth. I would love to know that it found such a great home."

"Thank you, Josh." She placed the vase back on the counter and looked around the kitchen. "I am really glad I have been able to stay in this house. It was important to me to stay here after Ellie's dad passed, and then especially once the arthritis got worse. The house I bought with my late husband when we were both just wide-eyed newlyweds, the house I cursed when the rain and heat got in, the house I pampered and spruced up when company came over, the house I brought my first and only child home to and the house where I raised her into the lovely woman she's become."

"She is a lovely woman, indeed." Josh walked towards the window with a view of Aunt Ruth's tree. It was glowing in the yard outside. "Did she decorate the whole tree all by herself?"

"Your Aunt Ruth started it with her a couple months ago, but Ellie has done most of it. She's worked really hard on it."

"It shows. It's beautiful."

"You know, your Aunt Ruth will be missed so much. I'll miss talking with her. She was such a special person."

"I know. She was." Josh said. "It's odd being in her house without her there."

"Ellie tells me she left you the house?"

Josh sat down at the table where Evelyn was divvying up small piles of raisins and cranberries. "She did, yes. Mighty generous of her, huh?"

"I'd say," Evelyn agreed. "Did it come with any special conditions or anything like that?" She asked, smirking to herself.

"You know it did!" Josh confirmed.

"Isn't that just like Ruthie?" Evelyn chuckled. "Keeping you on your toes even as she's getting fitted for her wings. I can't imagine it going to a better person. I know you have some decisions to make about it, but I trust you'll make the perfect choices."

"That makes one of us. I hope I—" Josh lost his train of thought when Ellie appeared with her coat in hand. She had also changed into a dress. Not just any dress. A shimmering black dress with long sleeves that hugged her waist and flowed out a bit above her knees. She was showing an awful lot of skin for someone who needed mittens. Josh's reaction was immediate and spontaneous. "Wow." He also had to remind himself to breathe.

Ellie smiled.

"Well," Evelyn said as she put the final touches on the dish she was preparing. "I am so glad you two are spending time together again. I remember making this for you almost every afternoon when you were here together. You two would build tents with blankets and watch movies inside the tent like you were camping."

Josh and Ellie huddled around the table to see that Evelyn had made the ants-on-a-log snack they used to enjoy with celery, peanut butter, raisins, and cranberries.

"Aw, Mom..." Ellie covered her heart with her hands.

"It's nothing much. Just a little something before you two head out."

Josh looked at Ellie and felt an overwhelming clarity in that moment. This was exactly where he wanted to be tonight. He knew Ellie did, too. "This is so thoughtful, Mrs. Holden. What a great memory." Josh took off his blazer, unbuttoned his shirt sleeves, rolled them up, and then dug in. He nodded and winked at Ellie. "We're not going anywhere tonight." Ellie didn't argue at all, so he knew he made the right decision.

"Do you need to call and cancel a reservation or anything?" Ellie asked.

"What makes you think I made a reservation?" Josh said. *Had he mentioned it?*

She looked at him with a look that said, Josh. Come on. Of course you made a reservation.

"It's fine. They'll probably just sit the next party." He was trying to play it cool and work on going with the flow a bit more, but it was also very against his nature to just let a reservation go without any notice whatsoever. It was a practice he had always avoided. It wasn't fair to the business nor to the other patrons. If you made a reservation, the business was planning on you being there. Everyone from the host to the cooks to the dishwashers to the bussers. A schedule was created, and a seating plan established based on what you told them. It was practically one step away from a formal, binding contract. What good was your word to anyone if you couldn't even be trusted to commit to a simple dinner reservation? "Maybe I'll cancel in the app, just to be safe."

"You know," she said. "Since we're in a kitchen, how about we tackle another one of Aunt Ruth's traditions?"

"Oohh..." Evelyn's curiosity was piqued. "What's left to do?"

Ellie began moving around the kitchen gathering utensils and some staple ingredients such as flour, sugar, and eggs. "We've already made homemade ornaments downtown..."

"Tomorrow we'll do a food challenge," Josh continued. "An eggnog sampling. Then we have to go caroling, bake cookies, and have a gift-wrapping race of sorts."

Ellie tossed an apron at Josh from across the room. "Let's bake." The excitement had Evelyn all giddy. "I'll get the good mixing bowls!"

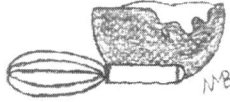

Ellie scooped flour into one of the large mixing bowls her mom had set out.

"Wait, what are you doing?" Josh said.

"Um...baking...?"

"But we don't even have all of the ingredients out."

"We'll get them as we go."

"No, no, no. We gather all of the ingredients, we measure out the proportions we need, and then we have everything we need ready and can quickly work through the steps in the recipe. That's how Aunt Ruth taught me and that's how I've always done it." Josh paused and looked around the kitchen. "Speaking of the recipe, where is that?"

"It's in my head," Ellie said as she collected measuring spoons.

"Whoa, whoa!" Josh was appalled. "That's not gonna work. What even is the recipe? Are we going to discuss that?"

"It's Aunt Ruth's favorite," Ellie said as she opened a drawer and dug around in it until she pulled out a wrinkled, stained piece of paper with handwritten notes on it.

"Double chocolate crinkle cookies," they both said as Ellie held up the recipe.

They paused. Josh sensed a silent acknowledgment that neither of them would invoke jinx powers.

"Fine," Ellie conceded. "We will get all of the ingredients ready. But I'm not measuring ahead of time."

"That's fair." Josh read out the ingredients they needed from the recipe and Ellie hunted them down.

"Let me know when you're ready for a taste tester," Evelyn said as she moved to the living room.

With everything they needed assembled, he and Ellie each began preparing their own batch of Aunt Ruth's favorite double chocolate crinkle cookies. Josh carefully leveled the flour in a measuring cup and then looked on in disgust as Ellie scooped a heaping cupfull directly from the container.

"You know," Josh said as he cracked an egg with one hand and expertly added it to his mixture. "You really shouldn't scoop the flour directly with your measuring cup. It will pack down the flour—hey!" Ellie slipped her bowl over top of Josh's as he cracked a second egg, so the egg went into her mixture instead of his. "Egg thief!"

Josh carefully added small amounts of vanilla extract to a measuring spoon until it leveled at exactly one teaspoon, but then Ellie purposefully bumped his elbow, so he spilled the whole teaspoon plus a little extra into his bowl. When all of the measuring and mixing and sabotaging was done, there was nothing left to do but wait for the oven timer to ding.

"Alright, we've got 11 minutes. What would you like to talk about?" Josh said.

"How close are you to really wanting to sell Aunt Ruth's house?"

"We're getting right into it, huh?"

Ellie nodded slowly as she leaned against the countertop. *She looks gorgeous.*

"I don't know." Josh sat down at the table that overlooked the tree in Aunt Ruth's yard.

Ellie joined him. "You know she wouldn't want you to sell it."

"Maybe not. Aunt Ruth was practical. If she knew that something was overvalued in the market, she could try to take advantage of that." They were quiet for a moment. "Sure, selling is a huge decision. But so is moving my life here. How do you like being back here?"

"It was really hard to be away from here when I went to college. At Plymouth State, I was with a lot of friends, but it wasn't everything that I wanted. I wasn't able to do much more than art history there, so transferring to an art college and being closer to home was so great. I wanted to come back here after college but got a job in Portsmouth. All this to say, yeah, it fricken' rocks here, Josh. I love it here. I love the people. I love being close to my mom. And we have the best pizza in this part of the country."

"Excuse me? That might be the most ridiculous thing you've ever said. More like the best pizza in the *whole country*. The deep-dish pizza at Pies 'n Fries is a slice of heaven on earth."

"See! You get it. You love it here, too."

Josh didn't *not* love it. He definitely liked it. There were a lot of good reasons to stay in Greenville. The housing market was strong, and property values seemed to hold pretty steady. So, it wasn't like he needed to time a seller's market just right. As far as work, he could probably work remotely. He knew that Jerry would not want to see him leave. But he could also try to get his own thing off the ground. Without a mortgage or rent, he could live on a small income for a while. Plus, he had some savings. Worst case, he'd always have the house that he could sell. And Ellie's podcast suggestion was not a terrible idea. Plus, Ellie was in Greenville.

It struck Josh that the lights were strung all the way to the tippy top of Aunt Ruth's tree. "How'd you get the lights all the way to the top? That tree must be, like, fifty-feet tall by now."

"Closer to sixty, actually. It's a bit of a team effort these days. Aunt Ruth knows someone at Greenville Electric, and they stop by to 'check her connection' with their bucket truck. While they're up by the wires, they wrap the first few strands around the top of the tree."

"You still use the Extend-O-Master 2000 to wrap the rest of it?"

Ellie chuckled. "We've actually upgraded it with the extender pack, so it's technically an Extend-O-Master 3000."

"Could we have just ordered an extendable pole online to help string lights on the tree? Sure."

"But why would we do that?" Josh picked up on Ellie's sarcasm. "Why would we do that when we could just get two 10-foot pieces of PVC pipe, glue the pieces together with a connector, hand saw another piece in half to make a handle, glue those pieces on, accidentally glue our fingers together, and then ruin our favorite shirt?"

"Right," Josh played along. "And if we had just bought one, who knows how lightweight it would have been. Then where would I have gotten my back problems?"

"Yeah. You would've had to get them from sitting too much or lifting heavy furniture like everyone else."

"At least we got to spend a day at your dad's hardware store finding all the supplies we needed."

"He gave us a pretty good deal, too."

Josh wanted to tell Ellie how sorry he was that he missed her dad's funeral. He thought about it a lot and regretted not coming back for it. "Ellie, about your dad—"

The oven timer dinged, and Ellie jumped up to grab the cookies from the oven. "Okay, mom!" Ellie shouted. "Come on in here and try them."

Josh got up to help Ellie with the cookies. They each picked a couple of the best-looking cookies from their batch and plated them on the kitchen table, Ellie onto a red plate and Josh onto a green plate.

Evelyn rolled to the table where two similar-looking plates of cookies awaited a taste test. "Alright, moment of truth. Let's see who's second best around here."

"Second best?" Ellie scoffed. "You mean first best."

"That's me, hon. You're both playing for second." Evelyn picked up a cookie from the green plate and took a bite. She chewed. Her deadpan reaction gave nothing away. "Hm. Interesting." Then she took a bite of a cookie from the red plate. She chewed. "Yup. Just as I suspected. I cannot pick a favorite."

"Come on, Mom! It's me, right? It has to be me."

Evelyn took a second cookie from the green plate. She winked at Josh as she turned away. "I'll never tell."

Josh and Ellie each grabbed a cookie from the others' batch.

"Mm, chewy," Josh said. He was impressed given her willy-nilly baking style.

"So chocolatey," Ellie added. "I'll take these down to Taylor's tomorrow. Otherwise, I will eat every last one of them."

Josh noticed that Ellie had some powdered sugar from a cookie on her nose. He reached over. "You've got a little sugar here." He gently brushed it away and then ran his hand down the side of her face.

"Get it?" She took a step towards Josh.

"I got it." He moved closer to Ellie, leaning into the passion of the moment. He felt the electricity between them. Which was interrupted when Evelyn popped back into the kitchen.

"You kids up for a movie tonight?"

Josh froze. Not ready for the moment to end.

"Sure, Mom. Of course," Ellie said. "Let me put a few things away first."

Josh helped Ellie put ingredients back to their places and move dirty dishes and utensils to the sink.

"Hey," Ellie said. "Earlier, what were you going to say about my dad?"

Josh couldn't get into all that now. He felt like the moment had passed. He'd have to broach it another time. "Oh. We had been talking about real estate, and I was just gonna say that he was great at real estate. A true real estate savant."

"Ha! A savant? He only bought two properties in his whole life."

"Okay, savant may be a bit strong. But he did great on that

building downtown, right?"

"Yeah, well, he wanted that specific building and had a number he could afford so he waited and waited for it to become available. And when it was, he didn't hesitate. He got it at the right price. Maybe you could find a place like that, store on the first floor, apartment upstairs, and then you could have your business there and earn some rental income from a tenant?"

"You two coming?" Evelyn called from the living room.

"What do you wanna watch?" Ellie asked and she turned off the kitchen light. "You feeling sentimental or hijinks?"

"Buzz, your girlfriend, woof," Josh quoted one of their favorite movies.

"We haven't watched "Home Alone" together in forever!"

15

RUDE AWAKENING

ELLIE – TUESDAY MORNING

ELLIE PEEKED INTO THE LIVING ROOM to see Josh still asleep on the couch before returning to the kitchen, where she and her mom went about their morning routine, making a light breakfast and having coffee. She assumed all the noise they were making would soon make its way out there and wake him up.

"Josh surprised me a lot last night," she told her mom. "It was so sweet that he wanted to stay in, and it didn't seem to bother him that he had made a reservation, and we would be skipping it. The Josh I remember from years ago would have been anxious about missing the reservation, regardless of how much he wanted to change plans and stay home. Maybe he was secretly freaking out, but he didn't show it. Either way, that was a lot of growth for Josh."

"People change, El," Evelyn said. "It was a pleasant surprise spending time with the two of you again," Evelyn said.

"I know. I had no idea he would be dressed so fancy," Ellie said. "I was still wearing the same clothes I had on all day! I panicked and rushed upstairs to change!"

"He didn't seem to mind," Evelyn said, raising her eyebrows in a playful way. "Luckily, you held on to all those dresses from Aunt Elizabeth."

"Mom! Stop."

"His jaw was practically on the floor, Ellie."

Ellie replayed the memory in her mind and recalled an audible 'Wow' from Josh. She smiled. *Mission accomplished.* She joined her mom at the kitchen table. "I did say something kind of mean to him, though. I said that Aunt Ruth wouldn't want him to sell the house."

"Oh, Ellie. That had to be hard for him to hear."

"I knew I was overstepping, but my emotions got the best of me, so I blurted it out."

"How did he react?" Evelyn asked.

"He was kind. He didn't shut down or get defensive. Another surprise, actually. I half expected him to give me a cold shoulder after that. But he didn't."

Ellie heard a phone ringing in the other room. She peeked in again and saw Josh fumbling around for his phone as it continued to ring. Lucky for her, he answered on speaker phone, so she was able to hear some of the conversation.

"Hello?"

"Josh. I'm glad I caught you. Were you sleeping?"

"Oh, hi, Shelbie. How are you—Sleeping? Me? No, I was just—"

"Sure. Listen, I'm having a virtual open house at your property in thirty minutes. Make sure it's ready to show. I'll be there in a few to set up.

"Oh, wow. An open house? Today? Wait, what's a virtual open house?"

"Get out of bed and get dressed, Josh. We are impressing some buyers today!"

Shelbie hung up and Ellie saw Josh place his phone down. He looked down at himself, fully dressed. "I am dressed..." Josh said to himself.

Ellie slipped back into the kitchen, out of Josh's sight.

"What is it, dear?" her mom said.

Ellie tried to shush her to avoid facing Josh at that moment, but it was too late. She forced a smile. "Heeeey, Josh. Good morning." She then busied herself pouring a cup of coffee.

"Morning, Josh. You sleep okay on the couch? I left a couple extra pillows for you," Evelyn said.

"Yes, I noticed," Josh said. "I did sleep well. I slept great, actually. Thank you for letting me stay. I just crashed out during the movie."

"Both of you kids did," said Evelyn. "When I went to bed, you were both conked out."

When Ellie woke up in the middle of the night, she was leaning on Josh's shoulder. She covered him up with a blanket and let him have the whole couch for the rest of the night.

"I hate to just rush out, but I got a call from Shelbie the real estate agent, and she wants to do some kind of open house."

"An open house?" Evelyn said. "The house isn't even listed yet. How are you doing an open house?"

Josh grabbed a coffee mug from the counter. Ellie didn't notice him reaching for her mug.

"She said it was a 'virtual open house'? Is that a thing? I don't know." Josh took a sip of coffee and grimaced.

"Sorry. That must be mine." Ellie swapped coffee mugs with Josh. "Isn't this moving a little fast? I mean, you aren't even sure you want to sell the house. I thought real estate agents want a signed agreement before they start working on a sale?"

"Right. I mean, I don't know. She did tell me she wanted to show her mom some initiative, so maybe she's just trying to be creative. I wouldn't mind seeing what the interest level is like. I was upfront with Shelbie about not knowing for sure what I'd do with the property. It couldn't hurt, right? To get some feedback from actual buyers? It's just research at this point, right?"

Ellie followed Josh back into the living room. "I guess..."

"Well, I should go." Josh said as he folded the blanket and tossed it onto the couch. "Can I take this?" He held up the coffee mug. "I'll bring this mug back to you later!"

"Sure," Ellie said to the front door after Josh closed it behind him. Her mind raced. Before she could spiral too far into an anxious pit of loneliness, her mom called out from the kitchen for Ellie's help.

"Ellie? Are you there?" Evelyn said.

Ellie looked out the window to watch Josh cross the yard through the snow as a car pulled into Aunt Ruth's driveway. *That was quick.* "Yes, I'm here, Mom." Then, much quieter, "Why am I here while everyone else seems to be there?"

16

SURPRISE OPEN HOUSE

JOSH – TUESDAY MORNING

WAKING UP ON A COUCH was disorienting enough. Never mind waking up to your phone ringing from who-knows-where. Josh's phone continued to ring as he slowly opened his eyes and felt around for the device. He started putting the pieces together when he realized he was on Evelyn's couch, fully dressed, and covered in the same blanket he and Ellie shared when he fell asleep during the movie last night.

The night went much differently and better than he could have ever imagined. Spending that quality time with Ellie and her mom was something Josh didn't realize he missed so much. Ellie brought a part of him to life, and he wanted to spend even more time with her. First, he had to find this dang phone. After tossing a couple of couch cushions, he found it and answered the call from Shelbie. Josh put it on speaker phone so he could replace the couch cushions while they spoke.

Shelbie explained she had an idea for some type of virtual open house and needed to see him right away. Josh didn't want to rush out of Evelyn's house, but he was really curious about what Shelbie had in mind for an open house. He had been clear that he wasn't ready to sell, and he definitely had not signed any papers yet. What could she possibly want to do?

Shelbie pulled into the driveway at Aunt Ruth's as Josh trudged through the snow across the yard.

"What are you doing playing in the snow? Let's get in the house," she shouted.

Josh unlocked the front door and let her in. "You know, Shelbie, this is a little confusing. What are you doing here? I'm not officially a client, and this house isn't even on the market."

"I know. But listen," Shelbie dropped her heavy bag and coat on a chair and took a deep breath. "I have these clients who live out of state. They haven't liked anything I've shown them, and I don't have much else for them to see. I need to show them something. They asked if I had anything that's not on the market yet that they could see. So I may have mentioned this place."

"Isn't that a little misleading?"

"They know the place isn't for sale. But for the right price..." she whizzed by Josh with a handheld vacuum. "Let's get some light in this place!"

Josh was hesitant. He was still riding the high of the time he spent with Ellie and Evelyn the night before. He didn't want to leave this place. He didn't want to sell this place. "I don't want to sell this place," he blurted out.

Shelbie was unfazed. She pulled a box of cinnamon rolls out of her oversized bag and placed them on the counter. "Do you have a plate for these?"

Before Josh could answer, she was off to another room. Josh plated the cinnamon rolls on a platter that was shaped like a snowman. Instead of plating the last cinnamon roll, he went to take a bite. Just as he was about to taste the warm, soft, delicious-smelling cinnamon roll, Shelbie slapped his hand. "No eating!"

"Why not? There's no one even coming here!"

"Atmosphere. Synergy. Balance. Aesthetic. Energy. It all transfers through no matter the medium." Shelbie moved to the living room and started to rearrange some of the furniture pieces.

Josh ripped off a piece of the cinnamon roll and snuck a bite. Had he just decided he didn't want to sell the house? Was he really going to stay in Greenville? It all felt very overwhelming. Maybe he needed to sit on it and continue to think about it. It certainly wasn't a bad idea, though. When he heard Shelbie start her video house tour, Josh made himself invisible.

After twenty minutes, Shelbie found him in the garage looking through boxes Aunt Ruth had stored out there. "Okay, good news and bad news," she said. "The good news is they loved the house."

"How is that good news?" he asked.

"The bad news is my mom called, and I told her what I was doing, and she got very upset. She wants to come here and see this place that I'm spending so much time on, which isn't even a listing. Will you be home later this afternoon?"

"I don't have any plans. I'll just be here cleaning out some things. Shelbie, I think your mom is right. I really am leaning towards not selling. I hope I haven't misled you in some way. Why don't you just explain to your mom how much you love interior design and focus on that?"

"Oh, Josh, you have never sounded so much like an out-of-towner as you did just now."

AN EPISODE

ELLIE – TUESDAY EVENING

ELLIE RETURNED HOME later that afternoon after working at Tay's. As she pulled her car into her mom's driveway, she saw Josh outside Aunt Ruth's. He was standing in the driveway talking to Jannie Turnkey and someone she could only assume was Jannie's contractor husband, Tucker. Ellie recognized Jannie from her advertisements all over town. Tucker must've been the one responsible for the super diesel pick-up truck that said TURNKEY CONSTRUCTION on the side.

Aunt Ruth's house was looking more festive than it had before. Josh had added strings of white lights around the porch railings and posts. "White lights..." Ellie mumbled under her breath. "He would use only white lights..." She was still upset with him about the open house. "So boring and plain. Kinda classic, though. Kinda pretty. UGH! Why am I complimenting him!" she said a little too loudly.

Josh, Shelbie, Jannie, and Tucker looked over at Ellie. Josh offered a half wave before the group returned to their conversation.

She tried to think of positive thoughts. She thought of the hot cocoa Aunt Ruth used to carry out for them while they played in the snow, and of the handmade ornaments she used to give to Aunt Ruth each season. She vividly remembered one of the earlier holiday seasons that she, Aunt Ruth, and Josh spent together. She was twelve years old, and she and Aunt Ruth were decorating the tree outside while Josh was being kind of a dyngus (Ellie's words) and tossing snowballs around...

Snow crunched under Aunt Ruth's boots as she trekked back to the tree from the nearby ornaments box. She was slightly out of breath from the brisk wintery walk, but also from digging through the box to find what she was looking for. Big puffs of cold breath came from Aunt Ruth's mouth in between her words.

"Josh, Ellie. Come over here and put this ornament on the tree together, my dears."

The "3 DAYS 'TIL CHRISTMAS" ornament spun as Josh and Ellie placed its ribbon onto a branch, officially marking it three days until Christmas as part of their Advent countdown tradition.

"It's perfect!" Aunt Ruth exuded with her hands clasped over her full heart.

Aunt Ruth loved this time of year with Ellie and Josh. She loved any time with Ellie and Josh. Even though Ellie was her next-door neighbor, she and Ellie had a very special bond; Ellie was as close to a daughter as Ruth had ever known.

"Aunt Ruth!" Ellie shouted, holding out what looked like either a deformed snowball or a ball of grocery store circulars she pulled from the tras—

"It's an angel ornament, Aunt Ruth!" Ellie shouted. "And I even wrote '2008' on it so we always know it was our handmade ornament for this year."

"Oh, dear, it is magnificent," gushed Aunt Ruth. "It belongs nowhere else but on our tree."

"I don't think we'd ever wonder if that was handmade or not..." Josh mumbled.

"Josh!" Ellie was aghast. "Quit being a dyngus! Don't you have a snowball launcher to play with or something?"

Aunt Ruth admired the handmade ornament for a moment, taking in the lopsided wings, crooked lines, excessively toothy smile, and saw what only the pure innocence of a child could create...a pure masterpiece. Aunt Ruth placed her hands on Ellie's shoulders and crouched down to eye level, "Ellie, the craftsmanship of this decoration is inspiring. It represents so much of the Christmas spirit we need these days." Aunt Ruth placed the ornament on a tree branch. "There, it's perfect," she said as she turned back to Ellie. "This will always be our special Christmas tree tradition."

"And I'll treasure our tree forever," Ellie said.

From afar, Josh shouted a warning, "INCOMINGGGGGGGGGGGGGGG!!!!"

SPLAT!

A burst of cold and wet interrupted Ellie and Aunt Ruth. Ellie quickly realized she'd been struck by a rogue snowball, and she knew exactly who was to blame.

"JOOOOOOOOSH!!!"

While a stiff, cold, and angry Ellie chased a giggling Josh around the fir tree, Aunt Ruth smiled and sang out of tune as she added more ornaments to the old branches.

🎵
O, Christmas tree...
O, Christmas tree...
How lovely are thy branches...
🎵

Ellie snapped back to reality when she heard her name.

"Miss Ellie! Miss Ellie!" Taniyah, Evelyn's nurse, hustled towards Ellie from her mom's house.

"What's going on? Is everything okay?" Josh asked as he jogged over from his driveway.

"Miss Ellie! Come please! It's your mom!" Taniyah said as she headed back towards the house.

"I'm coming!" Ellie sprinted after her.

18

NIGHTTIME CHRISTMAS MARKET

JOSH – TUESDAY EVENING

JOSH SPENT A QUIET AFTERNOON organizing Aunt Ruth's house. He decided to make a pile of the things he knew he could get rid of. That pile included an ashtray he made for Aunt Ruth when he was eleven. Or was it a teacup?

DING-BZZZ

He had forgotten that Shelbie would be stopping by again with her mom, Jannie. Josh welcomed them inside and offered them each half of the last cinnamon roll on the counter. Thankfully, they declined.

"Josh," Jannie began. "Shelbie has explained this situation to me. I am so sorry she has been treating this house like one of our listings.

It is gorgeous, though." Jannie looked around from where she was standing. "I love how you've decorated and how you have this furniture placed. The flow is perfect."

"That was all Shelbie, actually," Josh said. "She really does have an eye for interior design."

"When did you say this house was built?" Jannie asked as she slowly evaluated the rooms around her.

Josh followed her. "I think that I have decided to keep it and not pursue a sale. I don't think the timing is right and I am leaning towards holding onto the house—"

Jannie's phone rang, and she held up one finger as she answered. "Hi. Yes, I am at the Aspen Street house. Sure. See you."

"Sorry," Jannie continued as she ended her phone call. "This place would do great on the market, Josh. I think you should just consider all your options before you shut it down. Have you sold a property before? Capital gains on a property aren't taxed up to $250k if you're single. Are you single?"

"Actually, that's for a primary residence. I've just inherited this." Josh saw a spark of intrigue in Jannie's eye when he said that.

"Watch out for this one, Shelbie," Jannie said. "He's a feisty one. Let's step outside. Tucker is coming by."

"Who's Tucker?" Josh asked Shelbie as he followed them out the front door.

"Tucker is my mom's contractor husband. He probably wants to check out the bones of the house."

"Is Tucker your stepdad? Josh asked.

"No, he's my dad. Why?"

"Why do you call him your mom's husband and not your dad?"

"Hm." Shelbie thought for a moment. "I guess I've always described him relative to my mom because everyone in this town knows my mom. If I say, 'my dad, Tucker,' that doesn't tell people much. But Jannie Turnkey's husband? If a picture is worth a thousand words, then that's worth, like, at least double."

"That sounds kind of sad, Shelbie. I'm sorry you've felt like that. You shouldn't worry so much about how others perceive you or feel like you need to justify who you are like that." Josh picked up on the irony of him preaching about external recognition since he'd been chasing status and achievement his whole adult life. "I suppose I should listen to my own advice, too."

A giant pick-up truck rolled into the driveway as they got outside. A burly, bearded man in an insulated flannel shirt stepped down from the truck. "This the place?" He left his truck running and walked up to Josh with his hand extended. "Hi, Tucker Turnkey. Turnkey Construction. Nice to meet you."

Josh shook his hand, but felt like this was going a bit too far. "Listen, everyone, thanks for trying to help, but I really need to pump the brakes on this whole house sale thing. I'm going to take a little time and figure out what I want to do before I make a decision. I'm sorry to waste anyone's time—" Josh noticed Ellie pulling into her driveway next door. She looked upset. Josh offered a gentle wave and a half smile. He wished he wasn't talking with Jannie, Shelbie, and Tucker so he could go over and check on her. As he turned back to address the trio, he heard a commotion and turned to see Taniyah, Evelyn's nurse, calling for Ellie from her mom's house.

"What's going on? Is everything okay?" Josh asked as he jogged over from his driveway. He followed Ellie and Taniyah into Evelyn's house. Ellie asked Josh to wait in the kitchen as she disappeared down the hallway toward Evelyn's bedroom. He could hear voices from down the hall but couldn't make out what they were saying. He made small talk with Taniyah to give them privacy.

"How long have you been a nurse, Taniyah?"

"Twenty years, can you believe it? Some days, I cannot."

"How did you end up here in Maine? While that accent is beautiful, it does not sound like the Maine accent I've come to know."

Taniyah smiled warmly. "I always wanted to be a nurse and wanted to travel, so I applied to university all over the place. I was accepted into a few, but South Dakota State University was the most affordable. It turned out great because I found out that I love the cold winters. Growing up in Trinidad and Tobago, I had never seen snow. After my first year, I decided I would stay and then find a job in a cold place. I found a job in Maine right after I graduated, and I have been here ever since."

"That's amazing. What a great place to land."

"I love it. My family thinks I am crazy. They say, 'Snow blower? Who is the snow blower?' I have to tell them that the snow blower is not a person!"

They heard Ellie softly close Evelyn's bedroom door and quietly make her way into the kitchen.

"How is she?" Josh was concerned.

"She's okay," Ellie said. "She gets frustrated and overwhelmed sometimes and has a tough time calming down. She's good now, though. She's sleeping."

"She seemed on edge from the time I got here, Miss Ellie," Taniyah explained. "She did not want to eat, didn't want her medications, she did not want me to check her blood pressure, and she was becoming very irritated. Heat was not helping, cold packs were not helping and stretching was out of the question. I'm sorry, Miss Ellie. Normally, I would be able to handle an episode, but I saw you outside and you can always help her calm down."

"It's okay. Thanks for getting me, Taniyah," Ellie walked to the sink and splashed water onto her face.

Josh was trying to wrap his head around what had happened. "So, her arthritis flared, she lost her appetite, and had just had enough for today?"

"Yeah," Ellie sighed. "That's one way of glossing over it. This is when it's hard, Josh. There's no other way to put it. These are the hard days when she doesn't eat, or when she can't do something she could just do yesterday or even that morning, so she loses her temper and has an outburst. There isn't a formula or spreadsheet I can look at to plan or strategize. It's about being here and pushing through the hard stuff and staying by her side, trying to make her comfortable. You don't have to stay around for this, you know."

Josh felt silly for being so ignorant. "No, I want to." He moved close to her and grabbed her hands. You're supporting her and I want to support you. I was worried. I haven't been around a lot of hard situations like this. I want to do what I can to help and be supportive."

"Thanks for coming over," Ellie said. "I know you were in the middle of something." Josh sensed a tiny bit of sarcasm, or maybe annoyance, in her voice.

"Oh, that? That was nothing. It was more of a favor to Shelbie to help her with these really picky buyers. Then her mom stopped by to see why Shelbie was spending so much time on a property they weren't listing, then Jannie called her contractor husband, Tucker, because she liked the house so much. It was a whole thing. I made it clear as crystal that I was not planning on selling right now, and that I need more time to sort things out," Josh explained.

"Well, that's a relief. Jannie Turnkey can be very persuasive. I was kinda worried she would change your mind or at least convince you to let Tucker chop down that tree for firewood."

"No, Ellie, I meant it when I said I wasn't sure. I've really been enjoying spending time together. Speaking of which, I know we had plans, but I'm happy to just hang here with you if you'd rather stay close for your mom."

"Miss Evelyn will probably just sleep," Taniyah said. "You know they are doing the lighting display downtown tonight? You two should go out. I can stay late."

Josh shared a glance with Ellie. She started to tilt her head in a way that Josh could see an excuse coming.

"I mean," Josh said, trying to get ahead of Ellie's rejection. "We did plan on doing that. And that eggnog's not getting any fresher."

The Christmas market was bustling on this cold, crisp night. All the vendor tables were full, and the air was rich with the sound of holiday music and the scent of fresh wreaths and popcorn.

"Okay!" Josh was impressed. "I see you, downtown Christmas market! It does get better."

"I told you," Ellie smacked his arm playfully. "I'd love to gloat and rub it in your face, but we don't have time for that." She led Josh directly to the *Hut Chocolate Bar*, a hot chocolate station near the market entry with a lavish spread of toppings to customize your drink. "The *Hut Chocolate Bar* serves delicious hot chocolate, yes," Ellie grabbed two cups from the vendor. "But that's not the draw." Ellie signaled for Josh to join her around the side of the hut.

"Wait," Josh followed as he sized up the twenty-ounce cup filled only about halfway with hot chocolate. "This is only, like,—OH!" His eyes grew wide at the sight of an entirely unexpected world.

"As I was saying," Ellie continued. "What you really pay for is the toppings bar."

They walked upon a spread of white chocolate shavings, mint chips, mini candy canes, candy cane pieces, cinnamon, whipped cream, marshmallows, caramel, toffee, and more flavor syrups than Josh had ever seen in one place.

"I think we're just missing a pneumatic drill," Josh joked. "So, what's your strategy here? Keep it simple or go hard with the toppings?"

Ellie added a few marshmallows into her cup.

Josh faked an exaggerated yawn. "Boy, I almost fell asleep watching you create the most boring hot chocolate I've ever seen in my life."

"You're the 'go hard with toppings' type, I presume? You used to be just a whipped cream kind of guy."

Josh loaded his cup with shreds of white chocolate, mint chips, candy cane pieces, and then topped it with whipped cream. "If by, 'go hard' you mean make my hot chocolate delicious, then yes. I've grown a lot these last few years."

"I've noticed," Ellie said.

When his cup was overflowing with whipped cream, Josh sprayed some on top of Ellie's cup. "Hold on to that for me, would ya?"

That earned him a smile.

"What else does this market have? Josh asked. "Is it all downhill from here?"

"Are you kidding me?" Ellie replied. "You just wait. We're about to stumble upon one of the staples of the Downtown Christmas Market."

The hot chocolate sugar rush hit as they rounded a corner and were imbued with the sounds of four-person a cappella group serenading a small audience and passersby with a rendition of "The Christmas Song." Josh was in heaven.

🎵
Silent night, holy night
All is calm, all is bright
'Round yon virgin Mother and Child
Holy infant so tender and mild
🎵

Transfixed by song, everyone seemed to slow down around the quartet. Josh's arm became interlocked with Ellie's, and she leaned her head on his shoulder. It felt like the most incredibly perfect moment to him.

🎵
Sleep in heavenly peace

Sleep in heavenly peace
🎵

Out of the corner of his eye, Josh spotted a group of teenagers carrying a short stick with a decorative plant dangling from one end. One of the teens held a sign that said *Mobile Mistletoe - $2 Donation for the Kids*. Without Ellie noticing, Josh got their attention and signaled for them to come his way. The giggling kids broke Ellie's trance. It didn't take long for her to realize that she and Josh were standing underneath the mistletoe. Again.

"It's for the kids," Josh smiled sheepishly.

Josh leaned in and the two kissed. A sweet, lingering kiss.

"Ooooh!" the teens interrupted.

"Here you go," Josh deposited a five-dollar bill into their donation can. "Make sure all of this goes to the kids. You know, you're hurting your business by teasing your customers," he joked as the teens moved along.

"That was sweet," Ellie said.

"I'm sure it's going to a good cause. I should have asked for a tax receipt."

"I wasn't talking about the donation." Ellie gazed into Josh's eyes and then she kissed him again. This time, more passionately and uninterrupted.

In that moment, it was just Josh and Ellie in his tiny little world. The background blurred, and the a cappella singing was indistinct and atmospheric. He leaned back from her and the world around Josh slowly came back into focus. "Who's paying for that one?" he joked.

Ellie smacked his chest as they continued walking.

"Look!" Josh pointed out the booth with the Eggnog Sampler Flights.

"Do you know what time it is?" Ellie asked.

"I don't...but I can check for you...?" Josh was confused by this seemingly random question. He started to reach for his phone.

"It's nog o'clock, boi! Let's go!" Ellie sprinted towards the eggnog booth.

"Of course." Josh stood, a bit embarrassed for falling for it. "Of course it's nog o'clock. What other time could it be..."

Josh and Ellie stood at a two-top table, each with an eggnog flight in front of them.

Josh surveyed the five four-ounce cups of farm-fresh noggin. "What do you think? Go left-to-right or...?"

"Left-to-right seems the most logical," she said.

"Um...so, I know we're calling this a 'speed sampling,' but we don't really need to emphasize the speed, do we?"

"Hmm. Seems like maybe someone went too hard at the *Hot Chocolate Hut*, didn't he?"

"What? No. That's not it." Josh placed his hand over his stomach. "I mean. It doesn't feel great. It's just that, in these conditions, dairy, and especially egg yolks—"

"GO!" Ellie shouted and shot the first eggnog. She quickly moved on to the second cup. Josh scrambled to catch up. By the time Ellie started the third cup, Josh was right on her tail, and they both slammed down the empty third cup at the same time. They paused, holding the fourth cup in the air. Ellie had caught her breath while Josh was struggling; his stomach made a gurgling noise loud enough for Ellie and the small crowd that had gathered to hear. He made eye contact with Ellie, and simultaneously they nodded their heads: *3...2...1.* They chugged the fourth cup.

As they reached for the last cup, it was a paradoxical scene. Josh is nearly doubled over while Ellie pounded her chest, seemingly getting stronger with every 'nog. Josh mustered whatever strength he could, and he tapped sample glasses with Ellie, who drank it without issue to a wave of cheers from the small crowd. Josh took a slow sip and then placed the cup down. The crowd jeered.

As Josh slid his mostly full final cup across the table towards Ellie, he started a quiet chant, "Ellie...Ellie...Ellie..."

The crowd joined the "Ellie" chant and then erupted when she finished Josh's last cup in one quick shot. She raised both arms in victory and took a bow before the rowdy crowd dispersed.

"We really NOGGED that out, huh?" she joked.

Josh moved extra cautiously as he tossed the empty cups. "Oooff, that was tough. You did great, Ellie. Another tradition in the books."

"You did *EGG*-cellent, too."

"Your eggnog puns are making my stomach hurt even more." Josh joked, but he was mildly concerned about a digestive disaster ending his night in tragedy.

"Sorry." She was quiet for a moment. "I'll nog it off."

LIGHTING DISPLAY CEREMONY

ELLIE – TUESDAY EVENING

THE CROWD WAS FILLING IN at the end of the market where the lighting display was going to be presented. This was the end of Main Street with a wide-open grassy park area. On the back side of the park, the ground sloped just enough to make the perfect sledding hill after the first snowfall. The very front of the park was where the town put up a stage and presented their lighting show spectacular, which was, basically, hundreds of strands of white lights in the shape of a cone that stretched about twenty feet in the air.

On the stage, volunteers adjusted sound equipment and arranged decorations. Mayor Matt Mayer stood at a podium reviewing his notes and practiced his vocal exercises while flashing his wide, warm smile.

Mayor Mayer spotted Ellie in the crowd and waved for her to join him on the stage.

"Here," Ellie handed Josh her hot chocolate. "Can you hold this for a second? I'll be right back."

"Why aren't you up here?" The Mayor called as Ellie made her way to the stage. "This is official Christmas Planning Committee business. You should be up here."

"I had no idea!" Ellie felt terrible. "No one told me about this, I swear."

"Where's Todd? Todd!" The Mayor yelled.

Todd hustled to the podium.

"I want Ellie plugged into the CPC calendar. She didn't know to be here for the lighting display ceremony. This can't happen, Todd."

"Of course, Mr. Mayor. It won't happen again."

"Ellie, you can just make sure all decorations are in place here on the stage," Mayor Mayer said before returning to his voice exercises. "A tutor who tooted the flute," the Mayor spoke quietly, smiling. "Tried to tutor two tooters to toot. Too-t. Unique New York. Unique New York. Unique New York. B-i bikki bi b-o bo."

From the back of the stage, Todd offered an enthusiastic thumbs up to the Mayor when he had everything ready to go, then he made his way over to the podium where Mayor Mayer was about to announce the lighting countdown.

"Thanks, Todd," Mayor Matt Mayer said as Todd arrived. "We'll count down from five, right?"

"I think maybe we start with eleven?" Todd suggested. "Give everyone a chance to get their footing and really get going at ten. Then it's smooth sailing into single digits."

"You think?"

People in the crowd sensed that things would start to happen soon, so they started to fill in near the stage.

"Good evening, Greenville!" Mayor Matt Mayer announced to a smattering of applause.

Ellie and the other CPC members took that as their signal to exit stage right. Mayor Mayer nodded at Todd to signal for him to get off the stage, too. Todd nodded back affirmatively, interpreting this as a standard head nod, not taking the hint. He picked up on it pretty quickly, though, after Mayor Mayer gave Todd the "get outta here" thumb gesture, after which Todd promptly rushed to the back of the stage.

"It's time for one of our favorite traditions," Mayor Mayer continued to the crowd." But first, let's take a walk down memory lane and talk about what this means to our town, shall we? In 1914—"

"Great job up there," Josh said as he handed Ellie her hot chocolate.

"Hey guys. Hey, Josh," a familiar voice said from nearby.

"Hey, Shelbie!" Josh said. "What a surprise."

Ellie tried to disappear behind Josh, but it didn't work.

"Hi, Ellie, right?" Shelbie recalled.

"Yup, hi. Great memory you got there."

"So," Josh said quickly. "What are you up to?"

"I'm just here with my mom for the lighting show. I'm grabbing some hot chocolate for the both of us."

"Aren't you worried about missing the lighting show?" Josh asked. "I think it's starting soon."

Ellie and Shelbie both chuckled and then shared a glance. The three turned towards the stage where Mayor Matt Mayer was pounding his fist on the podium as he spoke. "...and the language of origin could not have been Slavic. I knew it. You knew it. We all knew it."

"No, he'll be at this for a while," Shelbie said confidently. "I have plenty of time. By the way, the decorations you've added to your Aunt's house are a nice touch."

"Way to go, Josh!" Ellie said as she offered a delicate shoulder punch.

"But," Shelbie continued. "My mom says to go easy on the

garland—it makes you look desperate. I say the more the merrier, though."

Josh shrugged as he casually scooped some whipped cream off Ellie's cup for his hot chocolate. "That's garland for ya."

"Before I go, the virtual open house went well, and they just may be interested in seeing the property in person."

"Already?" Ellie said louder than either Josh or Shelbie expected. "I mean, wow, you and your mom are good," she said much calmer.

"Yeah, wow, that's really...I wasn't expecting that," said Josh. "Because last time we spoke, I said I wasn't interested in selling it at this point."

"He seems really serious," Shelbie continued. "Wouldn't hurt to see some numbers, would it? Looks like the Mayor will start the countdown soon. I gotta run."

Mayor Matt Mayer's audiences were used to him veering off track a bit during his speeches, and they typically gave him some leeway, but Ellie sensed that this crowd was getting antsy for the lighting display. He must've too, because he sped things along. "...and that was the last time I used my airline credit card for an online purchase. Well, I believe it is time for the countdown." As a smattering of applause made its way through the audience, he invited the nearby town staff to join him on stage. "Alright, count with me now...11...10..."

A thoroughly confused audience looked around at each other. A few voices joined in.

"9...8..."

Mayor Mayer, ever with his finger on the pulse of his constituents, must've sensed that his countdown was taking too long so he sped up to get to the good stuff.

"7..6..5..4.."

The Mayor raised his hands as if he were conducting an orchestra.

"3!"

The magic of the holidays was effervescent as the whole audience joined in to countdown.

"2! 1!"

At the back of the stage, Todd flipped a switch and the lights illuminated in the shape of a giant tree. There was a simultaneous roar of cheers from the crowd. Just as the applause quieted down, someone in the crowd taunted the Mayor.

"Too bad it's not a real tree!"

Mayor Mayer looked directly at a particular individual in the second row knowingly.

"Clam it, Melvin!" the Mayor said.

The crowd broke into an impromptu version of "Hark! The Herald Angels Sing" and the singing swelled and drowned out the Mayor as he shouted towards Melvin from the stage.

"It's like you don't even appreciate all the technological advancements I've brought to the holiday light display. The UV emissions alone—"

Josh scooped more whipped cream from Ellie's hot chocolate mug onto his own.

20

AT HOME IN GREENVILLE

JOSH - WEDNESDAY

JOSH HAD ONLY BEEN IN GREENVILLE for less than a week, but he was settling into the flow of things well. He'd been enjoying spending time with Ellie, meeting new people around town, and honoring Aunt Ruth by completing the holiday traditions. While he was puttering around Auth Ruth's house during a quiet morning, he found a piece of paper on the floor that looked like it had fallen off the countertop. He opened it and saw Aunt Ruth's handwriting:

Gvl Comm College 10A.M. Wed. Prof. Coykendall

The odds were slim that the meeting was actually that day, but it seemed like a pretty good reason to get out of the house. Plus, if someone were waiting to hear from Aunt Ruth, he could at least make sure that they had heard about her passing. Josh looked up the staff directory to see where the professor's office was in the building and then found his way to the Greenville Community College campus. When he arrived, the scene was not at all what Josh had expected.

"I'm sorry, let me just make some room here," the professor said as he dusted off a chair and made a space for Josh to sit. The soft-spoken professor's office was small, with books stacked in almost every square inch of available space. "What can I help you with today?"

"My name's Josh and my aunt was Ruth Matthews. Did you know her?"

Professor Coykendall removed his glasses and placed them on his desk. "I did, and I'm sorry for your loss, Josh. I considered Ruth a dear friend."

"So you've heard?"

"I have. I was shocked when I heard the sad news. Your Aunt Ruth used to guest lecture in some of my classes."

"Really? She was an engineer her whole career, it seems odd that she would guest lecture in a poetry class." This was something he had never heard his Aunt Ruth talk about. It made sense, though. She had so much experience and she loved to share what she knew with people.

"While I'm mainly a poetry professor, sometimes I have to be a team player and jump in to cover other classes. I've spent my fair share of time in front of international business and engineering students. I found myself reaching out to people in the community with actual experience in the fields and multiple people recommended I invite Ruth to speak. After her first couple of talks, word spread pretty fast about her compelling stories from years of leading a global team of energy experts, and her experience as a woman in an industry that was mostly male when she started."

"She was an impressive person." Josh could imagine Aunt Ruth and her curious spirit settling in perfectly leading a college lecture.

"Indeed. No matter what the subject, she could always find a way to relate her life experience to whatever the students were learning. She was a natural teacher."

The two spoke about Aunt Ruth, and each other's careers until Professor Coykendall had to leave for an appointment. "If you're ever looking to put that finance knowledge to work," he said as they shook hands, "we could always use instructors. I'll put in a good word for you."

Josh was feeling inspired after hearing so many kind words about Aunt Ruth from the community college professor, so he decided to stay out of the house for a while. While spending the afternoon exploring downtown, he got a phone call from his friends back home.

"Josh! It's Dave and Mia," Dave said. "We're going bowling!"

"Cool," Josh said. "I'm just walking around downtown, taking it all in."

"Did we call the right number?" Dave said. "Who is this and what did you do with Josh Hanson?"

"Very funny."

"So tell us about this girl," Mia said.

"Ellie? Well, I've known her for a long time, but we fell out of touch for a while. We've been spending a lot of time together here and, honestly, it's been really great."

"Josh!" Mia sounded like she took the phone for herself and tucked away to a quiet corner of the car. "I know we've only known each other for a short time, and I've only ever talked to Ellie over the phone in a group convo, but I swear, if you hurt her, I will come for you. You better treat her like a princess, but better. A princess who unknowingly ascends to the throne in a country she didn't even know existed. I'm talking the full royal treatment, Josh!"

"Yeah, put yourself out there, Josh." Dave said in the distance. Josh noticed he was standing outside Rex's Grocery. "I hear ya. I'll do my best. You guys have fun. I've gotta run." He stepped into Rex's on a mission.

As soon as Josh entered Rex's, Rex himself came right out to Josh and offered a hearty handshake.

"Josh? I'm Rex. I was a good friend of your Aunt Ruth's. She talked about you a lot. I feel like I know you a whole bunch, but you probably don't know anything about me."

He was right. Josh knew very little about Rex. Aunt Ruth had mentioned him from time to time, but she never talked much about herself, so she never gave too many details. "You're right, I don't know very much about you yet. I know she liked stopping in here for groceries, and she raved about your cuts of meat. I've already been in here a couple times, and I love the place."

"That's good to hear," Rex said. "You know, I don't think your Aunt Ruth would mind me speaking for her and telling you that she and I were pretty close. Close friends, but I like to think more than that. I really cared about her."

"Wow," Josh wasn't sure what to say. "I had no idea you two were so close. I wish she had told me more. I suppose I could have asked more, too. I'm glad to hear she was close with you and had someone special in her life."

"I'll sure miss her." Rex was quiet for a moment. He made his way back behind the counter where he wiped it clean with his hand. "So, what brings you in today?"

"Well, I'm looking for some uniquely delicious-sounding snacks."

Rex led Josh down a nearby aisle. "I have some really great gingerbread sandwich cookies. They have actual pieces of candied ginger in the cookie. They're really special. Also, peppermint bark cookies. They're little mini sandwich cookies that have pieces of peppermint bark with cream frosting in the middle." Rex stopped and looked at Josh. "I have something else that I think you'd really enjoy." Rex led Josh to the counter and handed him a clear plastic bag with a gold twist tie on top. "These are my spicy mint chocolates with chili flakes. I make them from scratch myself. Go ahead and try one." Rex put his hands on his hips and waited for Josh to sample them.

Josh inspected one. It looked like a chocolate-covered espresso bean. He popped one in his mouth and chewed. "Mmm." And chewed. "Spicy. And crunchy. And there's the mint. That chili hangs around, too, huh?" Josh choked out the words.

"Yeah, the kids around town love 'em."

"Yeah, I bet." Josh couldn't bear to tell him that he thought it was more for pain than pleasure. "Well, as long as they're moving off the shelves!"

Josh grabbed a pack of the chocolate mint chili drops and chocolate dipped caramels, Ellie's favorite from when they were younger, then settled up with Rex. His next stop was to Pour it Up, a favorite stop for his Aunt Ruth.

Sandra recognized Josh as soon as he walked in. "Josh, what's taken you so long to stop in?"

Josh knew that Sandra and Aunt Ruth were good friends, but he had only met her a few times when he was younger. She had probably heard a lot about him from Aunt Ruth. "Hi, Sandra. I wasn't sure if you'd remember me."

"Remember you? You were my best friend's favorite nephew. We're kind of rivals." Sandra pulled Josh in for a hug. "You know, your Aunt Ruth always talked about how hard you worked, but looking at you here, you look just so calm and relaxed. Greenville looks good on you!"

"Thanks. It's been great being here."

"That Ellie." She lowered her voice. "I think she's sweet on you." Sandra smiled big. "I do. I think she's sweet on you, Josh."

Josh could feel his cheeks turning red. "She is a sweet one, isn't she?"

Sandra must have noticed him blushing. "I get the feeling you might be sweet on her, too, Josh."

He felt more than a little sweet on Ellie, but he wasn't about to admit that to the ringleader of the Lunch Ladies.

"Mmm-hm," Sandra nodded knowingly. "So, you here for the ego boost or did you want to shop a bit?"

Josh left Pour it Up with a few bottles that Sandra said would go great with a wintery mix of snacks from Rex's. With armfuls of snacks and some hand-picked toddies from Sandy's, Josh was excited to go to Evelyn's and surprise Ellie.

Ellie let Josh in, but only into the entryway. Taylor was over, and they were in the middle of wine time.

"What's wine time?" Josh asked.

"It's the time we have wine," Ellie said.

"Sometimes we also whine about things," Tay added.

"I brought snacks and more wine. Can I join?"

"No. Afraid not," Tay said. Ellie also shook her head.

"What? Why not?" Josh got it, this was their time, but he could try just a little bit to intrude.

"Sorry bro," Tay said. "But thank you for this." She grabbed the bottles of wine from Josh.

Josh handed Ellie the bag of snacks. "I guess you'll be needing these, too."

Ellie mouthed, "Thank you," as she smiled and turned away.

"I'll just let myself out," Josh said to himself as he craned his neck to see her disappear completely out of sight. "Enjoy the snacks!"

TOWN HALL BEFORE WORK

ELLIE - THURSDAY

On a morning when Ellie was scheduled to work at Tay's, she stopped at Town Hall to complete a little mission. She wanted to talk to Todd about the Christmas Planning Committee and see what events were coming up. If she were honest with herself, though, the real reason to visit Todd was to try to get him to hang out with and connect with Josh. She thought that if Josh could continue making friends in Greenville, maybe he'd want to stay. If she were to be really, brutally honest with herself, the *real* real reason to visit Todd was to see if there was anything she could do through the town to try to preserve Auth Ruth's tree.

As she marched up the walkway, she passed a small group of people dressed in winter clothes posing in various stages of stretches in a shoveled area in the front lawn.

"Good morning, Ellie!" Todd noticed her as soon as she walked in. "You here for Cold Yoga? They just got started out front. It was just a little idea I had. A little alternative programming to sitting inside all winter."

"Hi. Cold Yoga? No. Good idea, though."

"Just you today or will Handsome Josh be joining us, too?"

"Just me today, Todd. Actually, I was thinking. You two should hang out. I bet he'd appreciate it if you'd reach out. It doesn't sound like he spends much time with people."

"What? That's hard to believe. Josh is a great dude. Should I invite him to karaoke?"

"I definitely think you should invite him to karaoke," Ellie said, knowing it would be a hard "no" from Josh. If anyone could convince him to go, Todd could. "Hey, Todd, do you remember our conversation yesterday with Josh and the Mayor about doing a Christmas tree decorating contest?"

Todd reached for a notebook on the countertop and flipped it open. "Let me check my notes."

"Notes? You took notes?"

"Ah! Yes!" he said as he turned a page. "I have it right here. You said, and I quote, 'How about a tree decorating contest throughout the town.'" He closed the notebook and looked up at Ellie. "Then you stuck your arms up into the air like this," he said as he held his arms into the air above his head.

"That doesn't sound like me..." Ellie said, a little embarrassed, a little self-conscious.

Todd opened his notebook again to a page with the exact text he just read and a hand-drawn sketch that resembled a pretty decent courtroom drawing. "See, that's you. And that's you with your hands above your head. The short horizontal lines are meant to indicate movement."

Ellie leaned in for a closer look. "That's actually pretty good, Todd."

"Thanks," Todd closed the notebook and leaned on the counter. "I was on a jury once and sat near the court artist. I spent a good bit of the time watching them and the rest of the time doing my own sketches."

"Oh, cool."

"Yeah. The defendant was guilty as sin. Unfortunately, I got caught sketching so much they declared a mistrial."

Ellie's eyes went wide with surprise.

"ABC!" Todd said, unfazed. "Always be sketchin', right?"

"You mean A...B...S...?"

"Nah," Todd waved her off.

"Yeeaahh...so. Todd," Ellie tried to turn the conversation away from something incriminating and subpoena-worthy. "Per our last conversation, I was just wondering if there was some other way to move along the tree conversation, and maybe really focus on how to ensure that any tree that doesn't want to become the downtown Christmas tree doesn't have to? Specifically, the tree I showed you. Is there any way to make sure that tree stays put? That tree means so much to me. Aunt Ruth and I decorated it every year, and every year I'd make a new ornament. It was one of my favorite traditions. She just passed away, so I want to preserve this tree and our memories. She was such an influence in my life. I feel like she deserves a monument. What's the process for designating historical monuments? Is there a donation amount that would preserve it? Is there anything we can do?"

As Ellie spoke, Todd fished around for something under the counter and then pulled up a plot map book that showed all of the property lines throughout the town. "I'm sorry about your Aunt Ruth. I got to see her regularly around here. She was a great person." He opened the book right up to the street with Aunt Ruth's property. The map showed her property lines and one large triangle labeled 'TREE'. "Ah. Here we are. Yup, the tree is clearly on her property."

"Maybe we could fudge some kind of utility easement?

Something that would not allow digging?"

"We don't joke about those kinds of things here, Ellie," Todd said. "While I can't endorse your methods, I understand where you're coming from. I'm really moved by your story. Unfortunately, I'm powerless."

Ellie sighed, feeling slightly defeated, sad, and missing Aunt Ruth.

Todd looked up at Ellie sincerely. "But guess what?"

"What?" Ellie listened intently.

"I'm doing a tree survey."

"Great! How can that help?"

"It can't. I just wanted you to know. You know, get all the potential conflicts of interest out of the way up front."

"However," Todd continued, "if there's a petition I can sign, I'll definitely sign it. If it's any consolation, the Mayor seemed pretty psyched about your tree contest idea." Todd pulled out his phone to show a text exchange with Mayor Mayer. "See? This is the last message I got from him." Todd showed her a text that was simply a line of multiple Christmas trees followed by multiple flames: 🎄🎄🎄🎄🔥🔥🔥🔥. "Hopefully he didn't mean that his own tree was on fire."

Ellie cracked a skeptical half-smile.

"Before I forget," Todd grabbed a flier from nearby and handed it to Ellie. "Mr. Mayor wanted me to give you this. The Christmas Planning Committee is meeting tomorrow, and he'd like you to join us."

Right. The main goal of this trip. "Of course. Thanks, Todd. See you tomorrow, then."

Ellie helped Taylor wipe down tables at the choffee shop and talked through the scenarios of Josh inheriting the house or Josh possibly not inheriting the house. Partly to tell Tay, and partly just to hear it all out loud.

"Josh and I have to do Aunt Ruth's traditions or else Josh doesn't get the house. If we do all the traditions, he could end up just selling it anyway if he chooses to."

"If he keeps the house, though," Taylor said, "then you could both live there together happily ever after, right?"

"This is real life, Taylor. It's not some fairy tale where the boy and girl, who used to spend summer and winter breaks together, come back together to complete a bunch of holiday traditions so the boy can inherit the house and change his life for the better and then their lives are perfect and magical for the rest of time. It's just not like that, Tay."

Taylor must've noticed that the Lunch Ladies were intrigued by the new gossip and were swooning at the idea of that happily-ever-after love story because she included them in the conversation. "I think Ellie should just tell Josh that she'd like him to stay. Just put it out there."

The Lunch Ladies were a quartet of widows who spent as much time at Tay's socializing with each other as they could. What started out as four friends meeting for lunch quickly evolved into a daily routine of lunch, dessert, coffee, and lots of chit-chat.

"Estelle loves to hear all this gossip, so keep it coming!" said Laura, the jokester bookstore owner who liked to embarrass Estelle any chance she got.

"I do not. Stop that," Estelle scolded. She was the most reserved and private of the group.

"At least Ellie's got something exciting going on, unlike us four," grumpy Margery added.

"You know, Margery," said Sandra, the sassy ringleader of the crew, "I don't know how you can be so darn negative all the time when your family owns a candy shop! Do you know how many people dream of being able to walk into a candy store and help themselves to their favorite sweet treat whenever they please?"

"My doctor said that candy is not good for my hypertension," Estelle said without missing a beat.

"Anyway," Sandra said as she raised her coffee mug to take a sip. "Carry on, you two."

"What do you think, ladies?" Tay asked. "Should she tell Josh she wants him to stay in Greenville?"

"Who's this boy? Sandra asked.

"Is this Ruthie's nephew the math whiz from Philadelphia?" Laura asked.

"I went to Philadelphia once..." Margery added. "It was my first and *last* time in that city."

"Thanks for that, Margery," Sandra said and then turned her attention back to Ellie. "This is Ruth's nephew, yes?"

"Yes," Ellie answered. "He's an investment manager or something from north of Philadelphia."

Sandra nodded like she knew more than she was letting on.

"What is it?" Ellie asked.

Sandra pursed her lips, and the other Lunch Ladies busied themselves with their snacks and drinks.

Ellie scrubbed a table she had already cleaned and then turned her attention to the Lunch Ladies. "That can never happen, though, if Josh doesn't inherit the house, so we have to complete all the traditions. Then there's the issue of the tree! I want to keep the tree, but he doesn't. We need to agree on what to do with the tree in—"

The door chimed as Josh entered the choffee shop with the red and green plates of their leftover cookies. The Ladies, Ellie, and Taylor simultaneously looked at the door. Taylor broke into a smile. "Hi, Josh."

The table of ladies looked at Ellie, waiting for her to react.

"Hi...Josh..."

The Lunch Ladies were giddy with excitement.

Josh claimed a vacant table and set out the leftover cookies he and Ellie had baked. He had even made a sign that said, 'Free Cookies!' One by one, the Lunch Ladies made their way up for a complimentary dessert.

"Hi, Josh. I'm Laura. I knew your Aunt Ruth pretty well, and I miss her. I'm sure you do, too. She was one of the best people I've ever known." Laura nodded at the table where the other Lunch Ladies sat. "Present company included."

"Thanks for saying that," Josh said. "I do miss her, but being here has been great. I feel close to her."

Laura took a bite of a cookie from the green plate in front of Josh. "Mmm. This town needs someone who can make these cookies as well as Ruth did." She winked at Josh.

Margery stepped up to the table, hands clasped in front of her, looking indifferent.

"What do you think, Margery? Want to try a homemade cookie?" Ellie held out her red plate.

Margery took one from the plate and chewed. "These cookies are just like Ruth's."

"Aw, thanks," Ellie did a little shimmy, feeling proud.

"Hers were always too dry," Margery said and then walked away.

Ellie shrugged. "That's actually pretty good coming from Margery."

Ellie sat with Josh at the table for a little while longer. More people stopped by for a cookie, so Josh chatted and got to hear people talk about Aunt Ruth. At one point, he turned and looked at Ellie, grabbed her hand and squeezed. Ellie saw Tay out of the corner of her eye. Taylor looked at her with doe eyes and mouthed the words, "Tell him to stay." Ellie expressed her desire not to speak up via tiny, silent head and eye movements that only Taylor could understand. Ellie pursed her lips, knowing full well she should get that off her chest. That she should just say, *Josh, don't sell Aunt Ruth's house. Stay here in Greenville. I'm having a great time with you and want to spend even more time together. Let's take the leap and just see where this all goes.* Instead, she squeezed his hand and smiled back at him.

"Hey, El, ready to go?" Evelyn said as she rolled into the choffee shop. Ellie and her mom had plans to do some Christmas shopping that afternoon.

"Sorry, Josh," Ellie said. "I gotta head out. We have plans tonight."

"Oh, okay. No problem. I can handle things here," Josh said.

"Josh," Evelyn said as she grabbed a cookie from his green plate. "Care to join us? We're just doing some shopping downtown."

"You sure you don't mind?" he asked.

"I don't mind," Evelyn said. "Ellie, do you mind?" She looked at Ellie with a knowing smile.

"No, of course I don't mind," she said.

Their first stop was *Juniper Lee's Decor and Designs*, the local home decor store that specialized in decorations. They made their way up and down the aisles, picking up trinkets, shaking snow globes, and wind-up music makers.

"Mom, why don't you help me pick out some flowers?" Ellie said as they approached the flower counter.

"No, that's okay. You can choose, El," Evelyn said.

Ellie's mom used to love having fresh flowers in the house. Her dad would bring home fresh flowers at least once a week, and her mom would spend the next thirty minutes humming to herself while arranging them just right. Now, her mom just had cabinets full of empty vases at home. From years of watching her mom arrange flowers, Ellie knew the basics of a simple arrangement: a few flowers as the focal points, a handful of greenery, and then a couple handfuls of accent flowers. Knowing this, Ellie began to purposefully select an unbalanced arrangement, hoping her mom wouldn't be able to resist stepping in.

"Why are you choosing so much greenery?" Evelyn chirped. "And all of your flowers are the same height. Why aren't you—just give me that, please," Evelyn reached for the items Ellie had picked.

Ellie stood back, basking in her success, and watched her mother pick and choose just the right combination of flowers and greenery.

"Smooth, Ellie, smooth," Josh whispered in her ear.

She liked feeling his breath, so she stayed close and whispered back, "Do you think she realizes what I was doing?"

"Even if she does, I don't think it matters. It might have been the little nudge she needed to use as an excuse," Josh said as he bumped her shoulder with his.

As Ellie and Josh looked on, Evelyn explained to Juniper Lee why she chose the combination of flowers that she did. Evelyn was in her element, offering guidance and being helpful. Ellie could see a spark of life in her mom's eyes that she hadn't seen in some time.

"I'll be paying for that," Ellie said. "Don't you dare let my mom pay, Juniper Lee."

"I think this arrangement is on the house, Ellie. Your mom just taught me a trick that will save me so much time. Evelyn, if you're ever looking for some part-time work as a floral arranger, you come see me right away. I'd hire you on the spot," Juniper Lee smiled as she wrapped up the arrangement and packed in some flower food.

"We don't need all that, dear," Evelyn waved off the flower food. "I just mix up some sugar with apple cider. That's worked for me for years."

Juniper Lee stood with her hand on her hip, "Color me

impressed. What a good idea!"

Ellie stood back while her mom and Juniper Lee talked flower shop. Josh nudged her. "She kept your drawings up," he said.

"What's that?" Ellie had been entranced watching her mom, so she did not hear what Josh said.

Josh pointed at the wall behind the counter. "Your drawings of this building that you did when your dad owned it. I remember he had them framed and hung them up on the wall. Juniper had kept them up this whole time. That must feel good."

"Wow, I hadn't even noticed until you said that. Yeah, I guess she has."

The building they were in used to be owned by Ellie's dad. It was the building he bought for his hardware store, the building he had waited patiently to buy at the price he could afford. Once he owned it, he fixed up the apartment on the second floor and rented it to a tenant, and he opened his store on the first floor, making improvements to it over the years.

Josh leaned in for a closer look at one of the drawings. "Who's 'Elfie'?"

"Oh my gosh, I haven't heard that in years," Ellie moved in for a closer look. "Every year since I can remember, my dad would call me Elfie, starting Thanksgiving night until Christmas night. He called it my 'name decoration'. It was a special nickname he used only that time of the year. I must've drawn that picture during the holidays and signed it as Elfie for him."

"I can't believe I never heard that before," Josh said. "That is so sweet."

"It was sort of our little thing." Ellie stepped back from the counter. "Yup," she continued. "This is where my art career began. I didn't know I could draw until I started sketching this building. Honestly, even if I couldn't draw well, my dad probably still would have told me how great they were."

"He totally would have."

"Yeah. Yeah, he would've. I've kept sketching this building over the years. Every time someone new bought it or the business changed over, I'd sit on the bench across the street and draw."

"That's really cool—" Josh's phone rang. "Sorry, let me get this." He looked confused as he answered, but quickly recognized the caller. "Hey, Todd...oh, Ellie gave you my number, huh?"

Ellie recognized his glare, so she sheepishly slipped away down an aisle.

After he was done with his phone call, Josh found Ellie in the Christmas Village aisle, where she was working out how to fit a two-foot outdoor skating rink and hot chocolate stand into the two inches of space she had left in her village at home, but the math wasn't mathing. "Who was that?" she asked, feigning ignorance.

"Apparently," Josh said, "someone told Todd that I would *love* to go to karaoke with him. Any idea why Todd would think that I love karaoke, Ellie?"

Ellie was having a hard time keeping a straight face. She was pressing her lips together so hard she was afraid they would get stuck.

"Wow, that was so thoughtful of him. What'd you say?"

"I couldn't say no! He was so excited that he ended our call with 'konnichiwa,' for crying out loud. As offensive as that might be, I didn't have the heart to say no to him."

Ellie burst out laughing. She couldn't hold it any longer. "Aw, Todd. I'm sure his heart is in the right place. It'll be good for you to spend some time with a friend."

"A friend? I've probably hung out with Todd five times in my life!"

"Then it will be good for you to spend time with a future friend. When are you meeting him?"

"He said he'd be at Moriah's Light Ale House at 7p.m., and to come whenever I could. Does that place only serve light beer or something?"

"No, it's just a silly name that doesn't make any sense. It's better than Fitzy's, though. That place is a total dive, and they have the weirdest, nonsensical specialty drinks."

Josh zipped up his coat. "I guess I'd better go and start warming up my pipes. You should come! He didn't say if it was strictly a 'guy's night' or not."

"Maybe. I might have a song in me," Ellie said, "but I do have to be up early for work, though."

"I know what you were doing back there, with the flowers," Evelyn said as she and Ellie strolled back to the car.

"Who, me?" Ellie feigned innocence.

"It did feel good, though. Thank you. Maybe you could use a taste of your own medicine."

"What's that mean?"

"Maybe it's time for you to get back to something you're passionate about. What do you do that you love?"

"I love hanging out with Tay, and I love taking care of you..."

"Those are things for others, El. You're always doing things for everyone but yourself. I can say from experience now, it feels pretty good to pick up an old hobby."

Seeing her mom express even the slightest interest in flowers again took a weight off Ellie's heart. "Maybe you're right."

22

KARAOKE NIGHT

JOSH – THURSDAY EVENING

JOSH ARRIVED AT MORIAH'S LIGHT ALE HOUSE at 7:30p.m., just in time to see Todd perform "Wild World" by Cat Stevens.

Josh grabbed a seat at the mostly empty bar and waited for the bartender to notice him. He clapped as Todd finished and introduced the next singer.

"Hey, Josh!" Todd slapped him on the back. "Glad you could make it down!" Todd turned to the bartender, who was still looking at her phone across the bar. "Rachel! Two beers, please!"

Todd tapped Josh's bottle and took a sip. "So, what're ya gonna sing?"

"I'm not much of a karaoke guy, Todd. I know Ellie may have led you to believe otherwise—"

Todd had a look of disgust on his face. "Not much of a karaoke guy? Said no one, ever! Be right back!" Todd sprinted to the stage and grabbed the microphone from the singer who just finished their song. "Alright, thanks, Mike. Best version yet. Next up, a song I've been told was written about me." Todd winked at Josh. He then flowed through a flawless version of Salt-N-Pepa's "Whatta Man."

He's singing an awful lot of songs, Josh thought.

"Another beer, sir?" Rachel, the bartender, asked. *Better take it while I can.* "Sure, and one more for my friend, too." *My friend. That felt weird.*

Todd hopped back onto the barstool next to Josh, breathing heavily. "How'd I do?"

"Great. You do this a lot?" Josh asked.

"Once a week here, twice a month over at Shandy's. Once a month at Lonnie's. What about you?

"Karaoke? Nah. Hardly ever."

"No, I mean, social stuff. What do you do for fun with your friends back home?"

Josh thought for a moment. He was embarrassed to say not much.

"Gotta go! BRB!" Todd jetted back to the stage and kicked off a rousing version of NSYNC's "Bye Bye Bye."

Another song?? When Tood returned, Josh just had to ask, "Is there not a limit on the number of songs you can perform?"

"As the host, I have to fill in the spots where no one signs up. I mean, Tammy sings sometimes, but I can only hear her make a mess of a Whitney Houston song so many times—"

"When you said we should hang out and get a drink at karaoke, you actually meant you were hosting karaoke?"

"Right. I mean, six in one, half dozen of the other, right?"

"I think the saying is actually six *of* one, half dozen of the other."

"Ehh..." Todd thought. "I don't think it matters. Anyway, I hope the a cappella group shows up. That group of singers at the downtown market? They're part of a six-person a cappella group, and they rotate members as the quartet. Yeah, I'm pretty good friends with most of them. Their group's name is MAD BARs, because they're singers, you know? You want to know the coolest part? It's actually the letters of their names! Marc, Ali, Dustin, Britt, Antonio, and Ryan. Last week, they blew the doors off this place with a Nickelback song. Well, duty calls. Gotta do a Backstreet Boys song now, so it doesn't look like I'm playing favorites." Then he mouthed, "NSYNC is my favorite."

Todd got a break when a group of co-workers rolled in, celebrating someone's promotion.

"You gotta have time for *you*, Josh! Why aren't you making time to hang with your friends?"

"I've just sort of been head-down working. I really enjoy my job, so I've been really focused on that."

"I love my job, too. It's my dream job, but I think it's important to have hobbies, too. I feel like it makes a person more dynamic, more interesting, more—shoot! Gotta go! Hold onto your butt for this one!" Todd dodged patrons to get back to the stage and took advantage of every inch of the stage for a passionate version of Rachel Platten's "Fight Song."

23

FINANCE ROUNDTABLE @ TAY'S

ELLIE - FRIDAY

As OFTEN AS THEY COULD, Ellie and her mom met up once a week after Ellie finished a shift, and they would sit and have coffee together. When she first moved back home, it was every week, then it changed to every other week, then only days that happened to be an odd number and when their moods aligned with the moon phase. Lately, though, Evelyn had become one of the local transportation service's favorite customers since Ellie and Evelyn had been spending more time together outside the house.

Ellie sipped coffee with her mom while the shop bustled around them. "Mom, I heard about a freelance graphic design job with some company in Ohio."

"Oh? That sounds fun. Would you need to relocate? You know, it's okay if you did. I am doing just fine. I'm actually, what's the word? Try-ving?"

"You're thriving, Evelyn," Taylor said as she dropped off a couple of apricot ginger scones at the table. "Try-ving sounds like the phase right before thriving."

"Thank you, Taylor," Evelyn said. "I'm *thriving.*"

"So, Evelyn," Tay continued, "Are you all caught up on this ridiculousness between Ellie and Josh? All the traditions they're doing so Josh can inherit Aunt Ruth's house?"

"I think it's kind of adorable. I'm sure Ruthie is enjoying this." Evelyn playfully raised her eyebrows as she sipped her drink.

"Excuse me? What's that supposed to mean?" Ellie said defensively.

"On that note," Tay said as she exited, "I have work to do."

Ellie continued, "Don't think I didn't see that coy little smirk behind your coffee mug. Anyway, to answer your question, no, the job is remote. I am not sure I'd want to work any place other than here. It feels like my whole world is right here."

"They would really benefit from your skills. I know that," Evelyn said.

It had been a while since Ellie felt excited about getting back into graphic design projects. She picked up small freelance work that she could complete in a day or two, but getting back into a full-time role? Maybe she was ready. Something she was really interested in—

"Ooh!" Ellie jumped to her feet. "I just had an idea. Hold my latte." She made her way over to a table where the Lunch Ladies were sitting. "Hi, ladies. Are you up for helping me out with a little project?"

"What's in it for us?" Margery barked, while Sandy, Laura, and Estelle rolled their eyes.

"Of course, dear," Estelle said.

"Perfect! Thanks!"

Most of the table was giddy as Ellie rushed off. She pulled out her phone and moved behind the coffee shop counter near Taylor.

"Tay, I have an idea, but I'm going to need your help." Ellie worked feverishly on her phone as she spoke.

"O-kaaay...does it involve a horse?"

"No," Ellie continued working on her phone.

"Does it involve the beach?"

Ellie was unfazed. "No."

"Does it involve a timeshare?"

"No."

"Can you tell I'm thinking about a warm vacation?"

"No. There." Ellie tapped her phone one last time and then looked up. "Done." She turned her screen to Tay and revealed a simple but catchy flier design that Ellie had just created.

Taylor read it aloud as she spoke, "That's cool, El. But what exactly is the 'Greenville Finance Roundtable Today @ Tay's Choffee Shop'?"

Ellie tapped the "Print" icon on her phone screen, and the printer behind the coffee shop counter spit out multiple copies of the flier. "I am going to invite Josh down here for this afternoon's Finance Roundtable." Ellie grabbed a flier from the printer and handed it to Taylor.

"Pardon my ignorance, but what Finance Roundtable, Ellie?"

"The one you're hosting here in a few minutes."

"Ellie, you know I'm always down with your cosmic ideas - they're out-of-this-world! I just need to know what this is really about."

"Alright. Fine. I had this idea that maybe if Josh could experience what it would be like to work in this community, then maybe he would want to stay here. I just need some people to ask him some investing questions and then he can be his regular helpful self. Hopefully, he'll find it rewarding and fun, and he'll want to stay."

Taylor took this in for a moment and then nodded affirmatively before she addressed her customers. "Alright, people, get out your finance documents. Get your 401Ks, your W9s, your ICD10s, your Chapter 11s, it's investment roundtable time!"

"Thanks, Tay. Love you so much. I have to make a quick phone call." Ellie said as she stepped outside to make a vague call to Josh to lure him down to the choffee shop.

"Hey, Josh, could you swing by Taylor's? There's like, this investment get-together happening, and I think you'd really like it."

A corner of Tay's Choffee Shop had been transformed into Berkshire Hathaway's Annual Shareholder's Meeting - East. A few tables were pushed together, and a small group of elderly folks sat around with their eyes focused on Ellie, presumably waiting for the sign.

"They keep telling me to give them the sign when Josh arrives," Ellie said to Tay as she grabbed a carafe of coffee for the group. "What's the sign? What are they talking about?"

"Humor them, Ellie. This is literally the most exciting thing they've done in weeks. I'm actually worried Margery's heart might not be able to handle it."

The bell at the entrance door dinged as Josh walked through. Ellie looked over at the table—at the Finance Roundtable—and began to tap her head and then touch her nose. The group looked at her, confused, like they weren't even waiting for the sign. Ellie pointed towards the entrance door and mouthed *That's Josh!* This must've been the sign they were waiting for because all at once, and not at all suspiciously, the group focused their attention on each other and began chatting amongst themselves.

Josh spotted Ellie and walked towards the counter. "Hey! So, what's this all about?"

Ellie handed Josh a flier. The ink smudged when he grabbed it.

"Thanks for coming, Josh. So, there's this investment get-together, just like, a real casual thing with some folks who love to talk investing."

"Oh, cool. Great!"

"Yeah! It's today. Can you believe it? I thought maybe you could join the conversation, answer some questions, you know, do some of the stuff you like to do."

"Sounds like fun!"

Ellie led Josh to the corner where the roundtable participants had gathered. The chatter had already veered off course into medical appointments, but everyone quickly tightened up when Josh joined. Laura winked at Ellie.

"Alright. Hi everyone," Josh dove right into the conversation. "Has anyone heard about the proposed annuity changes that the S.E.C. and the F.I.R.A. are working together on?"

Josh spent the next forty-five minutes explaining the heck out of investment ideas to the group around the table. At one point, Ellie looked over to see Josh furiously punching numbers into an old school desktop calculator with the receipt paper. He was grabbing papers from one person, reviewing line items from another person— fully in the zone, as much as a finance person could be.

"You're bad, sister," Taylor said to Ellie while the two stood behind the counter and watched Josh dole out investment advice.

"He talks about his plan and how he's always been working towards it, but then when he talks about the stuff he'd like to do that he hasn't had a chance to do, he lights up. So, before he continues on his predefined, narrow path, he should at least look at other ways to go."

"I know that everyone grieves in their own way," Taylor raised her hand to stave off interruption, "but I just hope that this is at least 51% inspired by you genuinely wanting the best for Josh."

Ellie didn't immediately respond. She watched Josh and took Taylor's comments to heart. "Is he not having the best time right now?"

24

RIDING HIGH ON NUMBERS

JOSH – FRIDAY

LATER THAT DAY, after the Finance Roundtable event had come to a close, Josh and Ellie moseyed down the Main Street sidewalk with coffee cups in their hands. The town shops around them were decorated beautifully, and a tinny, bass-less version of Kelly Clarkson's "Underneath the Tree" played from beneath the snowcapped bushes.

"I feel so energized right now!" Josh said still riding the high of helping people with investment advice.

"You're glowing," Ellie said.

"I have you to thank. What are the odds, right? That I'm here for a random, pop-up investment chat? It was fun." Josh couldn't remember the last time he had the opportunity to sit around with people and discuss, debate, suggest...all without trying to wedge in a sales pitch. *Why wasn't this more common? Why is this the only place that does this sort of thing?*

"Yeah, about that..."

"You know," Josh cut off Ellie excitedly. "I'm really enjoying my time here in Greenville. It might be a sign that I should stick around a while."

Ellie was quiet, but he had a feeling that she would be okay with him sticking around for a while. Josh's phone dinged with a new text message.

"Hm. That's strange," Josh looked at his phone to see a new message from his boss, Jerry.

"What is it?" Ellie asked.

"Just a text from my boss. I haven't heard a peep from him since I got here. I just hope it's nothing important." Josh stared at his phone and read the text to himself.

> 💬 Jerry (boss): There's something we need to talk about. And it rhymes with 'demotion'.

His phone dinged with another text message from Jerry:

> 💬 Jerry (boss): Was trying to rhyme. Bad example. Let's talk about a promotion. Everything you talked about. Total autonomy."

Ideas swirled in his head. Jerry had never shown interest in the things Josh cared most about, like what was best for each individual and their financial situation. Jerry cared about the "macros," as he put it. "In business and in the gym." If Jerry was going to let Josh manage clients without hassling him, then this could be everything Josh had ever wanted. This was a lot to consider.

Through the noise in his head, Josh heard Ellie ask a question that sounded like it was about food, but he was too distracted processing what Jerry had mentioned. "Um, sure," he said, still looking at his phone and uncertain about what he'd agreed to. "That sounds fine." He started to compose a reply to Jerry:

💬 Sure, would love to talk…

He stopped and deleted what he wrote. After a thoughtful few seconds, Josh typed:

💬 Can we talk tomorrow?

A second later, Josh's phone dinged again.

💬 Jerry (boss): Baby spinach, greens, dill, tarter, onions. Balsamic Vinaigrette ON. THE. SIDE!!!

Ding.

💬 Jerry (boss): Sorry, wrong text. Talk tmrw.

"Hello? Earth to Josh," Ellie said. "You getting bombarded with investment questions from soon-to-be clients?"

"Not exactly. Sorry about that." Josh realized he had been ignoring her, so he tucked away his phone. "It's just some work stuff. It can wait."

Josh followed Ellie as she stepped up to the Hot Pretzel cart and looked around at the other food options. "They should call this the

Hot Corner or something. Look at all these hot food options."

Ellie stared blankly.

"What?" Josh was oblivious. He was not fully present, and he was bad at multitasking. He decided to explain to Ellie what the text messages from his boss were about.

CHRISTMAS PLANNING COMMITTEE MEETING

ELLIE – FRIDAY

AFTER THE FAUX FINANCE ROUNDTABLE, Ellie strolled Candy Cane Lane with Josh. She was pretty proud of herself for putting together such a successful ruse on-the-spot. There was a tiny bit of guilt starting to eat away at her, sure. But everyone involved actually got something from it. Everyone Josh talked to had real questions, and Josh got to give real advice and felt genuinely energized afterwards. It was clear to her that Josh needed to start his own investment firm. She just had to tell him the truth about the investment meeting first. Just as she built up the courage and was about to explain it to him, he cut her off, excitedly glowing about his time in Greenville.

Ellie weighed her choices in that moment. Celebrating too hard and too fast could backfire. Downplaying the excitement could be suspicious. Josh already knew she didn't want him to sell the house and leave, after all. Luckily, Josh's phone dinged with a new text message.

Continuing along the sidewalk, they neared a few street vendors selling hot pretzels, hot chocolate, hot dogs, and popcorn. "They should call this corner the hot pocket." Ellie joked. She noticed Josh was distracted, probably processing whatever those texts were about. "Because of all the hot items for sale here..." she mumbled. "Would you like anything to eat here? Pretzel? Hot dog?" She said a bit louder, trying to get his attention. It didn't work. "Uni? Shark fin soup? Wild unicorn?"

"Um, sure," Josh said, still looking at his phone. "That sounds fine."

"Hello? Earth to Josh. You getting bombarded with investment questions from soon-to-be clients?"

"Not exactly. Sorry about that." Josh tucked away his phone. "It's just some work stuff. It can wait."

Ellie stepped up to the Hot Pretzel cart and Josh followed.

"They should call this the Hot Corner or something," he said. "Look at all these hot food options."

Ellie stared blankly. Is he for real? I just said that!

Ellie and Josh shared a bag of popcorn at a small table in the Hot Corner Pocket, as they had agreed to call that corner of downtown. The table was adorned with a plaque that said:

THIS OUTDOOR FOOD COURT GENEROUSLY
DONATED BY JANNIE TURNKEY AND HER
CONTRACTOR HUSBAND TUCKER. VALUABLE AND
RESPECTED MEMBERS OF OUR COMMUNITY.

"About the text messages I was getting," Josh began. "They were actually about my job—"

"Oh!" Ellie interrupted. She had been wanting to tell Josh about the graphic design job she heard about and how she was feeling excited about the prospect. "I'm sorry, but you just reminded me of something. There's this company in Ohio looking for a contract graphic designer, and they reached out to me. It sounds pretty cool. I'm kind of excited about it."

"That's cool! A longer-term project you could really sink your teeth into? You know, Ellie, I feel like I may be stating the obvious here, but you don't really need to work a full-time job if you don't want to. If we invest—I mean, if you invest right, compounding will continue to do all the work for you."

"If *we*, huh?" She caught that little slip of the tongue. "Yeah, I know, but it's not about the money. I kind of actually want to get back to working more." Ellie had been thinking about what her mom said about having a hobby and doing things for herself. She really enjoyed working on design projects, but the effort to book a freelance gig was exhausting. The idea of a role where she could just do the work and not have to deal with all the other stuff around it was exciting.

"I'm surprised you would leave here for a job," Josh said.

"It's remote. Ohio? You think I would leave here for Ohio? Get real. Plus, I should probably keep working because I think I want to sell some of the stocks Aunt Ruth left for me." Ellie braced herself for a blizzard of investment lingo and reasons why this was a bad idea, but Josh surprised her.

"You know," Josh said with a smirk, "as your financial advisor, I have to warn you about the tax implications of liquidating part of an asset and how you'll have less of a dividend to reinvest each quarter, but as your friend, I'd simply ask which account you would like your funds deposited to."

"I said *interim* financial advisor," Ellie joked.

"What's the money for, if you don't mind me asking?"

"I want to buy my mom a cruise to the Bahamas for Christmas."

"That is incredibly generous of you, Ellie. Isn't it kind of close to

Christmas to get her signed up for a cruise, though?"

"I just mean I want to pay for it. She can pick when she goes. She would probably never buy something like that for herself, and she's made sacrifices for others her whole life. What's the point of sacrificing and putting things off if you never actually reward yourself or get the payoff? I don't want her to forget that even though things are a bit more complicated with her health, she can still live her life and experience fun and amazing things. And I'm not going to buy the travel insurance, so there's no way she can say no."

"Whoa, whoa, whoa, I know I'm still getting used to my newfound fiscal flexibility, but that's just bad decision making."

"Fine. I'll consider buying the travel insurance, per the recommendation of my interim financial advisor." Ellie felt good about her decision and was glad to have talked it through with Josh. She had always loved hearing about Aunt Ruth's travels. Even the trips that sounded like they were full of problems were at least great stories. Ellie was excited about this special gift for her mom. "I'm sorry, I think I interrupted you before. Were you saying something?"

"Right." Josh took a deep breath. "I wanted to tell you—"

Ellie tapped Josh's arm excitedly. "I swear I'm not doing this on purpose, but look!" She pointed across the street. "Carolers! We gotta go! We can check off caroling, Josh!" Ellie grabbed Josh's hand and tugged him across the street to join the carolers.

Inside a small Town Hall conference room, the Christmas Planning Committee had gathered. There was a table near the entrance covered in snacks and a large conference table in the middle of the room. A decorative Christmas tree in one of the corners made it extra inconvenient to navigate around the table, especially with the Mayor's Assistant and Photographer standing behind him at all times. Each member of the Christmas Planning Committee sat behind a placard with their name on it, and each member adorned the same Christmas tree pin on their shirt. The meeting commenced when Mayor Mayer gaveled them into session.

"Alright everyone, thanks for coming. We're here to discuss ideas for making our downtown Christmas celebration even better. As you can see..." The Mayor motioned to an easel at the other end of the conference room. "We have our meeting topics listed here. I'd like to have everyone around the table take a second to introduce themselves to the group, and then each read one item off the list. This way, we get the introductions and the agenda out of the way in a fun, creative way."

"Very nice, Mr. Mayor," Todd said. "Very efficient. Very creative." He nodded sternly.

"Yes, thanks, Todd." Mayor Mayer turned to face Ellie. "Let's start with you, Ellie. Introduce yourself to the group and read off the first agenda item."

"Okay," Ellie began. "Hello everyone, I'm Ellie Holden." She waved awkwardly. "This is my first meeting, and I'm really excited to be here."

Out of the corner of her eye, she could see Todd twirling his finger as if to say wrap it up.

"The first agenda item we'll be covering, um..." she squinted to read the first item, "is *Manger Scene with Real Baby*?" Ellie paused, having just read it for the first time. "Really? That doesn't seem like a very good idea—"

"Okay," the Mayor interrupted. "Let's not editorialize the agenda, mmmkay? Who's next?"

"Merry Christmas, everyone!" the cheerful woman next to Ellie said. "I'm Robin and this is my third year on the Christmas Planning Committee. Can hardly believe it! The next item on our agenda is

Live Reindeer." Robin held her smile as she looked around the room. "That's all it says. Just *Live Reindeer.*"

"Thanks, Robin," the Mayor said. "More on that later. And finally?" The Mayor motioned to the man next to Robin.

"Hey everybody, my name is Melvin Debby. I basically started this here committee."

"Okay, Melvin," The Mayor interrupted. "Just read the agenda, please."

"The next and final item on the agenda is *Real Life Snowman.* Real. Life. Snowman." Melvin turned to Todd. "I mean, is the science even there yet?"

"That's enough, Melvin." Mayor Mayer cut him off. "We have the start of some ideas. Some consider these good. Others consider these not-so-good."

The Mayor, Todd, and Robin simultaneously looked over at Melvin.

"Hey!" Melvin piped up. "I'm just askin' questions!"

"Anywho..." the Mayor continued. "Does anyone have anything else to add to the discussion?"

Ellie raised her hand. "I do have something that maybe we could discuss. What about paper ornaments made by kids in the community? The stores could hang them in their windows and—"

"Nah," the Mayor interrupted. "Too basic. We need bigger, flashier ideas. Aren't you a designer? Shouldn't your ideas be, what do they say in Silicon Valley? 'Out-of-the-box' and 'revolutionary'?"

"To the moon!" Todd gestured up into the air like a rocket.

Ellie slouched back in her chair.

Mayor Mayer leaned forward and gestured towards Ellie. "Didn't you have the real tree idea? Now that's a big idea."

"Actually," Ellie cleared her throat. "It was a tree decorating contest idea. A real community-building event."

"Oooh, I like that idea," said Robin.

"It's just that the tree in that picture is really important to me,

Mr. Mayor," Ellie explained. "Aunt Ruth and I would decorate it every year, and now that she's gone, I want to continue the tradition."

"I'm not trying to be insensitive, Ellie, so I want you to know that I am trying to say this as delicately as possible. It sounds like you're holding onto the past a little too tightly and you may be smothering the opportunities for growth and change in the future."

Ellie was taken aback. As rude as the Mayor's comments were, they were also pretty insightful.

"The big city has their biggest real tree ever this year," Todd added.

"Enough!" Mayor Mayer slammed his fist on the solid conference table. "I don't want to hear about that big city and their gimmicky downtown Christmas tree. I'm tired of being outshined." He tilted his head to Todd, uncertain. "Outshone?"

"Outshoned, I think?" Todd seemed unsure.

The Mayor stood up and began to gather papers and pack them up. "I am not going to be outdone by that city! Ohhh no. No, they don't. Not again. Todd, cut down that tree Ellie showed us and put it up downtown. STAT!" The Mayor stormed out of the meeting room, followed by his Assistant and Photographer Greg Grunberg, who grabbed a handful of snacks on his way out the door.

Ellie, Melvin, and Robin looked at each other wide-eyed. Ellie stood up and followed the Mayor out to the hallway.

"Um, sir," Todd said to the Mayor. "The downtown is still zoned for a tree and gathering space—"

"Well, good. Make it happen."

"But, sir, unfortunately—"

"Don't do it, Todd. Don't bring me bad news. Not on my special day."

Todd looked surprised. "Happy birthday, sir? I had no idea—"

The Mayor's Assistant shook her head, indicating that it was not the Mayor's birthday.

"It's just that," Todd continued, "downtown is zoned for a tree and gathering space, but there's now a formal process in place and we must hold an emergency hearing to vote on having a real tree again."

"He did it, folks," the Mayor looked around at other committee members who had gathered in the hallway and started a slow clap. "He brought me bad news."

Todd sheepishly continued explaining. "It's one of the protections enacted under the BRIGHT LIGHTS Act."

The Mayor nodded slowly. "Right, right, right... Beautifying Right In Greenville...Home cooking Tastes..."

Todd and the Mayor rattled off words, struggling to piece together the acronym that neither could remember.

"Help To Liquidity...Levitate..." Todd tried.

"Like...it...Gree...Great...forget it!" the Mayor said. "Schedule the emergency hearing, Todd. I have to start working the phones. This is personal. No more bad news, Todd." Mayor Mayer stormed off, followed by his Mayoral Assistant, mother, and Mayoral Photographer, Greg Grunberg, who snapped a photo of the Christmas Planning Committee contingent.

"Not now, Greg!" the Mayor shouted.

26

JINX FIGHT

JOSH - SATURDAY

INSIDE AUNT RUTH'S HOUSE, Josh sat on a stool at the kitchen island with a perfect view of the tree in the front yard. He was having that phone conversation with his boss, Jerry, that they both agreed to delay until the next day.

"It's everything you could want in a promotion, and it's all yours, Joshua."

"Wow. Yeah, it sounds great. It's just—"

"Great. Now that all the business stuff is out of the way. How're you doing up there, man? You hanging in there? Remembering your Aunt Nancy and everything?"

"It's my Aunt Ruth. Her name was Ruth."

"Right, of course. So you've been enjoying some time off around there?"

"A bit. I actually did get to talk investments the other day—"

"You pushing the Goliath funds? My man! Grief, shmief, am I right? Get some, Josh!"

"No, it wasn't like that. At all. It was more of an impromptu conversation, just a small group of locals in a coffee shop talking about the market and asking questions."

"Uh huh. The coffee shop where your ex-girlfriend works?"

"Yeah, but, I mean, it's not like that..."

"No, of course. Small town, sheer coincidence. Just happened upon an investment meeting. It's not like the one who doesn't want you to sell your house and leave is the one who called to tell you about this impromptu meeting or anything, right?"

"Right. Yeah, that'd be weird."

"Well, hey, I gotta run. Great talk. Real excited to get you back here and get settled into your new role, Mr. Director of Private Equity Asset Allocation."

"It has a nice ring to it. Hope it all fits on the business car—"

The phone line beeped from the ended call.

Josh was feeling unsure about things now. On one hand, a dream promotion just dropped in his lap. On the other hand, he had really been enjoying his time with Ellie and the others in Greenville. He was more open to making a change than ever. Maybe it was time to get back to real life. What he had been experiencing lately, it wasn't real. He was more like a visiting holiday tourist. It wasn't reality.

Outside in Aunt Ruth's front yard, Josh noticed a commotion from inside the house. He walked to the window and saw Ellie outside hammering a stake into the ground with a sign on it: ZONING BOARD OF APPEALS CHRISTMAS TREE SUBCOMMITTEE MEETING TONIGHT.

"What the heck is going on out there..." Josh mumbled as he grabbed his coat and headed out to the front yard. Outside, he found Ellie, but also an unexpected crew standing around Aunt Ruth's tree, including Todd, the Mayor, the Mayor's Assistant, his Mayoral Photographer Greg Grunberg, and a couple others he didn't recognize who were wearing Christmas Tree pins and reflective vests that said *Christmas Planning Committee*.

"Hey, Ellie. What's this all about?" Josh said as he approached Ellie, who was holding a hammer and yard signs promoting a Zoning Board meeting.

"Hey, Josh." Ellie squinted from the sun reflecting off the snow. "So, good news for you. The Mayor OK'd a proposal to put up a real tree downtown. But we have to have a town vote first to—"

"I'm sorry, what?" Josh interrupted. "Is that why they're over there looking at Aunt Ruth's tree? Do they think they can just take a vote and then cut it down?"

"I don't think it happens overnight like that, but I thought you'd be excited. This is what you wanted. You wanted to donate Aunt Ruth's tree."

She was right. He had been suggesting that. He wasn't so sure now, though. "It feels like things are happening kind of fast." Josh had even more to consider now that he had been offered this ideal promotion. Staying in town was not as straightforward anymore.

What if he needed to get back for his new role right away and sell the house really quickly? This whole tree process sounded like it could really slow things down. "I got a call from my boss. He wants to promote me."

"I'm not surprised. You're great at your job."

"He would need me back in the office as soon as possible. I might need to button up all this," Josh gestured towards the house, "as soon as possible."

"Wow, that's a sudden change of events. I thought you were having second thoughts about your career and about staying with a big company? Plus, we still have one of Aunt Ruth's traditions left to—"

"Come on, Ellie. This is real life." Maybe that was a bit too strong, but he didn't know what to say. The list of decisions he needed to make was growing. "I just mean that we can't pretend this is some fantasy and we're living in a snow globe."

"It is real life, Josh. This is real life. Aunt Ruth really wanted you to do these things. I know it seems silly to you because it's not time working up a corporate ladder, but this is real. Aunt Ruth spent her whole life climbing the corporate ladder. She lived alone her whole life and worked hard, and she was happy. You said it yourself; you've been working so hard to achieve success in your career, and you've done that, and you still aren't satisfied by it. I think Aunt Ruth knew that about you. She knew you needed more. I'm sure she knew this would be hard for you to do, but the least you can do, the very least, Josh, is see it through. Honor her last wishes and do her silly traditions and come to an agreement with me about this tree. After that, you can still choose to do whatever you want. But this is real life, Josh." Ellie sighed. "You can do whatever you want. It just seems so immature to leave—"

"Immature?? I'm not being immature! You're immature!"

"What!?" Ellie gasped.

Simultaneously, they yell, "You're immature!"

They stood in silence for an angry moment. He thought about how a jinx didn't feel right. She was probably thinking that too. It went without saying, he figured. They mostly avoided eye contact, but she caught him looking at her. He felt bad. He was mean, but so was she. They stood there without another word. And then she stormed off.

As inconvenient as it was, Josh needed to head back to the office to meet with Jerry. He packed his car for the road trip back to Danvers, PA. Maybe a long ride would help clear his head. He was still feeling frustrated after his argument with Ellie, a little embarrassed, a little guilty for getting so upset. He still did a bad job of communicating his emotions in the moment and felt sorry for being so mean to Ellie. Not being able to shove one of his bags into the trunk was not helping his frustration level. Something was sticking out. Inside one of the bags he had packed, he noticed an unfamiliar box. He opened the small, square, weathered box and smiled to himself when he saw the ornament. Josh walked over to the tree in the front yard. He took the handmade *Merry Christmas 2015* ornament out of the small box and hung it on the tree. Right next to the *JH + EH* that he carved into the trunk when they were teenagers. He thought back to the memory from ten years ago.

Spending school breaks at Aunt Ruth's was always the most fun time of the year. So many memories were made and traditions started. Every day was just the best day, but

Josh's heart always sank to its lowest point of the year when it was time to leave.

It was their last summer together before the first year of college. They were feeling all of the emotions. Ellie was excited. Josh was, too, but also feeling sad about having to leave. He was emotional, feeling like Ellie wasn't going to miss him. He didn't know how to express this. He wasn't mature enough to describe his feelings to her, so he pouted and whined and waited for her to figure it out and explain it to him and to herself. She got annoyed with him being a downer. Sure, she would miss him, but she wanted to enjoy the time they had together. She wanted him to snap out of it. They could be sad but also have fun. As the end of summer got closer, Josh got more and more distant and replaced words with grunting sounds. He hated when Ellie left before him, so Josh was distracting himself with analyzing pine needles on Aunt Ruth's tree while Ellie said her good-byes to Aunt Ruth before heading off for college. Ellie wanted a hug before she left, or a kiss, or a smile, or a hand. She would have even settled for a goodbye, but he couldn't be bothered to turn around and do that.

"Josh, why don't you come over and say goodbye to Ellie?" Aunt Ruth called out.

He was really engaged in how the smaller needles were at the front of the tree branch and the longer ones were at the back, so he just called out to Ellie without turning around. "See ya."

Ellie looked at Aunt Ruth and shrugged.

"It might be hard to appreciate this right now," Aunt Ruth said, "but some things just have to run their course. Some of the most beautiful and important plants have the sharpest of thorns. To protect themselves. You see?" They both look towards Josh. "They don't want to be hurt, so they isolate and protect themselves from others getting too close. They keep things that could hurt them at a distance."

Josh moved on to picking at the tree bark.

Ellie, still faced towards Josh, cupped her hands around her mouth so her voice carried, "I hate your guts and hope I never see you again!"

Josh still had his back turned to Ellie and Ruth. The sadness in his heart made its way to his head. His eyes welled up, but her comment made him laugh and then cry a little. With his back still turned, he raised a hand and offered a flimsy wave.

Aunt Ruth grabbed hold of Ellie and squeezed her hard and then walked her to her car to see her off.

With the coast finally clear and having finished his work with the tree, Josh turned around just in time to see her drive away. It was just him and Aunt Ruth now. And the freshly carved *JH+EH* surrounded by a heart that he had just finished.

Josh adjusted the *Merry Christmas 2015* ornament so the initials he carved those years ago were visible. Suddenly, he felt something plop against his back. He had felt that before. He turned around to see Ellie with another snowball in her hand, ready to fire. He chuckled. "Do you hate my guts and never want to see me again?"

VIRTUAL CHRISTMAS TREE SUBCOMMITTEE MEETING

ELLIE - SATURDAY

FROM INSIDE HER MOM'S KITCHEN, Ellie could see Josh outside, standing by Aunt Ruth's tree. She was taking her mom's advice to heart and trying to clear her head by focusing on a hobby she enjoyed. As Ellie sketched the tree, she had blocked off the spot where Josh was standing, unsure if she wanted to include him in the drawing or not. She considered drawing him with clown shoes or maybe even as a giant turd. As juvenile as it was, the thought actually did help her feel a tiny bit better.

"What's the meeting for?" Evelyn asked, acknowledging the pile of ZONING BOARD OF APPEALS CHRISTMAS TREE SUBCOMMITTEE MEETING TONIGHT signs at Ellie's feet.

"To vote on having a real tree again downtown," Ellie said without looking away from the window or taking her hand off her chin.

"Ohh, that sounds nice."

"They want to cut down Aunt Ruth's tree," she said, still staring out the window.

"I thought you were going to keep the tree safe?"

"It's impossible, Mom. I'm up against an unstoppable force. This Christmas Tree Subcommittee has more power than any government entity should have."

"Ellie, hon, this doesn't sound like you. What happened?" Evelyn rolled over to Ellie's side.

"Josh and I had a fight. He's leaving. He got a promotion and now he's probably selling the house and never coming back here ever again."

"This is not the Ellie I know. The Ellie I know always sees a positive side, always sees a way to make a situation better. What's got you so down?"

Ellie turned to face her mom. "Do you think I'm stuck in the past?"

"Why do you ask that?"

"The Mayor said something to me that really struck a chord. He said that I didn't want Aunt Ruth's tree cut down because I was holding onto the past, and by doing that, I was smothering the future. Am I just holding onto the past? Is Aunt Ruth's tree a symbol of the past that needs to come down so I can move forward? And Josh. We have a past. Am I just trying to relive that and get back to that?"

"First of all, let's be real, Ellie. It's too close to Christmas to cut down a tree, put it up downtown, and decorate it. I think you need to take a step back from everything and look at the bigger picture. Why are you upset?"

"Josh is flip-flopping. He said he enjoyed being here. Then one phone call from his boss and he's out there packing his car."

"Why is he doing that?"

"I know what you're doing, Mrs. Holden." Ellie knew the tricks from her mom's years as a counsellor all too well.

"Humor me."

"He's selfish and career-driven and blinded by the mirage of success."

"Why is he selfish?"

"Why is he selfish? He's unsure of what to do and has always followed his mind regardless of what was in his heart."

"What's in his head?"

"I don't know, Mom. I'm not in his head."

"Just try. Make an informed, irresponsible assumption."

"An outward image of success by achieving a certain level in his career."

"What's in his heart? Again, reckless assumptions only."

"It's not fulfilled by what he is doing. He wants to build his own business and have close relationships with people. Something other than just measuring his success by dollars and job titles. He also keeps people at a distance, even though he has people in his life who want to be close with him."

"It seems to me that the old Josh from years past would not have even told you about the promotion or shared some of the insecurities he was feeling."

"Maybe not." Ellie knew her mom was right.

"Maybe he's trying and he's not so good at following his heart. Unlike you, Ellie. You've always listened to your heart in spite of your head."

"That doesn't sound like a compliment, Mom."

"It's a delicate balance. I love the way you are. So much like your dad."

"What would dad do?"

Her mom sat quietly for a few moments. "I think he would tell you to get your butt out there and help a hurting soul. You're a helper, Ellie. You've always been."

"Wouldn't that make me kind of a pushover? Why do I have to be the one to fix things? Why can't he come find me?"

"You could look at it like that. You could also look at it as taking control of the situation and expressing your feelings on your terms. You can express that you won't put yourself in a position where you feel like a pushover, and that you want him to communicate with you better. You asked me if you were stuck in the past. It's not about holding onto trees or other things from your past. It's about what you want for the future. Do you want what's best for your future self? For Josh? For me? If, in your heart, you want the best, then your feelings and emotions are valid. You shouldn't question them. You should defend them."

Ellie did want the tree. Because of the past, sure, but also for the future, too. "Yeah...yeah!" Ellie got excited. "I think I just had a little breakthrough. I want to keep the tree, not just because I am holding onto the past, which, duh, but also because I want it to be part of my future. I want to make ornaments for it and decorate it and create new memories."

"Are we still talking about the tree?"

"Mom, stop it." She leaned in for a hug and noticed something that she had not seen until that moment. A vase holding flowers on the butcher block island up against the wall. "Mom! When did you do that?"

Evelyn must have known exactly what Ellie was asking about because she didn't ask any clarifying questions. "That's the vase Josh gave me. I called Juniper Lee and asked if she could put together a little winter arrangement for me. You know, just some poinsettias with red roses, maybe some white ranunculus, and then maybe fill it in with some sprigs of berries, balsam fir, and pinecones. She did a pretty good job, didn't she?"

"It's lovely." Ellie felt a wave of relief that her mom was showing the slightest interest in having flowers in the house again.

Evelyn rolled across the room and plucked a couple sprigs from the vase. "She was a little heavy-handed with the fillers, but overall, I agree."

"Thanks for talking, Mom. You're the best and I love you."

"You're welcome, sweetie. I never like to see you feeling down."

"I'm going to try to catch Josh before he leaves."

Josh hadn't noticed Ellie walking behind him yet, so she made a snowball and tossed it at his back. *Bullseye.* As he turned around, she made another snowball.

He chuckled. "Do you hate my guts and never want to see me again?"

Ellie dropped the snowball on the ground.

"I just want you to know," she began, "that I'm sorry for getting upset with you and being mean. I hope you are, too, because I don't want to be treated that way. I want to be able to communicate with you, and that goes both ways. That being said, I know that you have a lot on your mind, but I want you to consider something. When you think about a decision, are you making it because it's what you want or because it's what you think you should do? It seems like you've spent a lot of your life following a path that you've planned out, and maybe you've lost sight of what's in your heart. If logic is failing you and you feel unsure about a decision, then maybe you should follow your heart."

"I'm sorry, too. I feel really bad for hurting your feelings. You've been so helpful to me while I've been here. I need to go talk to my boss about this job. When I get back, I'd like it if we could finish the last tradition together? The gift-wrapping race? For Aunt Ruth."

"I'm like the Tom Petty of gift wrapping, so watch out," she said.

"I think you mean Richard Petty."

"Maybe...?" she was unsure.

Ellie walked Josh to his car. They hugged extra-long through puffy winter jackets. A jinx truce commenced. As Josh drove away, she heard "Runnin' Down a Dream" by Tom Petty blasting from his car.

Ellie walked to the tree where Josh had been standing moments ago. She saw the *Merry Christmas 2015* ornament that he added and their initials that he had carved. She traced the heart with her finger, like she had done so many times before.

Back inside her mom's kitchen, Ellie opened up her laptop and prepared for the virtual town meeting. She had her chamomile tea, her notebook and pen, and a plate of homemade shortbread cookies. She was prepared for anything.

Ellie joined the video call a few minutes before it started and could see people joining. The turnout was better than she expected— thirty-three participants for a last-minute vote to have a live tree downtown again. When Mayor Mayer joined, his Mayoral Assistant was leaning over his shoulder, presumably trying to unmute him. His Mayoral Photographer, Greg Grunberg, was nearby holding up his camera. "Not now, Greg," suddenly blared through Ellie's computer speakers as the Mayor came off mute.

Right away, there was another audible voice from an anonymous participant who had not muted themselves.

"Yeah, can I get that peppermint shake with no whipped cream and no cherry?" the meeting participant said.

The Mayor responded immediately, "Who gets their peppermint shake with no whipped and no cherry?"

Ellie wondered what Josh was up to and what his boss would offer him. She wondered if he would spend time with his co-worker friends on Sunday before his meeting Monday morning. She had a whole day planned with her mom: brunch, the movies, mani-pedis, the works. First, she needed to get through this meeting.

"Maybe we should begin with the Pledge of Fir-llegiance?" Todd said.

"Not now, Todd," the Mayor said. He then opened the meeting to public comments. Someone immediately raised their hand. "Yes," the Mayor said. "In the back, I see that hand."

However, the Mayor had everyone muted because of the peppermint shake incident, so when no one spoke up, he moved on to reading submitted comments. "Okay, we've got a letter submission from Ellie." He must've been feeling impatient because he glossed over most of the heartfelt parts. "There's some real sentimental stuff about Ruth Matthews in here...blah blah blah...and then finishes it off with a Christmassy quote. Nailed it, El. Anyone else?"

Next, as the Mayor was rushing to wrap up, he pressed a button and accidentally applied a filter that made his face look like a hamburger. "Woops. I must've hit a button somewhere here and I can't turn it off. Rest assured, I am not a hamburger."

Finally, the screen glitched and went black. The meeting ended abruptly and without any resolution.

28

JOSH AT WORK

JOSH - MONDAY

JOSH'S DESK LOOKED NEAT AND TIDY, just the way he left it. He made his way to Jerry's office, which took up two normal-sized office suites and featured floor-to-ceiling glass walls. Jerry waved him in when he spotted him about thirty feet away. As Josh approached the chair across from Jerry's desk, Jerry leaned back and crossed his arms. His signature plastic smile was in full effect.

"Joshuaaaa," he said like he was in a Budweiser commercial.

"Jerry, good to see you."

"Let's get right down to it. You'll have a team of up to three analysts reporting directly to you. You'll get to do what you love. Analyzing numbers. Your team will handle all the minutiae for you. You know, the client calls, the weekly reports, the quotas, all the stuff you don't need to bother with. Your team will do all that stuff. You just make sure the numbers work. Sounds great, right?"

"Yeah, I guess. What do you mean by 'make sure the numbers work'?"

"You know, rates of return, portfolio distribution, service numbers, you just get to look at numbers. The thing you love the most."

"Service numbers...as in fees associated with our funds?"

"Well, yeah. I mean, come on, Josh. We have a business to run here. We still have to make money."

"I do make money, Jerry. Nearly all of my clients' portfolios return a positive rate. I'm on an epic streak. Even you have to admit that much."

"Sure, you're a great stock picker, Josh, but we're paying out for the funds that we manage but don't own. It's an expense we can control."

"You want to insert a layer of entry-level sales dweebs between me and the clients to make sure they sell the Goliath Funds, is that right?"

"Have you seen the salary for this new role?"

Josh stood up and paced the office. He knew he was valuable to Jerry and the firm, but how valuable? How far should he take this? "This fantastic opportunity you've sold me on is not as autonomous, independent, nor perfect as you made it sound. It's the same job I have now, just a corner office, direct reports, quarterly revenue goals, and hardly any interaction with clients. The exact *opposite* of what I am looking for." As he heard the words come out of his mouth, he realized how much he didn't want it, and how much he didn't want to be there.

"And more money! Look, you can't live in this fantasy space where profits don't matter. You're on the track to success. Stay on track, Josh. Bountiful rewards await."

Josh crashed back into the seat. "Money costs too much," he mumbled.

"What's that?"

He cleared his throat. "A good friend named Chris Hill once said that money costs too much. Well, he feels like a friend. He's a podcaster I've listened to for a long time. Anyway, I didn't really get it until now."

"I don't get that at all. You could get yourself into real trouble saying stuff like that around here." Jerry popped a handful of almonds into his mouth and pointed at Josh while he chewed. "Quick way to get the S.E.C. breathing down your neck with comments like that, Josh." What are you saying? You don't want the promotion? You can stay in your current job at your small desk. We'll need to implement some goals, though, because—"

"I'll quit." Josh mustered.

"You'll *what*? Did you say you'd quit?"

"I don't think our values align, and I don't think I can serve in my role any longer. I quit. I resign. However, you're supposed to say it. I don't want to work here anymore."

"I don't have values, huh? You know what, Mr. High-on-His-Values-Horse? Just to show you how dumb you are, and to spite you, I'm gonna do you one last favor. I reject your resignation. You didn't even write a letter. Get with it, man. Have some decorum. For that, you're fired. We're downsizing your department. Organizational changes. Whatever we need to call it to get you a big, fat severance. And every time that severance check gets deposited, you're gonna think of me. And how great it is to make money. And about how right I was."

"I think severance is one lump sum deposit, actually."

"Yeah, you probably like that. Probably better for taxes, too, isn't it, Josh. Mr. Advantageous Tax Guy over here. With your tax-friendly distributions..."

"Actually, depending on the amount, it could be income I hadn't planned on, so it could *increase* my tax burden."

"Oh, I'm gonna make it hurt, Josh. You're gonna feel it in your taxes, alright." Jerry stood up and walked towards the office door. "I think we're done here."

As Josh left his office, the two shook hands. Josh didn't have any ill will towards Jerry. It was hard to stay mad at the guy.

Back at his desk, Josh packed his personal items into a small box. He jumped a little when he heard his desk phone ring.

"Hello, Joshua Hanson speaking."

"Hi, Joshua. This is Mrs. Lewis calling."

He smiled at the familiar voice on the phone.

"Ahh, Mrs. Lewis. So good to hear from you. Actually, I am glad you called. There is something I wanted to tell you."

Josh looked around the office before sitting down for more privacy.

"I'll be leaving Goliath Investments, Mrs. Lewis. This will be my last day here. But not to worry; you're in great hands. I'm sure your new account manager will reach out soon—"

"Joshua, I've stayed with Goliath Investments for one reason and one reason only. And you're it. Wherever you are going, I will be going, too. Is it a firm I know?"

"No, actually, I think I'll be going off on my own, starting my own investment firm—"

"Well, it's about time. I think that is great. I'll be moving my entire portfolio."

"Oh, wow. Really? Mrs. Lewis, as your long-time account manager, I can't advise moving your investments over to my new firm—"

"Will I have to login to an online thing-a-ma-jig to see my statements?"

"No, I won't have an online portal that you'll need to login to—"

"Then count me in. And I won't hear another word on it."

"Okay, I won't argue with you. It would be an honor to manage your investments with my new firm. I'll talk to you soon."

Josh hung up the phone and pumped his fist. He was psyched about his very first client.

A large office meeting must have just ended because a number of co-workers began filing back to their desks, including Dave, Mia, and Scott.

"Dude!" Scotty said, offering a fist bump. "We just heard you're leaving!"

"What happened? Dave asked. "Last we heard, a big promotion was on the table."

"I think we settled on 'organizational changes' as the official line, but we both realized it was time for a change."

"You're right," Mia said. "He is more diplomatic in person."

Josh laughed. "The truth is, I haven't enjoyed what I was doing for a long time. I don't even know what I was working towards. This work used to fulfill me and mean so much to me. While I was in

Greenville, I was barely working, but I felt more fulfilled than I had in years."

"I'm happy for you, man," Dave offered a pat on the back. "I'm kind of envious, actually. It takes a lot of guts to shake things up."

Hey, now that you're not working," Scott said, "you should definitely join my livestream. There's a shirts versus skins, last man—" he looked at Mia, who as staring sharply back at him, '—or woman standing, winner take all, losers walk, tourney."

"You have to play shirtless?" Josh asked.

"It's optional," Scotty said. "But I'm definitely playing shirtless."

"Hey," Josh addressed the trio, "when I finish packing up here, you want to go to lunch?"

The excited cheering and high fives they exchanged earned them dirty looks from multiple groups of cubicles nearby.

As Josh walked out of the office building with Scott, Dave, and Mia, Josh looked up at the GOLIATH INVESTMENTS sign on the building. He placed his box of belongings on the ground, made a snowball, and then chucked it at the GOLIATH sign. He nodded with satisfaction at the idea that he may have even made the lights flicker a tiny bit. The four continued to throw snowballs at the sign for the next five minutes until the building security guard came out and yelled at them to stop.

Over lunch, Dave, Mia, and Josh agreed to join one of Scott's livestreams once a week together, and the group planned to have regular calls during lunchtime to catch up. They decided to call it their "Lunch with the Boys. And Mia."

When Josh returned to Greenville, it was a bit late, and he was tired, but he saw Ellie at Aunt Ruth's tree adding more lights, and he couldn't resist. She hadn't noticed him yet, so he tossed a snowball at her back.

"No you didn't," she said as she turned around. Ellie put the strand of lights down and quickly scooped together a snowball, then fired it. Grazing his shoulder.

Before they knew it, they were exchanging snowballs, using the tree to defend against incoming shots. As they rounded the tree chasing after each other, they finally collided and crashed to the ground. Josh leaned over her face. "Truce?"

"Tru—"

He kissed her. He felt Ellie lean into him, so he continued kissing her and held her tight against him for a long time. It felt new and exciting, but familiar and comfortable. The two lay in the snow looking up at the stars. He was feeling relatively peaceful about his decision. Naturally, he couldn't help but question if he made the right choice, but so much had felt right during the short time he had been in Greenville. The heartfelt conversations with Ellie, meeting people around town who knew Aunt Ruth and who welcomed him as one of their own, and the finance meeting were really the icing on the cake. He had been wanting to connect with people in that way for a long time. Being in a place where people have those types of conversations, it was almost like fate. It went against so much of how he normally operated, but he was trying something new. He was following his heart.

"I'm not taking the job promotion. Actually, I quit."

"You *what*??" Ellie sat up.

"It just felt right in that moment. Something came over me and I just, I don't know, I did not want to be there. I wanted to be back here."

There was one tiny question he wanted to ask Ellie about. Ever since Jerry brought up how coincidental the finance chat was, he wondered how that came about and if there would be another. He didn't want to ruin the moment, though. Ellie had been looking out for him the whole time, so he felt good about how everything had happened.

"I am sh...well, I was gonna say that I'm shocked but maybe I'm not. I'm excited. I'm excited for you!"

"Yeah, me too. Thanks. Thanks for encouraging me and helping me realize this was a possibility. You're a real inspiration."

"That's why they call me Ellie the Inspiration."

"Ohhh...right. Yeah, that nickname makes sense now. Hey, they held that virtual tree vote meeting while I was gone, right? How'd that go?"

"That was an absolute disaster. Basically, the screen glitched and went black. And that was it. They ended without any resolution. They're going to hold another tree vote meeting in person. So many funny things happened that I have to fill you in on."

"Oh, good! Tell me all about it," Josh said as he lay back in the snow with his hands behind his head.

29

GIFT WRAPPING
EVENT

ELLIE - TUESDAY

ON THE NIGHT OF THEIR FINAL TRADITION, Ellie and Josh arrived at the gift-wrapping event early so they had plenty of time to grab a bite to eat. "How are you feeling?" she asked as they walked the few blocks to Pies 'N Fries.

"Pretty good. Stomach feels a little funny, but I think that's just because I'm hungry."

"I mean about your job, goof."

"Right. Yeah, good. As long as you didn't get the whole town in on a plot to trick me to stay here, then I'd say I'm feeling surprisingly calm about the change."

Ellie felt like she had a little explaining to do about how she organized the finance event and how she had been talking openly with Tay and the Lunch Ladies. Not a lot of explaining, but a little.

Maybe after they got some food in their stomachs.

At Pie's 'N Fries, they grabbed a slice to go and a box of Cinnamon Snough Balls.

"They're basically just Cinnamon Dough Balls," Josh said.

Ellie stopped in her tracks. "It's Christmas. They're different."

Lucky for Josh, his phone rang. He didn't know it, but that saved him from a whole speech on how Cinnamon Snough Balls were nothing like the Cinnamon Dough Balls that were offered the rest of the year.

By now, Josh knew to answer the calls from his friends. "Hello. I've got you on speaker phone."

"Josh! Ellie! It's Scott." "And Dave!" "And Mia!" the trio shouted over a noisy background.

"Hey, you guys!" Ellie shouted back at them.

"Josh, listen, we're at trivia and Dave thinks you would have known this question. Ready?

"Oooh, I love trivia," Ellie added.

"Yeah, Josh hates it," Scott said. "Okay, here's the question. In *Mad Men*, Don Draper works with clients whose stock prices are influenced by public perception. What financial metric reflects investor confidence and future growth expectations?"

"I haven't seen *Mad Man*, but it has to be price-to-earnings ratio, right?"

"I knew it!" Scott shouted.

"Thanks for the vote of confidence, Scott," Josh said.

"Well, no," Scott said. "I didn't think you'd get the answer right. I just said I bet you've never seen *Mad Men*."

"That's embarrassing, man," Dave added.

"You guys guessed P/E Ratio, right?" Josh asked.

The line was quiet for too long. Finally, Scott said, "Mia put debt-to-equity ratio. She blamed it on the pressure. Can you believe that? Okay, we gotta go, buddy. Talk soon!"

"How have you never seen Mad Men?" Ellie was shocked.

"I'm afraid to tell you some of the titles I have not seen yet."

They arrived at the Greenville Community Center a few minutes after the doors had opened. The function room had a dozen tables set up as gift wrapping stations. For a mostly bland, rectangular room, the environment was festive and jovial. Of the thirty-ish people in attendance, all of them were wearing fun holiday sweaters. Ellie and Josh stood out in their casual attire.

Sandra noticed them right away. "Hey you two! I'm so glad you could join us!"

"Hi, Sandy," Ellie gave her a warm hug. "Josh, this is Sandy fro—"

"Yes, of course," Josh offered a quick wave. "I know Sandy. She was at the investment roundtable at Tay's."

Ellie remembered that she had never gotten around to explaining that to Josh.

"Hi, Josh. It's good to see you again. You two can follow me." Sandy escorted Ellie and Josh to a nearby table that was stocked with gift wrap, scissors, tape, and a pile of toys that needed to be wrapped. "I wanted to let you know, Josh, that I took your advice and I spoke to my advisor about rebalancing my portfolio. Thank you for the suggestion, dear."

"Good! You know, I am thinking of starting up my own firm here in town. I'm hoping to become a regular at your group finance chats," Josh smiled at Ellie.

"Wow, look at all these toys!" Ellie interjected.

"I know," Sandy explained. "They were all donated and we're going to deliver them to the children who placed a star on the wishing tree downtown. Such a lovely thing. You know," Sandra leaned in for privacy, "an anonymous donor set up a fund with enough money to fulfill giving tree wishes for the next few years. My guess is that it was someone who was near and dear to each of our hearts."

"Aunt Ruth," Ellie whispered.

"Josh, maybe you'll stick around and help us grow the giving tree fund even more." Sandra offered a sly wink at Ellie as she turned to walk away.

"What was that?" Josh said. "It looked like a little wink, huh?"

"Was it? I don't know. She likes to wink, I guess. Hand me a toy, would ya?"

Josh grabbed a toy and placed it on the table. "Huh. You know," he lowered his voice, "it feels a little weird in here, right? Like everyone is kind of watching us?"

"I don't know, does it? Maybe we should have worn Christmas sweaters." Ellie glided the scissors across the wrapping paper.

"I love that," Josh said. "It's like an ice skate gliding across fresh pond ice."

"If you say so." She was trying to keep her cool, but inside she was starting to panic.

"You know," Josh said. "I was thinking about why I was having such a hard time enjoying myself here, and how good it felt to be around these people, and how good it felt to be around you. Things seemed to fall into place so easily."

"Yeah?" Ellie tried to focus on the task at hand, but she must have looked distracted.

"What?" he asked.

"Nothing. What?"

"You're just quiet."

"I'm focused. I love wrapping gifts." Woops. She knew that he knew that was a lie.

"You do not." Josh looked suspicious.

"Fine." She tossed the scissors onto the table a little too flippantly. "You do it." If the room wasn't spying on them before, they definitely were after that.

"Sure, I can help. I didn't expect you to do it all. I love wrapping gifts. What's the matter anyway?"

Ellie had grown agitated, mostly about keeping the secret about the finance get-together too long. "Josh, I need to tell you something."

Josh aligned the edge of the wrapping paper perfectly with the pattern so the seam was virtually invisible. "Can you hand me that tape?" he asked.

"That finance meeting at Tay's?" Ellie continued. "I made that up. It was just something I pulled together last minute."

Josh looked up from the gift he was wrapping. The edge of paper flapped up from the tightly folded position he was holding it in. "What do you mean?"

"I mean we've never done that before. It's not a regular thing they do, like I told you."

Josh looked befuddled as he was surely running back the whole scenario in his head. "Why did they do that?"

"Tay mentioned to them that—"

"Tay was involved, too!?" Josh shook his head. "So, what, you two just told everyone to play along? I knew Margery was being too nice." He motioned to Sandra, who was across the room. "Even Sandra, Laura, and Estelle. The whole crew was way too gracious. I should have known something was up. I would have noticed a finance meetup flier on Tay's bulletin board if there was one."

Sandra must have seen the commotion or heard her name because she arrived at the table and tentatively interjected. "Is everything okay over here?"

"Wow," Josh said with disbelief. He looked around the room at everything except Ellie. "I must have looked completely ridiculous being so oblivious. So, what else? A coordinated finance meetup, a random invite to join Todd at karaoke..."

"Hey," Ellie interrupted, "I told you that I gave Todd your number."

"Yeah, you're right, that wasn't secretive, but you were pulling the strings."

Ellie chuckled.

"What's so funny?" Josh sounded annoyed.

"It's nothing. It's just that you said strings and all I could picture was Todd doing his version of NSYNC's "It's Gonna Be Me." Now's not the time, I know," Ellie admitted.

Josh shook his head. "What else were the Lunch Ladies coopted for?" He looked at Sandra. "Were you and the other ladies polite to me just to make me feel welcome here?"

"Of course we were nice, Josh!" Sandra said. "We're friendly with almost everybody who comes to visit here!"

"Josh," Ellie said, "I never asked them to meddle and trick you into anything. I think you may be overreacting. I've only been looking out for you and trying to have fun." Ellie knew she was in a morally gray area with the finance roundtable, but her heart was in the right place.

"Maybe I am being paranoid and freaking out a little bit," Josh said. "You know that I don't handle change well. I don't know what you were doing, or if you were doing anything at all, but that uncertainty, mixed with the major life changes I've made...not a good combination. I don't know, Ellie. I feel silly. I feel like everyone was in on it this bit to make me want to stay here and move into Aunt Ruth's house and keep the tree and...wait a second..." Josh looked at Ellie with wide eyes. "Was this all just to make sure we kept the tree?"

"What? No!" Ellie denied the accusation strongly. She was shocked that he would jump to a conspiracy like that. "Now you're definitely being ridiculous."

"Okay, you two..." Poor Sandra tried to settle them down.

Ellie grabbed the tape off the table and finished wrapping the gift that Josh had left undone.

"At first, I thought maybe I was being paranoid," Josh said. "I could have been making connections that didn't exist and imagining the coincidences. Now I'm realizing the ultimate coincidence is how well this all played into your wanting to keep the tree."

Ellie placed the perfectly wrapped toy on the ground next to the pile of toys. "Josh, all the stuff we've done together has been real. I may have...maybe the investment group wasn't as ad-hoc as I made it seem, but all I did was throw a label on it. All the people, the conversations you had, it was all you. I asked Todd to invite you to karaoke because I wanted you to have a good time, and Todd really likes you! As for Sandra and the other ladies, I never asked them to do or say anything to you. Sure, they overheard some conversations at Tay's, and maybe Tay brought them in on a few of them, but not to trick you into staying here. I would never do something like that."

"Even to save Aunt Ruth's tree?" Josh asked.

Ellie sighed. "Of course I want the tree to stay, but this hasn't been some grand conspiracy that the whole town was in on."

"She's right, Josh," Sandra said. "I never heard Ellie discussing a single ruse. If anything, she was trying to keep us out of it all. Why don't you two go talk somewhere? I can finish up here."

Josh quietly nodded to himself. "It's okay. I'll go." He handed Ellie a piece of tape. "I think we've met our gift-wrapping obligation." Josh took one step before turning back to Ellie. "I quit my job. I thought there was a real chance to make a life here and start a business here. Now I'm afraid I've made a mistake. This is why I stick to logic. Clear, logical steps. I've gotta go."

Ellie stood at the wrapping table alone, shocked by the whirlwind of what had just happened. Sandra pulled her in for a warm, comforting hug.

"I've never tried to trick anyone in my life," Ellie mumbled into Sandra's vintage holiday sweater vest.

"I know, dear," Sandra comforted her.

Ellie felt bad about misleading Josh, even though that wasn't her intent. She wished he had stayed longer so they could have talked, and she could have explained that she was just trying to do something for him that she thought he would enjoy. Something different to get him out of the rut he'd been in. Ellie was disheartened that instead of facing his emotions, Josh had just left.

"Ellie, dear," Sandara said.

Finally, Ellie thought. She needed some supportive words of wisdom in this moment of sadness and frustration.

"I think your hair is caught in my brooch, dear."

30

A WILL AND A WAY

JOSH - TUESDAY

AFTER WALKING OUT OF THE GIFT-WRAPPING EVENT, Josh strolled aimlessly through downtown. It was a beautiful nighttime Christmas scene. Lights twinkled on bushes and trees, and most of the shops were closed, but they left their window displays glowing. The streets and sidewalks were quiet and smelled like cinnamon and nutmeg. He found a quiet place to sit with a view of the street. He was feeling so many emotions. He felt a little bit tricked but was also aware that he was probably just being paranoid. Most of all, he was feeling embarrassed about how he reacted. From Josh's perspective, parsing his feelings in a way that he could express himself in the moment was a superpower stronger than invisibility.

"Oh, Aunt Ruth," he said quietly to himself. "I wish you were here. I could really use your advice." He pulled out his phone and searched for an email from Mr. McGillicutty. He tapped the link to his Aunt Ruth's Will video and watched a couple minutes, then tapped the "Fast Forward" button a few times. The video jumped to out-of-context commentary by Aunt Ruth.

> "...a green thumb! So I said, you can put
> that green thumb in your b—"

Josh chuckled and then tapped "Fast Forward" again.

> "...who says, 'analogous to'?? Who talks
> like that??"

Josh fast-forwarded again. He stopped at a part in the video where Aunt Ruth's doorbell *DING-BZZZ*ed. She got up, and when she came back into view, a teenage Josh was with her; he just happened to arrive at her house while she was recording. Grown-up Josh teared up when he saw himself with Aunt Ruth. In the video, Josh sat down next to her. She looked at the camera earnestly, fully aware of what was happening, but teenage Josh had no clue. She pulled Josh close.

> "I'm just making a video for some time in
> the future. I'll stop in a minute. You know,
> Josh, it's important to take good care of the
> people in your life and do things for others.
> We come into this life alone, and most of us
> leave this life alone. It's all about the
> connections we make while we're here. That's
> what makes a full life."

Aunt Ruth discreetly wiped away a tear. Teenage Josh was oblivious to the emotions Aunt Ruth was holding in at that moment, but grown-up Josh could see how her eyes welled up and the forced smile she held so she would not fall apart.

"Can we go sledding or watch *Wild Wild West* or something?" young Josh asked.
"Absolutely! Let's go."

Aunt Ruth stopped recording and Josh's phone screen went black. "You're right," Josh whispered to the blank screen. "Thank you."

The next morning was quiet in the streets of downtown Greenville. Josh was out and about before most people had finished their first cup of coffee. He didn't sleep very well and just wanted to get some fresh air, so a crisp walk to see the town wake up felt invigorating.

He was surprised to see a town worker already doing road work before the morning traffic rush. He looked an awful lot like... *Todd? Yeah, that's definitely Todd.*

Josh crossed into the street. "Morning, Todd!" he called out, but Todd couldn't hear him since he had on big headphones that covered his ears. Josh lifted the headphones off Todd's head to surprise him. "Boo!"

"Whoa! Josh! You scared me there," Todd was startled. *Success.*

"What are you listening to?" Josh put the headphones over his ears and heard a deep, gravelly voice speaking.

"He grabs Penelope in his massive, farm-strong arms, and pulls her body close to his. Their hearts are both beating over one hundred beats per minute. Penelope longs for the taste of his lips—"

Josh hands the headphones back to Todd. "What the heck are you listening to, Todd??"

"Just a book," Todd said. "It's a farmhand romance. Farmance, some call it."

"Oh, cool." Josh handed the headphones back. Todd was standing next to a pothole equipped with a shovel, heavy work gloves, a wheelbarrow filled with asphalt, and, of course, a reflective vest. "What are you doing out here this morning? I didn't think they'd let you walk around in one of those town-issued reflective vests."

"They don't. I had to special order this from the internet."

"And the traffic cones?"

"They were a package deal with the reflective vest. Got an extra vest in the truck if you care to join in the fun."

Josh took in the scene. "Nah."

"What's wrong, man? I can sense the sadness on you."

"It's a long story." Maybe it was the fumes from the warm asphalt or just the weight of everything on his mind, but Josh felt comfortable opening up to Todd. "I'm just worried that I'm making some big changes in my life without really thinking them through properly. Ellie has been really supportive and trying to make me feel at home here, but also sort of primed the pump, so to speak."

"Niiiice use of farm hand lingo!" Todd raised a hand for a high five.

"She set up an investment conversation and made it seem like a regular thing that happens here, but in reality, it was just for me to get to talk to people and answer their questions."

Todd stuck his shovel into the pile of asphalt and then leaned on it with both hands. "You know what your problem is? You're too calculating with things. So what if she made up the meeting? It actually sounds really nice. You really met with people, right? You really helped some people."

"Yeah, I guess I did."

"Everything is what you make of it. Ellie is out there just making things happen. It's important to put your mark on things, to have a hand in making a place what you want it to be, to be part of the solution. You can sit in meetings all day, have conversations all day. You know how many calls I get about the potholes in the roads? They're endless. We have meetings every week about it. You know who's not in those meetings? The people who actually shovel the asphalt into the ground. We just sit around and talk about the budget, and the overtime, and all the details around it. At some point, someone needs to pick up a shovel and fill in the hole. You probably wonder why I've stayed here my whole life. It's because I can do this. I can have an impact. I can pull over on the side of the road and fill a hole to make this place a little better."

Josh took this all in. He thought of the time he had spent with Ellie and about how his Aunt Ruth loved spontaneity and taking big swings. He wished that were more innate in him. "I get it. She's done a lot for me. A lot of people in my life have done a lot for me. You're making a bigger impact today than you know. Thanks, Todd."

Josh rushed out of the street and straight into the Turnkey Real Estate office.

31

IN-PERSON CHRISTMAS TREE SUBCOMMITTEE MEETING

ELLIE – WEDNESDAY

ELLIE SAT QUIETLY ON HER BED, working on an animated graphic for the Christmas Tree Committee's real tree campaign. She hadn't spoken to Josh since the argument the night before at the gift-wrapping event. She had decided that it was up to him to reach out if he wanted to talk. He was the one who decided to walk away from their conversation, so he should be the one to initiate a new conversation.

Getting creative again felt good for her soul and her mind, even if the rest of her felt pretty crummy. She re-shaped branches, eyebrows, and sneakers, erased top hats, re-drew stars, and fussed over every other little detail, then she sat back and admired her work. She had created a little pine tree with big green eyes that lifted a branch and sniffed its armpit, then sighed with pleasure at its own scent. She posted the animated graphic to *Blah-Zam!*, a website where graphic designers and artists shared their creative work to get help or suggestions from the community. It started out as a place where amateurs could post their basic ideas (*Blah*) and then those with a more creative eye could spruce it up (*Zam!*), but the site had become more of a mainstream photo-sharing app. Ellie jumped a little bit when her phone *DINGED* with a text message.

Tay: Are you coming into work?

"Shoot! I lost track of time!" Ellie rushed to get herself together.

During a break from the choffee shop rush, Ellie printed a batch of "Tree Vote" fliers. "It just felt really good to design something again," she said to Taylor. "Even something as simple as a little Christmas tree."

"I saw it. I loved it. You're so good at coming up with ideas like that. Your post is getting a lot of love. It's got like, 300 zammies."

"Really?" Ellie looked at her phone to see all the love on her post. She wasn't quite a viral sensation, but she felt satisfied. *DING*. A notification popped up:

Josh Hanson liked your post and left a comment.

Ellie tapped the notification and read Josh's comment.

"Everyone loves a real Christmas tree."

She felt the slightest sense of relief from the angst that had been constant since last night. She didn't even realize she was smiling until Taylor interrupted her thought storm.

"What are you scheming?" Tay said slyly.

"I think I have an idea. You don't need me, right?" The choffee shop bell jingled as Ellie rushed out the door.

Since the virtual subcommittee meeting went so poorly, the Christmas Planning Committee, in conjunction with the Zoning Board of Appeals, organized a public Christmas Tree Subcommittee meeting at the Town Hall. Ellie and the rest of the CPC planned to present their idea to once again host a real tree downtown, which could be selected from within the community. Then they planned to open the meeting to public comment. Finally, the committee would vote on whether or not to allow a real tree. That was the plan, anyway.

Ellie sat with the other voting members of the CPC in chairs that had been set up at the front of the packed meeting room. She tapped her foot nervously as she watched community members file in and find an open seat. Normally, the open comments portion of these forums was for the residents who were attending, not for members of the committee. However, Ellie had decided she would do something special for this meeting and planned to make a speech in honor of Aunt Ruth and on behalf of every person who held tight to the past but wanted to shape their future.

Thanks to the elevated platform she was sitting on, Ellie spotted her mom and Taylor right away when they arrived, and she pointed to the two seats she was holding for them in the front row. Jannie

Turkey and her contractor husband, Tucker, greeted each person they walked by on their way to their seats. The Lunch Ladies found a row where they could all sit together. Sandra and Laura joked with each other, while Margery looked like she was being held there against her will. Estelle sat at full attention with great posture, occasionally shushing the other ladies. Most of the seats around the room had been taken and Ellie felt like Mayor Mayer would be starting soon. Suddenly, she saw Josh walk in. He looked around and smiled when their eyes met. Ellie started to smile, too, but quickly turned her head. She wanted to smile and wave and call him over but didn't want to give him the satisfaction. *Immature? Maybe. But this time, he could be the one to step up for once and—*

"Hey, Ellie," Josh said as he put his hand on her knee and leaned close to her ear. "Can we talk for a minute?"

Her shaking leg settled, and all of the nerves left her body. She felt a wave of calm, and a flutter in her heart. "Yeah, sure. I guess."

She led Josh to a corner of the room where they could talk somewhat privately. At least this way, the townspeople might catch only every other word.

"Before you say anything," he said as she stood with her arms crossed, "I want to tell you that I'm sorry. I'm sorry for how I treated you last night while we were wrapping gifts, and I'm sorry that I left. I'm still working on expressing my feelings in the moment."

Finally, he takes ownership of it! "Yeah, you should be, Josh. You really ticked me off."

"I know. You were right, I overreacted. I mean, I still wish you had just told me sooner..."

Ellie tilted her head, anticipating a backpedaling campaign, but it never came.

"I will admit, I don't think you could have told me ahead of time because I probably would have said no and called it a crazy idea..."

She uncrossed her arms from in front of her, a slight concession that she was considering accepting his apology but wasn't ready to say it with words quite yet.

Josh reached out and held her hands with his. "I hope you can forgive me and that we can keep spending time together, and I hope I'm still welcome here in this town."

She took a step closer, so their lips were almost touching. "Of course, you're welc—"

BANG! BANG! BANG!

Mayor Mayer gaveled the meeting into session from the lectern on the stage.

"I forgive you," Ellie whispered before she and Josh slowly slinked to their separate seats.

"Good evening," the Mayor began. "On behalf of the Christmas Planning Committee, I'd like to thank you, our most civic-minded and holiday-forward members of this community, for joining us here tonight. We all know why we're here. I trust that everyone's had a chance to review the minutes from the previous meeting. So, if there are no objections, I'd like to skip right to the public comments portion. First up," Mayor Mayer did a double-take at the agenda as if it was the first time he was seeing it. "A member of our committee, Ellie? This is unusual, but come on up."

As Ellie made her way up to the podium, she felt her nerves jumping again, but she was determined to deliver a heartfelt message. "Thank you, Mayor Mayer." Ellie placed her note cards down in front of her on the lectern and adjusted the microphone. "As many of you know, Ruth Matthews, a beloved member of this community, passed away recently. I wanted to share with you a quote from her last Will and Testament. She said, 'Of course, my favorite tradition is decorating the Christmas tree for everyone to see. That brings everyone holiday cheer.'" Ellie looked up to see many members of the audience nodding in agreement. "Voting for a real tree is a way for me to honor Aunt Ruth's memory, honor the wonder of the season, and it would be a symbol of the strong feelings I have…" Ellie looked around and found Josh in the audience next to her mom and Tay "…the strong feelings I have for the special people in my life. I do hope that we can all work together to select the right tree, while respecting those who do not wish to have their tree cut down. Thank you."

Amid a subtle and respectful amount of applause, Todd attempted to start a chant. "TREE! TREE! TRE—" which he quickly stopped when he caught a fierce glare from the Mayor.

Mayor Mayer stepped to the lectern again. "Well, I believe that concludes the public comment portion. Let's move on to the vote, shall w—"

"Not so fast, Mr. Mayor," Melvin interjected. "I am not a fan of ad-hoc rule changes nor bias in the arguments. The Mayor is clearly pro-tree, and per Ellie's comment, we don't even have a section that defines how a tree would be selected." Melvin looked around to his fellow committee members. "The proposal's incomplete and we already know how he's going to vote. I think that everyone should put aside their preferences and vote based on the issues presented. As a result, I am abstaining from voting and request that both myself and the Mayor be replaced with neutral voting members."

Mayor Mayer shook his head and organized the papers in front of him. "Well, well, well," he said. "Just as I suspected. Melvin's out. Look, a tent pole of my election campaign was that I would never abstain from a vote, so no can do, Melvin. No can do. I made a promise to the people."

Todd stepped up to the lectern and discreetly whispered something to the Mayor, who nodded, and then announced, "Um, folks, we're going to take a five-minute recess." He gaveled out of session. "Adjourned. No. I mean, paused. Uh, break. You know what I mean. We'll be back in five."

While most of the attendees talked amongst themselves, Todd and Mayor Mayer huddled in a corner.

Ellie popped into an open seat near her mom and Josh. "I wonder what this is all about."

"Yeah, who knows," Josh said, craning his neck to see what the Mayor and Todd were doing. "Hey," he shifted focus back to Ellie. "You did really great up there tonight!"

"Thanks. It wasn't too cheesy?"

"I think I saw a tear stream down Todd's cheek. It was perfect."

"Alright, folks," Mayor Mayer announced. "Sorry for the delay. Unfortunately, I am getting word that a bylaw exists in the Christmas Planning Committee Handbook. There's a rule that every committee member must participate in a committee vote, otherwise no member will participate. I mean, I knew about it; I know all of the rules and bylaws, of course, but I was just reminded. Unfortunately, this basically tables the real tree issue for the year."

The audience groaned.

"So," Mayor Mayer continued, "there won't be enough time to get a new vote, cut down a tree, put it up, and decorate it all in time for Christmas." As Mayor Mayer lifted his arm to gavel the session to a close, he froze midair when he heard a faint beeping noise coming from outside. "What's that? Is that someone's car alarm? Did you double-park again, Todd?"

A yellow light flashed through the windows with every beep.

"I can tell ya exactly what that is," Jannie's contractor husband, Tucker, said as his well-worn bones slowly creaked into a standing position. "That right there is the sound of a backhoe backin' up."

"Good ear," the Mayor said, impressed.

Never one to be outdone by someone with actual knowledge, Todd jumped in. "Probably, what, like a Kubota? John Deere?"

"Nah." Tucker shut him down. "That right there is a CAT."

"Right, right, CAT was my next guess..."

Suddenly, the whole room looked towards the door to see Shelbie, who rushed in and was panting heavily. She looked around the room and finally spotted Josh. He looked at her eagerly. She nodded excitedly and gave him two thumbs up.

Josh grabbed Ellie's hand. "Come with me." He led Ellie to the front of the room and addressed the crowd. "Excuse me. Everyone. I have a very special surprise." The audience went quiet. "We may not be able to chop down a tree and put it up downtown, but thanks to the SHADE AND GATHER provision in our downtown zoning bylaws..."

Both Mayor Mayer and Todd mumbled incoherent sounds that may or may not have included the letters that spelled out 'shade and gather.'

Josh continued, "...We are able to add greenery to our downtown." He turned to face Ellie. "There's an addition to our downtown that I'd like you to see," he said to her.

32

TREE LIGHTING

JOSH - WEDNESDAY

SOMEHOW BETWEEN THE WALK FROM TOWN HALL to the lighting display stage, the audience had doubled. It felt like nearly the whole town had ended up gathering by the stage at the lighting display, but instead of the lighting display infrastructure, there were two bucket trucks from the electrical department stationed on either side of the stage propping up a large tarp.

Josh led Ellie onto the stage. Todd gave Josh a thumbs up from the back of the stage when the microphone was ready.

"Ellie. Residents of Greenville." He looked to the sky. "Aunt Ruth…"

Ellie looked slightly concerned. "Josh, did you cut down Aunt Ruth's tree?"

"Hold that thought," he whispered.

Josh turned to the crowd. "I'd like to present to you, our brand-new downtown Christmas tree!" The town workers in the bucket trucks dropped the tarp to reveal a freshly planted three-foot-tall Douglas Fir seedling. Its branches weighed down with a string of lights and two handmade ornaments Josh bought from June at the downtown Christmas market.

A light gasp from the audience was followed by a louder "Ooooh," when Todd plugged in the string of lights.

"This is so sweet, Josh," Ellie said. "It's beautiful."

"I think that Aunt Ruth's tree belongs right where it is. And now you have another one to keep an eye on and decorate throughout the years."

"Do you think you'll be able to stick around and help me?"

He smiled. "I wouldn't want to be anywhere else."

What a majestic night, Josh thought. A glowing tribute to the town, to Ellie, and to Aunt Ruth. The audience started singing an impromptu, transcendent version of "O Christmas Tree."

Josh nodded to a group of teens nearby, who stepped forward holding their Mobile Mistletoe over Josh and Ellie. The two kissed big, huge, gigantic ones in front of the tree.

Ellie pulled back slowly, "Thank you for not cutting down Aunt Ruth's tree."

"You mean like some—how did you put it? 'Like some infected pine and leave it to die on display in front of the whole town'?"

"Yeah, exactly."

Mayor Mayer, Jannie, and her contractor husband, Tucker, stood at the front of the crowd near the stage.

"They can't just cut through red tape and put up a real Christmas tree," the Mayor whined. "Can they??"

"It's my park, Matt," Tucker said without taking his eyes off the tree. "It's got my name on it. I can plant a tree." He nodded to a dedication plaque near the tree that read:

THIS PARK GENEROUSLY SPONSORED BY
JANNIE AND HER CONTRACTOR HUSBAND TUCKER

"Unless," Tucker continued, "you'd rather me tarp that hole I got in your roof right now while I dig that tree back up. Might be a few weeks before I can get back over to your house to re-shingle—"

"Nope," the Mayor replied swiftly. He then shrugged at the Christmas Planning Committee members. "It's his park."

33

MEETING WITH JASPER

ELLIE – THURSDAY

ELLIE AND JOSH SAT ACROSS FROM JASPER MCGILLICUTTY inside his law office. Once again, he pressed the "Play" button on a laptop and spun it around so they could see Aunt Ruth sitting on her couch, talking to the camera.

> "Obviously, you two are together now. As you should be. You have your very own holiday traditions now, too. By now, I'm sure I've seen how everything ended up, and I suspect I am happy as can be. Ellie, Josh, I love you both. Thank you for playing along. You have no idea how happy this makes me. Or maybe you do. You both know me pretty

well. There is just one more thing. Merry Christmas, you two. Jasper, Merry Christmas, and take it away."

"One more thing?" Josh was confused.

"We did everything on the list," Ellie added. "And we proved everything to you. We made ornaments, we made cookies—"

"We made *delicious* cookies," Josh added.

"Some of us..." Ellie side-eyed Josh, "crushed the eggnog challenge."

Josh hung his head shamefully.

"Caroling and gift wrapping," Ellie held up five fingers. "That was everything."

"Yes, that's correct," Jasper confirmed. "You have successfully completed everything you needed according to the Will document, so this isn't another task for you." Jasper closed the laptop and signaled for them to wait one minute. He disappeared to the back room.

Ellie thought about the rollercoaster she had been riding over the past ten days. Aunt Ruth passing away was so sad and unexpected, but getting reacquainted with Josh and getting to do all the of holiday traditions made this season special. She was feeling surprisingly optimistic about what was to come. Ellie looked at Josh and wondered what he was thinking about. He was probably thinking the same thing, too. At that moment, Josh reached over and grabbed her hand and smiled. *Yeah, he was definitely thinking the same—*

"I hope he remembers to take the napkin off before he comes back out this time," Josh joked.

She could have smacked him. Lucky for Josh, Jasper returned carrying a small, gift-wrapped box. He placed the gift on the desk in front of Ellie and Josh.

"This," Jasper said, "is for both of you."

"What is it?" Josh said as he and Ellie stood to their feet.

"This is something that Miss Ruth wanted you both to have. You can open it here if you'd like."

"Shall we?" Josh looked at Ellie.

Ellie carefully pulled the hand-tied bow apart and unwrapped the box. As she opened the box, she could see the shape of the object inside, and her heart filled with emotions. She held up the ornament for Josh to see. Two interlocked hands with the words "Our First Christmas" scrolled across the bottom.

"Wow," Josh admired the ornament. "For the tree she knew you would never cut down."

Ellie cleared the lump in her throat. "It's perfect."

"And that concludes our business on this matter," Jasper said. "I don't suspect you will have any trouble figuring out what to do with that gift from Miss Ruth." Jasper winked as he closed a manila folder.

Ellie and Josh exchanged handshakes, hugs, and well-wishes with Jasper. The bell atop the door jingled as they left the law offices of Jasper L. McGillicutty.

Inside Josh's living room, she and Josh stood next to a potted seedling. After the grand romantic gesture of revealing the newly planted seedling downtown, Evelyn pointed out that the tree probably would not survive the winter and suggested moving it inside for the extra cold months. So that's what they did. Ellie and Josh dug up the fir tree, which looked more like a branch with twigs sticking out of it, and placed it into a pot and inside Josh's living room. Ellie reached into her coat pocket and pulled out a small gift box. "I have something for you," she said as she handed it to him. "I thought of a better celebrity couple name for us."

"What's wrong with *Team Jellie*?" Josh asked. He opened the box and smiled as he pulled out an ornament that featured a large Christmas tree in the middle with Ellie on one side and Josh on the other, and the text *Team Jollie* scrolled across the bottom. "Team Jollie...I love it, Ellie." Josh looked into Ellie's eyes. "I love y...your...your gift."

Ellie smiled. It could have been the roaring fireplace or the extra layers she was wearing, but Ellie felt a wave of warmth rise through her body. "I love...yours, too."

Together, Ellie and Josh placed the ornament on the tree near the five other custom ornaments they made together: Master Ornament Maker, Eggnog Speed Sampling Champion, Dueling Caroler, Evelyn's Favorite Baker, and World's Best Gift Wrapper.

The two kissed and then admired their first Christmas tree. Josh joined Ellie as she began to hum the tune to "O, Christmas Tree."

Merry Christmas!

(34)

PUT ANOTHER EPILOGUE ON THE FIRE

JOSH – SEVEN MONTHS LATER

IN THE QUICK SEVEN MONTHS since Josh had parted ways with Goliath Investments and moved to Greenville, his personal investment consultant business had grown beyond the "try-ving" phase and was fully thriving. He had clients all over town. In no small part, due to the monthly finance roundtables he hosted at Tay's, the library, the bookstore, and beyond. Occasionally, an impromptu investment discussion would start up at the Pour it Up wine store, but Josh tried to discourage people from making financial decisions at wine tastings. Just another one of the "fiduciary responsibilities" he liked to talk about in his roles as an adjunct professor at Greenville Community College, a role that Ellie encouraged him to take on, and one he was truly loving. At first, most of the questions were about his Aunt Ruth's stories, but they've found a balance and were now almost fifty percent finance-related.

Josh was hurrying to wrap up some business on a rare Saturday afternoon in the office so he could make it downtown in time for the tree lighting ceremony. Thanks to another bright idea from Ellie, the town was celebrating their new downtown Christmas tree with a Christmas in July Spectacular, an event that Mayor Mayer promised to make an annual town tradition as soon as he heard the suggestion. Ellie had suggested that the town re-plant the three-foot seedling balsam fir that Josh had been caring for in his living room since Christmas. Right away, she and Todd began throwing out ideas for an entire Christmas in July celebration. Parade, snowmachines, Northern Lights projected into the sky, an actual sleigh and reindeer flying over Candy Cane Lane, and on and on. The Christmas Planning Committee settled on a downtown window display contest and a tree lighting ceremony. As a concession, the Mayor declared that when the tree lighting event was over, the mass exodus would be referred to as the Greenville Christmas in July parade.

Josh arrived just in time for the community candle lighting. Ellie handed him a candle, and he watched as Mayor Mayer passed the flame to his new Executive Assistant and Campaign Manager, Todd Samsonite. It had been a really big year for Todd so far, as he also got an opportunity to try out for the MAD BARs, the a cappella group in town. The feedback was great, but the group didn't want to change their name. They let him fill in sometimes, when they were short a singer, but Todd had to tell people his name was Antonio.

Todd leaned over to pass the flame from his candle to Josh. "Merry Christmas, Josh," Todd said.

"Merry, Christmas, Todd."

Josh turned to Ellie with his candle. Ellie had been busy the last seven months. She took a full-time graphic design job, but one that allowed her to work remotely and gave her the flexibility to keep up with the priorities in her personal life. She also started getting requests from local businesses around town to draw their storefronts. To help make the process as seamless as possible, she set up a simple online store where business owners could choose the type of drawing they wanted, upload a photo, and complete all of the payment activity without Ellie having to lift a finger. Before she knew it, she was getting orders from small businesses all over the country for sketches of their storefronts. The extra money went a long way in helping to pay for the additional days Taniyah was hired to help her mom during the week. While Ellie was spending a lot of time at Josh's house next door, they still gathered at Evelyn's at least one night a week for movie night and an indoor campout.

"Merry Christmas, Ellie," Josh said as he lit her candle.

"Merry Christmas, Josh."

Ellie turned to her mom, Evelyn, who had a four-legged companion named Bobo with her. With all the extra support from Ellie, Josh, and Taniyah, Evelyn had run out of excuses for not bringing another foster dog into the family. Within a week of welcoming Bobo into her house, she filed the paperwork required to request full adoption. Evelyn had also been busy preparing for her cruise in the fall. She was shocked by the unexpected and generous gift from Ellie and, just as Ellie had predicted, her mom initially tried to talk herself out of going. Ultimately, she agreed when Ellie said that she and Josh would be going, too.

"Merry Christmas, Mom," Ellie said as she offered the flame.

"Merry Christmas, El."

Evelyn turned as Shelbie leaned down.

Shelbie was now running her own home staging and interior design business, working with seemingly every real estate agent in and around Greenville. Josh suspected that, initially, agents hired her so they could make a good impression with her mom, Jannie Turnkey, in hopes of scoring some referrals when Jannie had too much on her plate, but Shelbie continued to recruit new clients and had formed an impressive reputation of her own in the interior design space. She had even made it into the final rounds of selection for an interior design contest that would be filming in Los Angeles.

"Merry Christmas, Shelbie," Evelyn said.

"Merry Christmas, Mrs. Holden."

Shelbie turned to her mom, who was in the middle of a phone call, so Shelbie lit hers and her contractor husband, Tucker's, candles.

Jannie Turnkey was as busy as ever. Josh had heard some gossip around town that Jannie was considering a run for Mayor, an unexpected development that would surely throw a wrench into Mayor Mayer's plans.

"Merry Christmas, Sandy," Shelbie said as she reached across to Sandra's candle.

"Merry Christmas, dear," Sandra lit her candle and then shared the flame with the other Lunch Ladies, which had become more than just a moniker. Sandra, Laura, Margery, and Estelle hosted a daily radio show on the local public radio station. Every Monday through Friday from 11 a.m. to 2 p.m., the group graced the airwaves of 89.7 FM to chat, take callers, and promote local businesses around their community. Sandra walked her candle over to Tay, who was busy serving drinks at Tay's Hot Choffee Stand, the latest expansion of Tay's business.

"Merry Christmas, Tay," Sandra said.

"Merry Christmas, Sandra."

"The candles are looking beautiful, everybody," Mayor Mayer said, "so let's go ahead and get started with the countdown. Ready? 11...10...9..."

As the crowd joined the countdown, Josh took Ellie's candle and handed both his and hers to Sandra and Laura, who had moved nearby.

"8...7...6...5..."

Josh turned to Ellie and then kneeled down on one knee. "Ellie?" Josh said.

"4...3..."

Josh's heart felt like it was pounding out of his chest. He opened the small box that he had retrieved from his office before arriving at the tree lighting and revealed a ring. A near colorless, half-carat round diamond with impeccable clarity, attached by a white gold band with pavé-set diamonds along the sides. He had gotten Evelyn, Dave, Mia, and even Scotty's approval before deciding that the ring was the one. Each of them re-enforced what he had already known in his heart.

"Ellie, I want to spend every day, week, month, and year together with you."

"2...1!"

Josh pulled the ring out of the box and tried to hold it still in front of him, despite his nerves. "Will you marry me, Ellie?"

Her reaction was everything Josh had dreamed of, and more.

"Now, Greg! Now! Get the shot!" the Mayor shouted excitedly as the crowd erupted into a raucous version of "O, Christmas Tree."

ACKNOWLEDGMENTS

A very special thank you is owed to the members of the Bramble Jam+ community who contributed their time and skills to this story.

For reading messy drafts and providing invaluable feedback: Kira Romens, Summer Nettleman, Lee Hodo, Emily Petraglia, Lynn Austin, Whitney Wilder, Holly Goodfellow, Nicole Beatty, Laura Schinner, Rina Saltzman, and Diana Herald. We all now share the weight of any typos, gaps, and inconsistencies in this story.

For creating hand-drawn illustrations for our pages: Lee Hodo, Lynn Austin, Tia Horn, Diana Herald, Ethan Herald, Jonah Herald, Emily Petraglia, Nicole Beatty, Rina Saltzman, and Fiona Furman. Check the sketches index at the end of this book to see the incredible work our friends provided.

Merry Christmas,
Bran, Dan, and Brian

SKETCHES INDEX

The Bramble Jam+ community contributed so much to this story, including artwork that was used throughout. Here you'll find a list of the art and the artist as it appeared in the story.

Emily Petraglia

Emily Petraglia

Lynn Austin

Lee Hodo

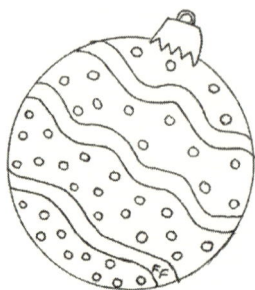

Fiona Furman

Emily Petraglia

Rina Saltzman

Emily Petraglia

Emily Petraglia

Tia Horn

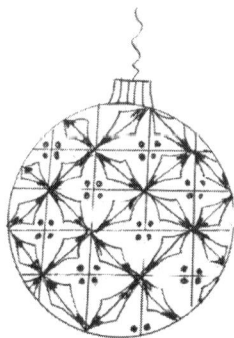

Rina Saltzman

Emily Petraglia

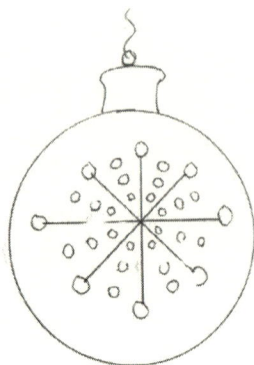

Rina Saltzman

Diana Herald

Emily Petraglia

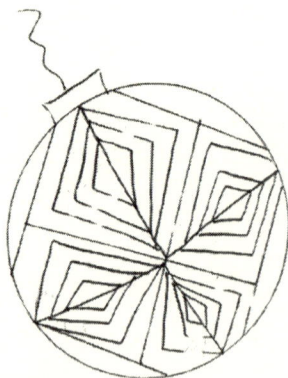

Rina Saltzman

Lee Hodo

Nicole Beatty

Emily Petraglia

Lynn Austin

Nicole Beatty

Tia Horn

Tia Horn

Rina Saltzman

Nicole Beatty

Fiona Furman

Diana Herald

Ethan Herald

Rina Saltzman

Jonah Herald

Rina Saltzman

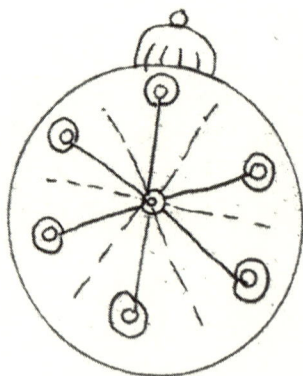

Rina Saltzman

Tia Horn

Jonah Herald

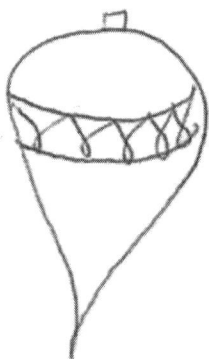

Emily Petraglia

Diana Herald

Tia Horn

Lee Hodo

THE AUTHORS

Brandon Gray

Bran loves love, peppermint mochas, and the Orlando Magic. Also the magic of the season and regular magic. All magic, really. He's the co-creator and host of the *Deck the Hallmark* podcast and has written two books: *I'll Be Home for Christmas Movies* and *When's it Gonna Be Christmas Again?* When he's not watching Hallmark Christmas movies, writing Christmas songs, or spending time with his family, Bran runs a podcast network with his best friend Dan.

Daniel Thompson

Dan followed the typical track of teacher turned principal turned basketball coach turned podcaster. He co-created and hosts the *Deck the Hallmark* podcast and has written two books: *I'll Be Home for Christmas Movies* and *When's it Gonna Be Christmas Again?* When he's not at the movies, he's spending time with his family and running a podcast network with his best bud Bran.

Brian Herald

Brian hosts the *Deck the Hallmark* podcast with his good friends Bran and Dan. He worked as a technical writer for more than fifteen years and has published four children's books with his sons in the series *The Adventures of Nino and Tenna*. Recently, he has been writing screenplays and adapting screenplays into holiday rom-com novels.

Carissa Bowser – Illustrator

Carissa is a life-long artist who has illustrated children's books, designed marketing and branding campaigns, and painted murals around her homebase of Travelers Rest, SC. See more of her work at victorygardenstudio.com and @victorygardenstudio.

DECK THE *Hallmark*

Find *Deck the Hallmark* episodes wherever you listen to podcasts,
and watch our episode videos at:
youtube.com/DecktheHallmarkPodcast

Join our mailing list to keep up with all the fun!
🎄 deckthehallmark.com 🎄

Connect with us on the socials!
🎄 @deckthehallmark 🎄

Want even more Deck the Hallmark? Join Bramble Jam+ for
access to exclusive content and the best community on the internet
(and maybe even real life).
🎄 bjn.supercast.com 🎄

Photography by Holly Fite of Mellonberry Photography

May we be the first to wish you a Merry Christmas!

24346987R00156